THE SILENCE OF THE FLANS

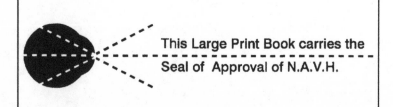

AN EMERGENCY DESSERT SQUAD
MYSTERY

THE SILENCE OF
THE FLANS

LAURA BRADFORD

WHEELER PUBLISHING
A part of Gale, a Cengage Company

GALE
A Cengage Company

Farmington Hills, Mich • San Francisco • New York • Waterville, Maine
Meriden, Conn • Mason, Ohio • Chicago

LIBRARY OF CONGRESS CATALOGING-IN-PUBLICATION DATA

Names: Bradford, Laura, author.
Title: The silence of the flans / by Laura Bradford.
Description: Large print edition. | Waterville, Maine : Wheeler Publishing, 2017. | Series: An Emergency Dessert Squad mystery | Series: Wheeler Publishing large print cozy mystery
Identifiers: LCCN 2017015014| ISBN 9781432839741 (softcover) | ISBN 1432839748 (softcover)
Subjects: LCSH: Murder—Investigation—Fiction. | Large type books. | GSAFD: Mystery fiction.
Classification: LCC PS3602.R34235 S58 2017 | DDC 813/.6—dc23
LC record available at https://lccn.loc.gov/2017015014

Published in 2017 by arrangement with The Berkley Publishing Group, an imprint of Penguin Publishing Group, a division of Penguin Random House LLC

Printed in Mexico
1 2 3 4 5 6 7 21 20 19 18 17

In memory of my great uncle Ray.
Spending time with him was
an honor and a joy.

ACKNOWLEDGMENTS

To say I'm enjoying Winnie and the gang in these Emergency Dessert Squad Mysteries would be an understatement. They make the time I spend at the keyboard, bringing them to life on the page, an absolute joy from start to finish.

A huge thank-you goes out to Lisa Kelley, Lynn Deardorff, and Eileen Pearce for helping me brainstorm some of the same dessert names Winnie brainstorms with her friends. These ladies listened to my crazy ideas and played along like champs.

I'd also like to thank my editor, Michelle Vega, and my agent, Jessica Faust. This book marks the publication of my twenty-fifth book, a milestone I'm proud of for many reasons.

And, last but not least, I'd like to thank you — my readers. Whether you're just now finding me through the Emergency Dessert Squad Mysteries, or you've been reading my work (such as my Amish Mysteries) for a while, the fact that you're here — with this book in your hand — matters to me.

I love to chat with my readers. I can be reached via my website: laurabradford.com.

CHAPTER 1

Winnie Johnson capped her pen and tossed it onto the wicker table, narrowly missing the black rook poised to capture the white queen.

"Whoa, I'm sorry, Mr. Nelson. I guess I wasn't thinking."

"*Winking?* You want to learn how to do some winking?" The seventy-five-year-old former sailor extracted the pen from the middle of the chessboard and set it on the edge of the table closest to Winnie. "I can teach you how to do some winking."

She tapped her finger to her ear and waited for her housemate to turn his hearing aid up a notch. When he did, she set the record straight. "I said *thinking,* Mr. Nelson. I wasn't *thinking* when I tossed my pen onto the table just now."

"Seems to me you've been thinking *too* hard, Winnie Girl." Hunching forward, he slid the black castle-like piece four spots to the left and then collapsed back against his chair with exhausted elation. "Now *that* was a move."

"You're playing *yourself,* you old fool." Bridget O'Keefe, their next-door neighbor, paused her hand midway down the spine of the brown and white tabby cat on her lap and shook her head. "Winnie asked for your help today, Parker. You do realize that, don't you?"

Elation turned to consternation as the elderly man took in, first, Winnie and, then, Bridget. "I came up with Baked Alaska-Bound!"

Bridget's snort of disgust was so sudden and so loud that Lovey woke from her sound slumber and narrowed her eyes on Winnie.

Hissss . . .

Raising the cat's narrowed eyes with a glare, Winnie hissed back, earning herself a second and louder hiss from Lovey and a soft tsking sound from Bridget.

"*What?* She hissed first," Winnie argued. "I'm not even the one who disturbed her just now! That was you, Bridget, with your reaction to what Mr. Nelson said!"

Mr. Nelson patted the top of his thigh and smiled triumphantly at Bridget as the cat abandoned the eighty-something's lap in

10

favor of his. Once Lovey was settled, tummy side up, he brought his attention back to Winnie. "Now I realize this is something I've never said before, but . . . well . . . Bridget is right." The second the sentence was out, the man scrunched his nose and made a face befitting someone who'd tasted something utterly awful.

Winnie laughed. *"About . . ."*

Shaking his head in one last burst of theatrics, Mr. Nelson pointed at the purring animal gently rolling around on his lap. "Lovey is never going to accept you if you keep hissing at her like you just did."

"I only started hissing back when it became apparent she has no gratitude for the fact that I'm the one who feeds her, and waters her, and sleeps on the couch just so she can have my bed!"

"Give it time, Winnie Girl."

"It's been well over a month now, Mr. Nelson. How much more time does she need? She's a *cat.*"

"She'll come around. You wait and see." Glancing back at the chessboard and the answering move he was surely itching to make, Mr. Nelson mumbled something under his breath and then focused again on Winnie. "Now, about this brainstorming you wanted to do today . . . You *did* write

11

down Baked Alaska-Bound, didn't you?"

She opened her mouth to answer but closed it as Bridget took center stage. "Just how many people in Silver Lake do you really think are going to Alaska, Parker? One? Maybe two? Do you really think that's worthy of a spot on Winnie's menu?" With a dismissive flick of her hand (and the dramatic wince that invariably followed), the woman uncrossed her swollen ankles and readied her stout frame to stand. "Fortunately, for Winnie, *one* of us brought along our creativity this afternoon. As a result, I predict my Couch Potato Candy will be a crowd favorite in no time."

"No one *likes* potato candy, Bridget." Mr. Nelson rubbed Lovey behind the ears and then scrunched up his nose again. "Have you ever had potato candy, Winnie Girl?"

"I can't say that I have."

"Do yourself a favor and keep it that way." This time, when he gestured toward Winnie's notebook, he used his non-cat-rubbing finger. "How 'bout something for a flu? Or when you're feeling all hot and achy —"

Hot?

From a flu —

"That's it! Mr. Nelson, you're a genius!"

Mr. Nelson puffed out his chest with pride. "Ah, Winnie, you shouldn't."

"You're right, she shouldn't." Bridget yanked the hem of her housecoat across the top of her vein-ridden upper shin and then pinned Winnie with an indignant stare. "You're calling *Parker* a genius?"

"Yes! A rescue squad surely needs something for someone with the flu!" Winnie recovered her pen from its resting spot beside one of Mr. Nelson's captured pawns, slipped off the cap, and began to write. "Lava-Hot Fever Cupcakes or — no! I'll make it Lava-Hot Fever Mini Bundt Cakes and they can come in all sorts of varieties — dark chocolate, milk chocolate, white chocolate . . . Whatever the customer wants."

A quick flash of his tongue in Bridget's direction was followed by yet another puff of Mr. Nelson's chest and a slow nod at Winnie. "Unlike potato candy, *that's* somethin' folks would actually want to eat, isn't it, Winnie Girl?"

Bridget scooted forward on the rocker, rose to her feet with nary a grunt or groan, and turned, hands on hips. "I declare you insufferable, Parker Nelson!"

Declare?

"You sit there, playing chess with yourself for hours on end and —"

"Wait," Winnie said, waving her hands

13

between the pair. "Say that again. Please."

Bridget removed her left hand from her hip and used it to point at the man seated in front of her. "Gladly. You are insufferable, Parker Nelson!"

"Did we really need to hear that again?" Mr. Nelson asked, peering around Bridget to afford a better view of Winnie. "My hearing aid is on full volume."

Again, Winnie waved her hands. "No. No. Not that part. The other part. About declaring . . ."

"Oh. Right." Bridget narrowed her eyes on the cat-stealing elderly man. "I *declare* you insufferable, Parker Nelson."

"I declare," Winnie repeated. "Yes! I — I D'éclairs!"

Bridget slid her irritation onto Winnie. "*What* do you declare?"

"I don't know. Anything!" Powered by another burst of enthusiasm, Winnie turned the page of her notebook and began to write. "A pregnancy, an engagement, a promotion — anything!"

"I don't understand."

She looked up from her latest menu addition and gave in to the smile she felt building inside her chest. "Éclairs. Only I'll call them I D'éclairs. The customer can decide what they're declaring."

Mr. Nelson hooked his index finger underneath Lovey's chin and gently guided the cat's sleepy eyes up and onto his own. "How can you hiss at someone who smiles like that, you silly girl?"

"Because Winnie hasn't *been* smiling like that these last few days," Bridget said. "She's been quiet — too quiet, if you ask me. Maybe her sciatic nerve is acting up. I get quiet when mine is acting up."

"Can you let me know when that's happening? Because I'll need to hit the store for some blankets before all them folks in hell snatch 'em all up." Mr. Nelson slapped the side of his leg and laughed — a big hearty sound that only deepened the reddish hue now branching out across Bridget's otherwise pale complexion. "Get it, Winnie Girl? The day Bridget is quiet is the day hell will have officially frozen over!"

Winnie stopped writing. "Sure, sure, I get it. But I *have* been smiling . . ." When Bridget shook her head, Winnie maneuvered her own around Bridget's midsection to get a better view of a still-chuckling Mr. Nelson. "Haven't I?"

Bridget reached down, plucked Lovey off the elderly man's lap, wrapped her arms around the cat, and proceeded to whisper something in its ear. The fact that Winnie

15

was able to pick out *Parker, deaf,* and *senile* among the whispered words was a pretty good indication Bridget hadn't found the whole hell-freezing-over thing nearly as amusing as Mr. Nelson had.

Eventually, though, Bridget returned her focus to Winnie. "Now, don't worry, dear. Parker and I know what's wrong. And we're here for you. Just like always."

Tightening her hold on her now-capped pen, Winnie ping-ponged her attention between her aging friends. Sure enough, their faces both sported the same concern.

For her.

"Nothing is wrong. I swear." Winnie stood, crossed to the porch railing, and then turned and leaned against it so she could see both of her friends at the same time. Only now, their concern had morphed into something that looked a lot like skepticism. "*What?* I mean it! Nothing is wrong. Sure, getting the Emergency Dessert Squad off the ground is exhausting in some ways, but it's proving to be a whole lot of fun, too. I mean, think about it. I'm still baking just like I've always wanted to do, and now, because of the whole ambulance theme, I'm getting to come up with all these crazy names and new recipes. I'm living my dream. Truly."

The skepticism moved to Bridget's eyebrow as she exchanged a knowing glance with Mr. Nelson.

"What?" Winnie heard the exasperation on the edges of her voice and did her best to rein it in. *"What* am I not doing? What am I not saying?"

Bridget lowered herself and Lovey into Winnie's chair and began to rock ever so gently. "We may be old, and Parker, here, might be nearly deaf, but we're not blind, Winnie. Not yet anyway."

"I don't understand." And it was true. She didn't. Mr. Nelson and Bridget might as well have been speaking in tongues . . .

"That young man of yours hasn't been coming around the last week or so," Bridget said.

Mr. Nelson nodded. "I could talk to her if you want. See if something I say might make a difference."

"Her?" Winnie echoed in confusion. "Who's —"

"The daughter," Mr. Nelson clarified. "Your young man's daughter."

Bridget's dramatic exhale had Lovey on her feet and off the elderly woman's lap in less than a second. "What do you think you can say or do that is going to get through to a sixteen-year-old girl, Parker? Sit on a whoopee cushion and hope the sound of a seventy-five-year-old man pretending to pass gas makes her grow up and start thinking of someone other than herself? Please. Let's pose solutions that actually have merit."

"And you think setting Winnie up on a blind date with the nephew of someone in your crocheting group has merit?"

Winnie parted company with the railing, her hands splayed outward in front of her chest. "Hold on a minute. Jay not coming around the last few days isn't because of any *problem.*"

"Does that mean the girl is thawing to you?" Mr. Nelson asked.

She stopped herself, midsnort, as Lovey looked up at her from the porch floor and hissed.

Blinking through the threatening tears, Winnie looked over her shoulder at the ambulance parked in her driveway and willed its Emergency Dessert Squad logo to help steady her breath. At thirty-four years of age, Winnie was blessed with a whole posse of good friends. Granted, the majority of them were over the age of seventy (if they were even still living), but still, they'd brought her a good deal of happiness. Her relationships with men, however, had been a different story.

That had all changed, however, when she met her first Emergency Dessert Squad customer, Jay Morgan, six weeks earlier. The business professor at Silver Lake College had placed an order as a way to check out Winnie's one-of-a-kind business idea. And from that first moment, they'd clicked. The only snafu in the mix? Jay's sixteen-year-old daughter, Caroline.

"Winnie?" Bridget prodded.

Inhaling the courage she needed, she returned her focus to Mr. Nelson and his lingering question. "No. There's no thawing." She swallowed back the lump now threatening her ability to keep speaking and forced herself to continue, her voice vacillating between raspy and downright difficult to hear even by her own ears. "But that's not why Jay hasn't been coming around."

She closed her eyes in the wake of her own words — words she wanted to believe more than anything else. Yet try as she did to buy what she was selling, there was no ignoring the voice in her head that kept posing the same two questions over and over again . . .

Why *hadn't* Jay come around?

Why *hadn't* Jay returned either of her calls over the last thirty-six hours?

A familiar, staccato thumping let her know

Mr. Nelson was en route to her side, cane in hand. Still, she kept her eyes closed for fear he'd see her tears. "She'll come around, Winnie Girl, you wait and see."

"You mean like Lovey has?" She hated the sarcasm in her voice and did her best to soften its impact by squeezing the man's hand.

"Sometimes the heart takes a while to catch up with the head, Winnie Girl. Especially when there's still hurt at play."

"Hurt?" she asked, opening her eyes.

"Yes, hurt. For Lovey, it's the loss of Gertie. I don't care what anyone says, animals form attachments to their owners and their routines every bit as much as the owners form attachments to them." Mr. Nelson squeezed her hand, only this time he didn't release his grip until he was sure he had Winnie's full attention. "Yes, you've given her a nice new home with ample sun spots to roll around in, and yes, you feed her every day. But you're still not Gertie."

Her deceased friend flitted through her thoughts and necessitated another round of rapid blinking to keep the tears at bay. "And I'll never *be* Gertie, Mr. Nelson. I'm just the person Gertie tasked with caring for Lovey."

"That's right. But Gertie was sharp as a

tack until the day she passed. She chose you to be Lovey's new momma for a reason. When you find yourself doubting that, think about that vintage ambulance she left you, too. That's worked out, hasn't it?"

She could only nod. Without the second bequest and the opportunity it afforded to start her Emergency Dessert Squad, Winnie would have been forced to hang up her measuring spoons and baking pans for good. Maybe Mr. Nelson was right. Maybe Lovey would come around in time . . .

"Jay's daughter isn't much different," he continued. "Only her hurt is even bigger. Her mother walked out on her when she was in kindergarten, right?"

"Yes."

"And it's just been her and her dad ever since, right?"

"Yes."

"Maybe she's just slow to warm up. Like Lovey."

She made a face. "Lovey warmed up to you and Bridget without any difficulty."

"She'd seen us before. When we spent time with Gertie."

"If you go with that logic, Lovey had seen me before, too. Many times." Winnie tugged her mousy brown ponytail over her shoulder and fiddled with the ends as she took Mr.

Nelson's words a step further. "Here's the ironic thing. Lovey and Caroline hit it off the second they met. Likewise, they both despised me the second I showed up."

"Why don't you share a drop of whipped cream from one of your desserts with Lovey the next time you have a little left over. See what happens." Mr. Nelson shifted his weight from one leg to the other with the help of his cane and then tapped the index finger of his free hand on the tip of Winnie's nose. "As for that young girl, I'm not saying her being territorial is okay, because it isn't. But it's a little understandable in light of her background, too. So just keep being yourself, Winnie Girl, and eventually your light will shine through the hurt. For Lovey, and for that young fella's daughter."

She cleared her throat of its on-again, off-again lump once and for all and studied Mr. Nelson through the renewed haze in her eyes. "And if it doesn't? Shine through, I mean?"

"You walk away." Bridget stood, shuffled her way to the railing, and flanked Winnie on the other side. "Just like you did when that good-for-nothing landlord of yours raised the rent on your bakery. You were devastated when you closed Delectable Delights for good. I saw it. Parker saw it.

But here you are — back on your feet and better than ever."

"I wouldn't go that far," Winnie whispered.

"Okay, so maybe not better than ever — yet. But you're on your way. Of that I have no doubt. Nick Batkas did you a favor making it so you couldn't afford that lease. You might not have known it at the time, but he did. You mark my words." Bridget hooked her finger under Winnie's chin and turned it so they were eye to eye. "As for the rest of us, all we can do right now is hope and pray that our elected officials get wise to Mr. Batkas before our wonderful little town slips past the point of recovery."

Winnie felt Mr. Nelson stiffen beside her. "What's that scoundrel up to now?"

Mindful of the fact that she had information Mr. Nelson and Winnie lacked, Bridget took a moment to remove her glasses, wipe them with a soft cloth from the pocket of her floral housecoat, and then reposition them atop the bridge of her bulbous nose. "I think the more appropriate question, Parker, is what is he *not* up to . . ."

CHAPTER 2

She'd just cracked the spine on the paper-back mystery novel she'd been waiting to read for days when the phone began to ring. For a split second she considered ignoring it and letting the call go to voice mail, but she couldn't. She wasn't wired that way. Besides, her personal cell phone wasn't always just for personal use these days.

Sighing, she flipped the book onto the arm of the overstuffed chair and crossed to the kitchen. A glance at the caller ID screen yielded a familiar name and a mental image so clear the woman may as well have been standing in front of her at that very moment.

"Hey, Renee, what's up?"

Renee Ballentine was, in a word, nuts. She was also funny, creative, loyal, supportive, beautiful in an eccentric, quirky kind of way, a hardworking if not punctual employee, a devoted single mother to her ten-year-old son, Ty, and a great friend. The fact that she was relentless when it came to Winnie's lack of interest in dating (until Jay, of course) and flirted shamelessly with Mr. Nelson despite their forty-year age difference, were really just minor flaws in the grand scheme of things . . .

"Whatcha doing?" Renee asked in her usual on-the-go breathless manner.

"Talking to you."

"Ha. Ha. Funny."

Winnie walked to the front window and peeked out at the comings and goings on Serenity Lane. Halfway down the street she spotted Peggy Landon, Serenity Lane's oldest resident, in an animated conversation with Mr. Nelson. Hands were moving, canes were swinging, and a folded newspaper rose up between them every few minutes.

"Winnie?"

At the sound of her name, she shook her head and wandered back to the kitchen table and its bench seat. "I was actually getting ready to read that book I bought when I dragged you through Silver Lake Books that one day."

"I don't remember going into the bookstore with . . ." Renee's voice trailed off only to return with an audible hint of shock. "Wait. That was like *three months* ago. You haven't read that yet?"

Winnie dropped onto the bench and ran her finger across the cover of her idea notebook. "Let's take stock of those three months, shall we? When I wasn't at the bakery, I was home trying to figure out how to *keep* the bakery. And then, when the money we thought Gertie had left me turned out to be an ambulance, I was kind of consumed by other things — like how to pay my rent and eat."

"An ambulance *and* a cat."

"Excuse me?"

Renee sighed in her ear. "When the money we thought Gertie had left you turned out to be an ambulance *and* a cat. You always forget the cat. No wonder Lovey is reluctant to embrace you."

She snorted. Loudly. "You are kidding, right?"

"No."

Pulling her finger off the notebook, she surveyed her immediate surroundings — the hammock-like bed attached to the window-sill, the matching food and water bowl atop a princess placemat, and the living room blanket that had once been Winnie's favorite now covered in brown and white fur. "Have you been wearing blinders the past six weeks, Renee? Lovey has all but taken over

26

my entire apartment."

"She's waiting for your love, Winnie. She's waiting for your love."

"How much more love does she need?" Winnie dropped her forehead onto the table and groaned. "Actually, can we talk about something else? Please?"

"Sure. Why, when the troublemaker is otherwise occupied, is Jay holed up in his office instead of there with you? Are you two really that inept at the notion of seizing opportunities?"

She jerked her head up so hard she nearly fell over the back side of the bench. "Wait. How do you know Jay is at his office?"

"Because Ty and I went for a bike ride a few hours ago and we passed him as he was pulling into the faculty parking lot. The troublemaker wasn't with him."

Pivoting on the bench, Winnie stood and made her way back into the living room, the book she'd been so eager to read no longer holding any allure. "You really need to stop calling Caroline that. I'm afraid it's going to stick."

"As it should." Renee laughed and then got back on point. "Anyway, when he saw us, he stopped and rolled down the window. He looked absolutely wiped out, Winnie, like he hasn't slept in days. Is everything okay with him? Has he been sick?"

"I — I don't know."

"You don't know?" Renee echoed. "Why not?"

Winnie swallowed. "Um, because we haven't talked in a few days."

Silence filled her ear for so long, Winnie actually pulled the phone from her cheek to check the connection.

Nope, Renee was still there . . .

"Renee?"

"What am I going to do with you, Winnie?"

"*Do* with me?"

"Yes. You have a guy who is crazy about you. And you, by some miracle, actually seem interested in him as well. Yet just when I think I can step back and let you handle things from this point on, you say something like that."

She felt her lower jaw begin to slack and did her best to bring it back in line with the rest of her mouth. "Say something like *what* exactly?"

"That you haven't talked to him in a few days."

"I haven't," she repeated.

"I heard you the first time. What you've failed to say, though, is why. Did you have a fight?"

28

"No."

"Did you say something about the kid that irked him?"

"No!" She reclaimed the chair she'd abandoned to take Renee's call and let her head loll back against the cushion. "He — he hasn't called."

"So you call him!"

Minus the voice, it was the same sentiment she'd heard in her own head countless times over the past few days. "I don't want to force myself on him."

"Why not?"

"Hmmm, maybe because his kid hates me? Maybe he's decided he's not interested? I don't know, take your pick."

"See, I'm leaning more towards you're a loon."

There's that . . .

To Renee, though, she said, "He hasn't called, Renee. At all."

"Okay, so he hasn't called. That doesn't mean he's not interested. In fact, based on the way he looked a few hours ago, I'd say he hasn't called because something else is going on. Something that's stressing him out."

She tightened her grip on the phone while she mentally dissected everything Renee had said thus far. "Like what?"

"I don't know, Winnie, maybe one of the half dozen or so things that make being an adult difficult — bills, teenagers, ex-spouses, work, et cetera, et cetera."

It made sense. It really did. But still . . .

"What happens if it's what I said? That he's lost whatever interest he may have had in me?"

"Then you pity him and you move on. The latter of which you can't do if you stick your nose in a book and opt to guess instead of know." Renee stopped and took a distinctive inhale. "C'mon. You're Winnie Johnson. Never in all the time I've known you have you balked at a challenge. You're tough. You're resilient."

Tough . . .

Resilient . . .

Before she could formulate a response, Renee continued, "Based on what he said, he's going to be in his office for the rest of the evening . . ."

One good thing about making a run out to Silver Lake College on a Sunday evening was the overabundance of available parking spots that were a rare commodity during normal school hours. Still, Winnie took her time as she drove up one row and down the next, visually scouring every utilized space for confirmation that Renee had, indeed, been right.

She rounded the corner and headed down the last row, her gaze immediately drawn to the four-door white sedan tucked beneath the branches of one of several dozen Bradford Pear Trees that had graced the campus with their gorgeous white flowers for the last several weeks.

Gathering her courage in one large breath, Winnie pulled the ambulance into the spot next to Jay's, cut the engine, and stared up at the Cully Business Building and, in particular, the lone lit window on the fourth floor.

Not for the first time since she hung up the phone with Renee, she found herself questioning the spurts of conviction that had propelled her to tear through her favorite cookbooks and her pantry for just the right icebreaker. Though why there was suddenly ice that needed to be broken between her and Jay was a complete mystery.

She rose upward in her seat and studied her reflection in the rearview mirror. Somehow, despite being surrounded by desserts nearly twenty-four/seven, her face was still slim, a by-product of the high cheekbones she'd been blessed with, no doubt. The turquoise-colored shirt she'd opted to change into before loading Jay's surprise into the Dessert Squad was a near perfect match for her eyes, and the soft pink lipstick she'd applied before actually pulling out of the driveway was still in place despite the occasional lip nibbling she'd caught herself doing as she left Serenity Lane and headed toward the college.

"I guess I'll do," she mumbled as she swung her focus onto the passenger seat and its four-legged inhabitant. "Now, the only question is what to do with *you.*"

Lovey sat up tall and peered out the front windshield.

"It's a school. You can't come in." She knew she sounded like an idiot explaining herself to a cat, but there she was, doing it anyway. "Fortunately for you, it's just shy of seventy degrees out so you should be fine in here with the window cracked for a few minutes."

Lovey's mouth dropped open and her narrow pink tongue rolled outward like a carpet. When her yawn was done, she blinked at Winnie.

"I don't know why you insist on tagging along every time I go out on a call. It's silly, really." She pulled the key from the ignition and opened the door. "Besides, you can't stand me, remember?"

She stepped out onto the pavement and made her way around to the back of the ambulance and the Éclair-mounted stretcher visible through the vehicle's narrow rectangular window. With any luck, by the time she actually stepped inside Jay's office, she'd actually know what she was declaring . . .

With a practiced hand, she unlatched the back door, swung it open, and pulled the stretcher out and onto the ground. Once the wheels were locked into place, she retrieved her rescue bag from its holding spot inside the cab and slung it over her left shoulder for the walk across the parking lot.

Despite being one of at least a half-dozen academic buildings on campus, the Cully Business Building's white columns and commanding presence had become the trademark of the school, appearing in most if not all of the college's brochures. During the school day, a smattering of students could be found studying on benches and blankets scattered around the south side of the building, while others took a moment to enjoy a little Frisbee and football fun on the large green space referred to as The Commons on its north side.

Dodging a Frisbee that narrowly missed

her éclairs, Winnie rounded the corner and entered the building through the doors on the south side. Six weeks earlier, she'd never been inside the Cully Business Building. Now, though, thanks to a few deliveries, she knew her way around without having to consult the silver-plated directory halfway down the hallway. Instead, she went straight to the elevator bank and waited for the now illuminated button to heed her call.

Once inside, she pressed the number 4 and did her best to ignore the butterflies that were flapping their wings a mile a minute inside her chest. Oh, how she wanted to convince herself she didn't care if Jay liked her as much as she liked him. But to do so would mean she was lying to herself, and that accomplished nothing.

Renee was right. Sitting around, waiting for Jay to call, was silly. He'd either be happy to see her or he wouldn't be. If the latter proved to be the case, she'd douse her sorrows in chocolate and move on . . .

The elevator doors swished open and she guided the stretcher into the hallway beyond, her gaze traveling down its length to the fifth room on the left. Even from where she was standing, she could tell the door was open and that someone was inside. But beyond that, she had no idea what he was doing or why he was there on a Sunday evening.

A student meeting perhaps?

No, there were no voices spilling out into the hallway . . .

Catching up on e-mails?

No, there was no tap-tap of the keyboard . . .

Swinging her gaze to the right, she noted the empty receptionist desk and the utter silence of her surroundings. If she waited long enough, she suspected a member of the campus security team might emerge from the elevator or the stairwell at the end of the hall to conduct a routine sweep, but for now it was just Winnie and one unsuspecting business professor.

She continued on her quest, the wheels of the stretcher remarkably quiet as they rolled along the standard office hallway carpet. Two feet from the door, she inhaled sharply, squared her shoulders, and finally settled on the proclamation that would go with her rescue dessert. Yet as she wheeled everything into view and opened her mouth to make her declaration, she found that she was unable to speak.

For there, seated behind the large mahogany desk with his forehead resting on the unusually cluttered surface, was the classically handsome man she never tired of looking at even if his current facedown position made seeing him difficult. Still, she soaked in what she could (the light brown hair with the sprinkling of gray near his temples) and mentally filled in what she couldn't (strong chin, blue-green eyes that sparkled when he smiled, six-foot frame, hands that seemed to swallow hers whole . . .), the image soliciting a small sigh from between her lips.

Jay's head snapped up at the sound to reveal the same blue-green eyes she saw in her mind's eye. Only the pair now trained on Winnie weren't sparkling, and he wasn't smiling.

"I . . . uh . . ." She backed up against the stretcher. "I'm sorry. This was obviously a — a bad idea."

His palms came down on the desk and he rose up out of his chair and onto his feet. "Wait! Don't go. Please."

She held her own hands in place atop the stretcher and waited to speak until she was sure any and all hint of emotion was under tight control. Then, "I heard you were working. On a Sunday. And that you seemed a little" — she paused, swallowed, and then continued on — "stressed. So I thought maybe a rescue was in order."

Even as the perfectly logical explanation

left her lips, she couldn't help wanting to pull her hand off the thin mattress and smack herself in the head. Really, what had she been thinking? Maybe the reason Jay had seemingly dropped off the face of the earth the last few days was because he wanted to . . .

The smile she adored slowly made its way across his mouth but stopped short of his eyes, which were now cast downward at the plated dessert in the center of the stretcher. "Those look like éclairs."

"They're I D'éclairs." She heard the slight shake to her voice and took a moment to get it under control. "For when someone needs a declaration."

"I D'éclairs," he repeated before bringing his focus back to Winnie. "That's awesome."

Unsure of what to say, she simply nodded.

"So?" he prodded. "What's the declaration?"

She waved his question aside and, with it, the words she'd settled on as she wheeled her not-so-smart idea closer to him. "Let's just skip that, okay?"

In a second, his hand was around hers, holding it tight. "No. Please. What was the declaration?"

A barrage of answers designed to protect

her heart and make her look less pathetic flitted through her thoughts, one after the other . . .

I D'éclair you're a fabulous teacher.

I D'éclair you're working too hard.

I D'éclair —

"You know what?" The rasp of his voice broke through her mental litany of possible answers and brought her attention back on him. "I think I'll take this one."

Releasing his hold on her hand, Jay lifted the plate of éclairs off the stretcher and held them toward Winnie. "I D'éclair you . . . and Lovey, apparently, are —"

She spun around in time to see Lovey jump out from under the stretcher and begin to sniff her way around Jay's office.

"Lovey! I told you to wait in the car!"

"She's fine, Winnie. Really."

"She's not fine," Winnie argued. "She's a menace and a stowaway."

He cleared his throat and lifted the plate still higher. "Winnie Johnson, I D'éclair you a sight for sore eyes."

"You do? I — I am?"

He drew back ever so slightly. "You doubt that?"

Stepping away from the stretcher, she wandered past him and farther into the office, unsure of what exactly she was doing short of putting a little distance between herself and an atmosphere that suddenly felt uncomfortable. "You stopped calling this past week. I didn't — and still don't — know what to think."

"Winnie, I'm every bit as interested in you now as I was last week." He carried the plate to his desk and set it on top of a mound of papers and grading books. Then, turning around, he reached out and stopped her aimless wandering. "Something you need to know about me is my inability to detach from my students. Sometimes, it's a good thing. Sometimes, like now, it's not."

Before she could make sense of what he was saying, he made his way around his desk and sat down, carefully removing his grade book from beneath the plate of éclairs as he did. "Graduation is three weeks from yesterday. If I do my job the way I should — and the way I believe I'm supposed to — Alicia Worth will not be getting her diploma."

"Alicia Worth?"

"Yes." He glanced down at the grade book and then leaned back in his chair, clearly exhausted and troubled. "This girl is . . . difficult. Most of that is her own doing. Her priorities are in all the wrong places."

Slowly, Winnie lowered herself onto the

chair across from him. "Okay. So if she fails to graduate, it's because of her, not you. Everyone has a choice to apply themselves or not. It sounds like she's made her choice, Jay."

"You're right. She has." He laced his fingers and brought his palms between his head and the back of the chair. "And if it was just Alicia in this equation, I'd see failing her as a learning opportunity. But she's not."

"She's not what?"

"The only one in the equation."

"I don't understand."

"The only reason Alicia is in college at all is because of her grandmother. And the whole time Alicia has been here, that woman has been hoping and praying something would connect with this kid. Something that would motivate her into giving a damn about life." He tipped his chin toward the ceiling and exhaled a troubled breath. "Alicia's grandmother is months, if not weeks, away from dying. She has cancer."

She considered his words and found herself on the doorstep of his quandary. "You want her to see Alicia graduate, don't you?"

He dropped his gaze back down to hers, his expression one of pain and turmoil. "I know it's wrong, but I want her grand-mother to be able to leave this earth with a sense of peace, you know? But Alicia, she won't even meet me halfway. I gave her an extra credit project that would have had her interviewing a local business owner about their company. She just had to talk to the person and write up a report. If she'd done it, I would have passed her. But she didn't even bother to try. And on top of that, she blew off the group project that was due on Friday and I can't pretend that away when there are three other students who know she did nothing."

It was a lot to take in. But even as Winnie tried to, her thoughts were already skipping ahead to a solution. "How about an inten-sive internship with a local business?"

"I couldn't get something like that off the ground with less than three weeks to go."

"I could."

He stared at her. "You lost me."

"I can't pay her, but I can certainly give her some hands-on experience. Heck, maybe she could even help with some of the marketing ideas Renee and I have been wanting to work on but have to keep shelv-ing to attend to other things."

A flash of hope lit his eyes momentarily before disappearing just as quickly. "I can't ask you to do that, Winnie."

"You didn't. I offered."

"But this is Alicia Worth we're talking about," Jay protested, bringing his hands back down to the desk. "She's . . . *trouble.*"

Shrugging, she plucked an éclair from the plate and held it out for Jay to take. "I run the Emergency *Dessert Squad,* not the New York Stock Exchange. How much trouble can one college girl really cause?"

CHAPTER 3

The bathroom door had barely latched closed before Renee's lilac-colored fingernails were digging into Winnie's upper arm.

"Look, I realize I'm the one who all but pushed you to track Jay down yesterday afternoon, but I didn't intend for you to jeopardize your business in the process," Renee whisper-yelled. "That girl is a disaster!"

Winnie pulled free of Renee's death grip and motioned Renee to follow her to the far side of the kitchen. Once there, with the refrigerator humming to her left and the wall clock ticking just over her right shoulder, she dropped her own voice to a murmur. "She just got here. You can't know that, Renee."

"Did you see the way Lovey glared when Alicia got within five feet of her?" Renee's emerald green eyes widened at the memory, only to narrow in on Winnie once again.

"Cats know, Winnie. And Lovey knows."

"Lovey reacts that way to me, too," Winnie reminded. "Does that mean *I'm* a disaster?"

Renee paused, considered Winnie's question, and then forged on. "When Lovey glares at you it's — it's . . . different."

"Different?"

"Yes. It's — it's more . . . *loving.*"

She couldn't help it. She snorted. Which, in turn, earned her an elbow in the rib cage.

"Winnie, shhh . . . I don't want her to hear us."

"You're being ridiculous right now."

Renee's overly tweezed left eyebrow rose halfway to the wispy bangs that completed her wash-and-go pixie cut. "Did she not ruin Parker's chess game the second she stepped onto the front porch this morning?"

Closing her eyes against the image of Alicia's tattooed wrist reaching across the tabletop chess board and placing Mr. Nelson in checkmate, she shrugged. "It was a good move."

"Did she not insult Ms. O'Keefe by saying the muffins she brought Parker had seen better days?"

"I —"

Renee's hand shot up in the air. "And did she not look down at Lovey's toy mouse after stepping on it and say, 'Tough break, cat'?"

"Okay," she whispered back. "So she's not exactly sensitive."

Lowering her hand to her side, Renee shifted her weight across her stilettos and copped a gentler, if not still flabbergasted, tone. "Can't Jay just doctor the grade book if he wants her to graduate so bad?"

"He wants her to earn it, Renee."

"But why here? We haven't been in business long enough to take a chance on someone ruining it."

It was a valid point and one she'd entertained at least a half-dozen times since Alicia stepped onto the porch just after nine o'clock. But she'd promised to do this. For three weeks. And once she'd convinced Jay it would be okay, the stress that had been oozing out of his pores when she arrived at his office, éclairs in tow, had virtually melted away in front of her eyes.

She couldn't go back on her offer now . . .

A distinctive click from the opposite side of the room let them know their new intern was on the way out, their brief window of privacy now a thing of the past. "We'll get through this, Renee. I promise."

Alicia came around the corner, stopped halfway into the kitchen, blew a wisp of purple-tipped hair off her forehead, and then pointed at the refrigerator. "So, um, got any beer?"

"We're working, Alicia." Renee pinned the girl with a glare and then widened it to include Winnie. Yet somehow, the meaning behind the glare that was directed at Winnie was vastly different than the glare that was aimed at Alicia. Which was preferable, though, was a toss-up.

Sweeping her heavily ringed hands toward the empty kitchen table, Alicia twisted her mouth into a knowing smirk. "I could get used to this kind of doing-nothing job —"

The ring of the main phone cut the college girl off mid-sentence and sent Renee scrambling for the phone. "Emergency Dessert Squad, please state your emergency."

Alicia rocked back on her sandal-clad feet and crossed her arms in amusement. "She can't be serious . . ."

"She can and she is. This is what we do, Alicia." Winnie moved in beside Renee and followed along with the details making their way from Renee's ear to the order pad in front of them.

Recipient: Melinda B. Tully

Problem: Time to hang it up. End of the road.

Requested Genre: A pie.

46

<u>Suggested Rescue Dessert:</u> Something with blueberries.

Winnie narrowed in on the first and third lines and threw out the first thing that came to mind. "Blueberries . . . blueberries . . . wait! I got it! Would blackberries be okay?" Winnie whispered in Renee's free ear. "We could go with Fade to Black-Berry Crisp! That would tie the theme up well and my blackberry crisp was always one of the bakery's most popular items, remember?"

Renee looked from the pad, to Winnie, and back again, shaking her head in wonder as she repeated the suggestions to the caller. Like clockwork, her shake became a nod and she returned her pen to the order form to record the caller's requests.

<u>Approved:</u> Yes.

<u>Location:</u> Bryant Hall Dormitory — suite 218.

<u>Time requested:</u> Deliver after last class (3:30 p.m.).

She left Renee to take the payment details over the phone and made a beeline for the pantry, the list of ingredients she needed finding its way through her lips. "For this, we need sugar, cornstarch, lemon juice, cooking oats, ground cinnamon, brown sugar, flour, cold butter, and of course, the blackberries." Glancing over her shoulder,

47

she motioned Alicia toward the refrigerator. "I'll need two cups of blackberries and butter. I'll get the rest."

"I don't bake," Alicia said.

"For the next three weeks you do." Winnie gathered up the items she needed, carried them to the small center island Mr. Nelson had installed for her, and then gestured toward the refrigerator once again. "Two cups of blackberries. We need to get this crisp made, into the warming bag, and out to the customer sometime in the next hour."

Alicia yanked the fridge open and stared blankly at the stocked shelves inside.

"Blackberries — in the crisper drawer. Butter — in the butter compartment to your right." She heard the exasperation in her voice and instantly regretted it. Alicia was here to learn. From Winnie.

Like a robot suddenly recognizing its commands, Alicia grabbed the carton of blackberries and the butter and carried it over to Winnie. "So what is this going to be when you're all done?"

"When *we're* all done, it's going to be a blackberry crisp."

"What's a —"

"Do you know where this dorm is located or should I pull up a campus map on the computer?" Renee asked as she returned the phone to the cradle and retrieved the order pad from the table.

Winnie combined the sugar, cornstarch, water, and lemon juice into a small bowl. "I know where it is. We delivered something there the first week or so."

"We're making this for someone at the college?" Alicia asked.

"That's right." When the mixture was at the desired consistency, Winnie set it aside and moved on to a second bowl and the remaining ingredients. "Alicia, I need you to measure out a half cup of oats and a quarter of a cup of flour while I take care of the brown sugar and the cinnamon."

Alicia took a step back and blinked. "Measure?"

"Is there a problem?" Renee snipped.

"Um, I, um . . . maybe I know the person this is going to. And if I do, maybe I know her schedule."

"Pick up the cup with the lines and fill the oats to the half-cup line, and then the flour to the quarter-cup line, Alicia." Renee glanced down at the form in her hand and then back up in time to supervise the intern's wary contributions to the blackberry crisp. "There you go . . . See? It's not so hard."

Alicia peeked over the edge of the bowl

and then leaned against the counter. "There. I baked. Now can I have a beer?"

"No!" Winnie and Renee said in unison.

Groaning, Alicia slunk her way over to the table and dropped onto the closest chair. "This is going to be a long three weeks, isn't it?"

"Yes, yes it is," Renee groaned. "For all of us."

If Alicia caught the meaning behind Renee's comment, it didn't show. Instead, she stretched her legs outward and released a long, drawn-out yawn. "So . . . who's . . . the one . . . getting the cake?"

When Renee refused to answer, Winnie stepped away from the mixing bowl and took the order pad in her friend's hand. "Melinda B. Tully. And it's a crisp. A blackberry crisp."

A yelp of amusement propelled Alicia upright in her chair. "Melinda? Melinda Tully? Are you serious?"

"Is there a problem?" Renee traded the pad for the one-quart baking dish Winnie had set on the counter and began to grease its sides and bottom, her irritation over Alicia's presence evident in the rigor with which she applied the shortening. "Because if there is, you could always give up on the notion of interning here."

Winnie waited for the pan to be done and then poured the blackberries into the bottom, taking control of the conversation as she did. "I take it you know our customer, Alicia?"

"Unfortunately, yes."

Realizing she'd forgotten to preheat the oven, Winnie corrected her mistake, and then poured the ingredients from the first bowl onto the berries. "So why don't you like her?"

"It's like Oprah said . . . let me count the ways."

Winnie paused her hand on the butter she was about to add to the second bowl and looked first at Renee, and then Alicia. "Elizabeth Barrett Browning said that, not Oprah."

Alicia swatted at the air. "Oprah, Elizabeth — whatever. What difference does it make? The words are still the same, right? Anyway, Melinda is beyond annoying. She's always lurking around with that notebook of hers and listening to private conversations that have nothing to do with her. Half the time you don't even realize she's there until she plasters it all over campus."

"All over campus?" Renee echoed.

"She writes the *Caughtcha* column for the college rag and she's caused an awful lot of

51

problems for an awful lot of people." Alicia balled her hands together and thumped them down on the table, narrowly missing the baking dish. "One of the guys I hang out with got kicked off the soccer team last spring because of her, and another friend of mine — Moira — she lost her job at the dining hall because of a story this chick wrote when we were freshmen. And if she doesn't make good on her promise, this whole last-ditch internship thing might not mean a hill of beans if . . ." Alicia's words trailed off momentarily, only to pick back up in a different, angrier spot. "She's ruthless, that's all."

Winnie sprinkled the mixture from the second bowl onto the berries and then carried the pan to the oven. Once it was safely inside and the timer set, she turned back to the college student still seated at the table. "Well, you're going to have to shake off your problems with this girl because you're accompanying me on this delivery as soon as the crisp is done and we've settled on a time."

"You want me to go *with* you to bring her this thing?"

"That's what Winnie just said, isn't it?" Renee gathered up the dirty measuring cups and spoons, dumped them into the empty bowl, and then deposited them on the table in front of Alicia. "For now, though, it's time to get all of this washed and put away so we're ready for the next order when it comes in."

Alicia's mouth gaped open. "Y-you want me to *wash dishes*?"

"Yup."

"I thought I was delivering a crisp to Ms. Snoop."

"You are. *After* you wash dishes."

Winnie was just wiping out Lovey's water dish when she heard the knock at her front door. Startled, she glanced at the stove's digital clock.

Ten fifteen.

"Winnie Girl, are you up?"

Mr. Nelson . . .

Setting the clean bowl on the counter next to the sink, Winnie crossed to the door, disengaged the lock, and flung it open to find both Mr. Nelson and Bridget staring at her from the top step of the interior staircase. "Is everything okay?" she asked before stepping back and gesturing her friends inside.

"We should be asking you that, dear." Bridget preceded Mr. Nelson into Winnie's apartment and then waited with obvious impatience as her cohort caned his way in at a much slower pace.

"You should?"

"Of course. It's a terrible thing. Truly terrible. But we're here for you no matter what, isn't that right, Parker?"

Mr. Nelson used his cane to point into the kitchen. "Got any pie in there, Winnie Girl?"

"Parker!" Bridget stamped her foot once, twice. "Don't you know not to pour salt in a person's open wounds? This is not the time to bring up Winnie's baked goods!"

"Salt in my wounds?" Winnie repeated. "What are you talking about?"

Bringing his cane back down to the floor, Mr. Nelson took a step closer to Winnie. "You're taking it mighty well, Winnie Girl. And I'm proud of you. You've landed on your feet before and you'll do it again."

"Unless the ME comes back with poison. Then she'll be behind bars and shackled to a bedpost." Bridget grabbed hold of her left wrist and held it gingerly. "There must be a weather front coming in because my wrist has been aching all day."

Winnie could feel herself staring. Yes, she knew it was rude, but she couldn't help herself. She had absolutely no idea what they were talking about . . .

"I hope you know, if it comes to that, I'll smuggle Lovey into the visiting room just so she can see you." Mr. Nelson reached out, pushed a strand of hair behind Winnie's ear, and then caned his way into the living room. "So where is she?"

"Sh-she?"

"Lovey," Bridget interjected before following Mr. Nelson over to the couch. "I don't think you can bring cats into prisons, Parker. Then again, I think Bessie Bakerfield's second grandson — the one from her banker son — might be a prison guard. Maybe he'll make an exception for a friend of his grandmother."

Clicking his tongue against the back of his teeth, Mr. Nelson looked around the room, his gaze skirting the cat bed beside the fireplace, the blanket-draped armchair, and the window hammock before landing back on Winnie. "I don't see her anywhere."

"That's because she's on my bed. Sleeping."

Bridget brought her hands to her cheeks and squealed. "See? We told you she'd warm to you, dear."

It felt good to laugh even if it had a sarcastic edge to it. At least, at that moment, she knew what was going on. "She hasn't warmed to me, Bridget, just my bed. And I say this because if I try to get *in* my bed while she's in it, she hisses until I leave."

"Oh."

"Are giving her whipped cream like I suggested?" Mr. Nelson asked as he sank onto the armchair that sat at a removed angle from the couch.

She nodded and slowly ventured her way over to the couch. "I am."

"Are you putting it on the end of your finger?"

"Why? So she can bite it off?" Winnie sat down on the vacant cushion next to Bridget and hugged a throw pillow to her chest. "Lovey still hates me. Nothing has changed."

Bridget clucked again. "You've been through so much, dear. And it just keeps going and going."

Mr. Nelson fussed around with the remote control and then tossed it onto the ottoman at his feet. "So no sign of the men in blue yet?"

That did it.

She was tired of being ten steps behind the conversation . . .

She set the throw pillow on her lap, hiked her calves up and onto the sofa between her and Bridget, and cut to the chase. "I have a feeling I'm supposed to know what the two

56

of you are talking about with shackles and prison and the trials and tribulations of being me . . . but I don't. So could one of you tell me what's going on? Because I've pinched my thigh twice now since you arrived and I know this isn't a dream."

A gasp from her right brought her attention onto Bridget and the woman's paler than normal skin tone.

"Bridget? Are you okay?"

As if she hadn't spoken a word, the elderly woman looked across the hooked rug at Mr. Nelson and slowly shook her head. "She doesn't know, Parker."

Mr. Nelson cleared his throat but said nothing.

Shifting her feet back onto the ground, Winnie stood and looked from Bridget to Mr. Nelson and back again. "I don't know what?"

Bridget opened her mouth to answer but closed it as Renee burst into Winnie's apartment, wide-eyed and out of breath.

"Winnie?" Renee slammed the door behind her and dashed into the kitchen, stopping in her tracks as she saw Winnie in her peripheral vision. "Oh. Good. You're here."

"Where else would I be?" she fairly shrieked.

Tossing her purse and car keys onto the

57

table, Renee strode into the living room and threw her arms around Winnie. "I was so afraid they'd have come and taken you away."

"Taken me —" She stopped, took a deep breath, and extricated herself from Renee's grasp. "Okay. Enough. All of you. What on earth is going on? Why are you all here?"

She saw Renee's emerald green eyes leave her face and travel over her head to, first, Bridget and, then, Mr. Nelson.

"She doesn't know yet," Bridget said between *tsk*s.

"Oh geez." Renee tilted her chin up, stared at the ceiling for a moment, and then returned her gaze to Winnie's. "Melinda B. Tully is dead."

She waited for more but there was nothing. Instead, she filled in the gap with the only question she could find. "Who is Melinda —"

And then she knew.

"I — I . . ."

"Her roommate found her dead on the floor of her dorm room about three hours ago," Renee added.

Something about Renee's expression sent a chill down Winnie's spine. "Wow. That's awful. What happened?"

Renee exchanged a funny look with

Bridget, yet neither of them answered.

Winnie turned to Mr. Nelson. "What aren't you guys telling me?"

Reaching up, he felt around for the clip-on bow tie he generally wore whenever Renee was around and then looked away, swallowing hard as he did.

"Renee?" she tried again.

"They aren't sure just yet, but they suspect she was poisoned," Renee whispered in a voice choked with emotion.

"Okay, so . . ."

Bridget stepped forward, grabbed hold of Winnie's hand, and squeezed. "With your crisp, dear."

"With my —" She stopped, looked at Renee for confirmation she didn't want, and then pulled her hand free of Bridget's. "This is *so* not funny."

"No one is laughing, dear." Bridget shuffled over to Mr. Nelson's chair and slowly winced her way down and onto the edge of the armrest. "No one at all."

CHAPTER 4

Quietly, Winnie pulled the outer door closed behind her and all but tiptoed her way past Mr. Nelson's apartment. Chances were, her friend was tucked away in his bathroom, slathering on cologne in preparation for the noon newscast and his daily sighting of the Channel Five weather anchor anyway, but one could never be too careful. Especially when that one wasn't fit for company.

She trailed Lovey up the stairs and through the partially open door at the top. "I'm back," she called, her voice flat. "Any sign of Alicia while I was gone?"

"*Shhhhh . . .*"

Tossing the empty rescue bag onto the kitchen table, Winnie took stock of the less than clean kitchen and then turned toward the living room. There, huddled up on the couch, were Renee and Mr. Nelson, their collective gaze ricocheting between Winnie and a commercial for a car dealership on the outskirts of Silver Lake.

"Renee?"

"The noon news is about to come on," Renee explained, leaning around Mr. Nelson and offering a half nod–half shrug at what Winnie imagined was the tangible incarnation of her brain's confusion. "I know the kitchen looks bad right now, and I'll take care of it, I promise, but I got a little sidetracked while you were gone, and then Mr. Nelson showed up out of the blue. Next thing we knew, it was time for the news to start and, well, here we are."

"And Alicia?"

"No show, no call."

"And the hits just keep on coming, don't they?" She felt Lovey's tail swish against her leg en route to the food bowl but she kept her focus firmly on her friends. "Anyway, do we have any orders we should be working on right now?"

Renee's green eyes left hers and settled briefly on Mr. Nelson. "No. No more orders."

"*Yet.* There are no more orders *yet,*" she corrected. "Which is why this kitchen really needs to be cleaned, Renee. So we're ready when the next one comes in."

The image of the car giant, best known for commercials involving scantily clad

61

women, faded from her peripheral vision, taking Renee's attention with it. Following suit, Winnie turned and watched as the Channel Five logo claimed the screen and then slid up to reveal the station's noon anchors, wide-eyed and ready to shower their viewers with a collection of stories assembled by a team of faceless and no doubt underpaid reporters.

"Welcome to Silver Lake's most reliable twelve o'clock news show. I'm Seth Dreyer . . ."

The camera pulled back from the forty-something former Silver Lake High School football star and panned in on the petite blonde seated at his elbow. "And I'm Karen Rogers. Let's get to our day's top stories, shall we?"

A full-screen picture of a young girl took center stage while Seth's voice narrated. "The entire Silver Lake College family is grieving the loss of one of its superstar students this afternoon. Melinda B. Tully was just weeks away from graduation and her dream of being a full-time reporter for the award-winning *Cincinnati Ledger*."

More than anything, Winnie wanted to turn away, to busy herself with a kitchen that needed to be cleaned, and a pantry that needed to be inventoried, but she couldn't.

Instead, she inched her way over to the armchair Lovey had yet to claim and sat down, transfixed by the twenty-one-year-old smiling out at her from the sixteen-inch screen.

Slowly, she registered the basics (strawberry blond hair, wide-set brown eyes, a smattering of freckles across the bridge of the nose) as the female anchor picked up the story. "That dream came to an end sometime between six and seven o'clock last night when Melinda's roommate found the girl dead in their dorm room.

"Today, officials are trying to piece together the why — a why that has them looking closely at a delivery service we told you about right here just a few weeks ago."

She heard Renee's gasp as Melinda's face disappeared from the screen and an image of Winnie's Emergency Dessert Squad took center stage.

"Back then, we told you about Winnie Johnson, the former owner of the now defunct Delectable Delights," Seth said, taking back the anchor baton. "Unable to keep up with the rising cost of rent downtown, Johnson was faced with the need to find a new career. But a bequest from a friend in the form of a vintage ambulance gave Johnson and her baking talents new life. Yet now, just several weeks later, the Emergency Dessert Squad, as Johnson aptly named her mobile bakery, has been identified by students at Silver Lake College as the delivery service who visited Tully just hours before her death. In fact, sources on the ground are reporting that a half-eaten dessert, atop a plate emblazoned with the Emergency Dessert Squad logo, was found next to Melinda's body."

This time, the gasp Winnie heard was her own as her Dessert Squad was replaced on the screen by a shot of her pushing a dessert-topped stretcher across the parking lot outside Bryant Hall Dormitory.

"That's my Winnie Girl," Mr. Nelson boasted with pride.

Before she could respond, before she could even truly breathe, a man in his early fifties and fiddling with something in his ear, came into focus, the familiar gray stone exterior that was Bryant Hall at his back.

"We take you to Rick Byrum, on scene at Silver Lake College. Rick, what can you tell us? What is the climate on campus today?"

Pulling his finger from his ear, the on-camera reporter assumed a serious face. "Good afternoon, Seth. Yes, I'm standing here, live, outside Bryant Hall where Melinda B. Tully's body was found less than eighteen hours ago. Her parents arrived here late last night and I spoke with them briefly. Here's what her father had to say . . ."

Jack Tully, according to the name across the bottom of the screen, cleared his throat and pulled his wife close in a sidearm hug. "Melinda was our — our pride and joy. She lit our lives from the moment she was born. Our lives will never be the same without her."

Winnie tried to blink away the tears she felt forming, but it was no use. Her heart ached for the couple even as their taped image was, once again, replaced by that of the live reporter. "And that's the sentiment we've been hearing all day today, Seth." Rick motioned for the cameraman to follow him over to a group of students standing around watching the newsfeed. The camera swung left to reveal a familiar face with its accompanying purple-tipped hair.

"This is Alicia Worth, a student at Silver Lake College." Rick held the microphone out to Alicia. "Did you know the victim?"

Alicia's momentary hesitation led into a nod, her eyes wide. "Melinda and I started at the college at the same time. She was my friend. I — I can't believe she's — she's . . . gone." And just like that, two large tears ran down the girl's face. "We — we were supposed to graduate together in less than three weeks."

"Isn't that the girl who was here yesterday?" Mr. Nelson pulled his wayward hand off Renee's knee and turned to Winnie. "The one who ruined my chess game and told Bridget her muffins were stale?"

She felt her head moving in something resembling a nod, but she couldn't be entirely sure. All she really knew at that moment was that Renee was staring at her with the same anger now raging inside Winnie.

"That conniving little weasel!" Renee rose onto her stilettos and tugged her form-fitting V-neck into place. "First she fails to show up for work on her second day, then she ignores my calls and texts trying to find out where she is, and now she stands in front of all of Silver Lake and *lies*?"

Mr. Nelson took a slow inventory of Renee's legs and then leaned against the back of the couch with a satisfied smile stretching across his weathered face. "Seems to me the reason she ain't here or answerin' calls is because she's mourning her friend's death. Give her time, she'll come around. But when she does, keep her away from my chessboard!"

Winnie opened her mouth to speak but closed it as Renee marched over to the television and then turned back to first Winnie, and then Mr. Nelson. "Oh no. There's no mourning going on with that one. None at all. Those tears you saw just now? Those were crocodile tears. Alicia despised Melinda Tully. She stood right there" — Renee pointed into the kitchen — "and told us that just yesterday morning . . . while Winnie was making that damn blackberry crisp they were . . ."

Something about the way Renee's words trailed off into a strangled inhale sent an answering shiver down Winnie's spine. "Renee? What's wrong?"

"I know we were watching her like a hawk during the prep process, but was she alone with the crisp at any point during the delivery phase?" Renee, realizing Mr. Nelson was trying to catch a glimpse of the weather girl now plastered on the screen, stepped to the side, her eyes still locked on Winnie's.

"I don't think so but it's certainly possible. I *did* tell Jay I'd make her work while she's with us as that's kind of the goal, you know?"

As if on some sort of autopilot setting, Renee wandered across the living room, the clack of her stilettos fading momentarily as she encountered the hook rug, and headed into the kitchen. Halfway to the center island, she stopped, made a quick detour over to the table, and sat down in front of Winnie's favorite notebook and pen. "We need to remember everything she said yesterday on the subject of Melinda. Every last word, every expression, every snide comment."

"We — we do?" Winnie stammered, confused. "Why?"

"Because it's only a matter of time before people start asking all sorts of questions about you, and me, and the Dessert Squad. You heard the newscast just now, Winnie. You're going to be looked at for this. By everyone."

She closed her eyes against a reality she knew to be true yet still couldn't quite comprehend.

Me? Winnie Johnson?

A suspect in a murder?

It was ludicrous. Absolutely ludicrous . . .

"It might be too late for the Dessert Squad, but I refuse to sit back and watch your character be smeared for something that anyone with half a brain knows you're incapable of doing."

She shook herself free of the mental pity party setting up in her head and forced herself to focus on her friend and the pages

68

of notes the woman was writing at warp speed. "Why does it matter what Alicia said yesterday? She's obviously got issues. Jay warned me about that when I agreed to take her on as an intern."

Renee stopped writing and stared at Winnie. "Think about it. One minute this kid is talking about how much she hates your customer, and the next she's crying crocodile tears over that same customer's death. I mean, c'mon. Do the math. Don't you find it all just a little suspicious?"

"Suspicious?" she echoed, only to smack a hand to her mouth as the meaning behind Renee's diatribe hit her with such conviction she actually stumbled backward, knocking Lovey's favorite sleep toy to the floor.

"It's about time you caught up." Renee lowered the tip of her pen back down to the notebook and continued writing. "It's her or you, Winnie, and I'll be damned if I'm going to sit back and let this be pinned on you."

CHAPTER 5

If Winnie didn't know better, she might actually think she'd been cast as the lead character in one of her favorite cozy mystery novels. After all, the police officer seated across the kitchen table from her was hanging on her every word, her loyal sidekicks were within earshot waiting for an opportunity to ride to her defense, and Lovey, the prerequisite feline, was snaking around the legs of all parties involved.

But she did know better.

She, Winnie Johnson, was being questioned in a death — a real death. And as far as *her* reality was concerned, the police officer wasn't drumming his fingers, her sidekicks hadn't interrupted even once, and Lovey kept looking up at her and hissing every time they made eye contact.

"Let's take it from the top again, Miss Johnson." Thomas Wyatt, Silver Lake Police Department's lone detective, pushed the plate of cookies he'd almost singlehandedly annihilated off to the side and leaned forward against the table. "How did you know the victim?"

"I didn't. She was merely my customer this one time."

"Your customer for what, exactly?" he asked.

"My business — the Emergency Dessert Squad. This Melinda B. Tully had an order for a rescue dessert and I delivered it to her dorm."

He jotted a few notes, though why, she wasn't sure. They'd already been over this. Multiple times. "Now, walk me through the entire delivery one more time."

She bit back the sigh she felt building and, instead, hit the mental rewind button on their conversation. "Once the crisp was ready to go, I gathered my things into my rescue bag and headed out the door with my new intern, Alicia Worth."

"And it was just the two of you?" he asked as he gestured his crumb-ridden hand over his shoulder in the direction of the afore-mentioned sidekicks. "No one else?"

"Renee never goes out on a delivery. She stays here and mans the telephone —"

"The dispatch center," Renee corrected from her spot on the living room couch. "I stay here and man the dispatch center and get everything spick and span for the next rescue."

Winnie swung her gaze back to the detective, nodding as she did. "With the exception of yesterday, I make all the rescues alone."

Mr. Nelson hobbled over to the table, reached his hand in front of the detective, and liberated one of the last two remaining cookies for himself. "That's not exactly true, Winnie Girl."

Detective Wyatt's eyebrow hiked upward. "Oh?"

Confused, she peered around the suited man to take stock of the flannel-wearing one just over his left shoulder. "I'm *always* alone, Mr. Nelson," she insisted.

"No you're not."

Her heart began to hammer inside her chest with such force she feared it could be heard on the opposite side of the table. Was the senility Bridget was always accusing Mr. Nelson of having truly kicking in?

"Parker is right," Bridget said, stepping into place beside Winnie's housemate. "Lovey has accompanied you on just about every one of your rescues since you started."

The detective looked down at his feet and then back up at Winnie. "You have a cat riding along with you on your dessert deliveries?"

"I, uh —"

"She sits up front, in the passenger seat," Renee rushed to explain even as she checked the current time on her phone and stood. "Far from the actual dessert."

"Anyway," Winnie continued, "Alicia and I drove across town to Silver Lake College. We accessed the campus via the entrance on the south side and drove directly to the parking lot behind Bryant Hall. I parked. We got out of the ambulance. I pulled the stretcher out of the back and we went into the building."

"Where was the pie?" the detective asked.

It was a question he'd asked every time she retold the story, prompting her to answer it the same way she had the first three times. "The *crisp* was on the stretcher. In the center, to be exact."

"Go on . . ."

Resting her elbows on the table, she tented her fingers beneath her chin and stared up at the ceiling as she found herself back in the elevator of the dormitory in question, the round numbers above the silver door lighting up as she and Alicia rode up to the second floor. When they reached Melinda's floor, the door swished open and Alicia led

73

the way down the hall, looking back periodically at Winnie and the crisp-topped stretcher.

"If I don't get an A in Mr. Morgan's class for this delivery, I give up."

She winced all over again at the slight squeak to the stretcher's front left wheel and remembered making a note to talk to Mr. Nelson about it when she got home. But she hadn't. Now she had to wonder if she'd even get to . . .

Lowering her chin back down to her fingertips, she met the detective's gaze and shared Alicia's comment aloud. When he offered no response in return, she put him into the conversation it had sparked. "When I questioned Alicia on why she thought her grade should go from an F to an A because of one delivery, she referenced how much she despised Melinda."

The detective leaned his gut into the table, narrowing his eyes as he did. "Miss Worth was interviewed by the local media during their noon newscast. She didn't *despise* the victim, Miss Johnson. She was *friends* with the victim."

Renee threw her hands up in the air, the various bracelets on her left forearm clanking against one another. "She was interviewed by the *local media*? Are you kidding me?"

"They'll probably run the interview again on the five o'clock news," Mr. Nelson interjected. "Though that cute little weather girl just does the noon show."

"I don't care if they rerun that interview every second of every day!" Renee marched herself over to the table and stared down at the detective, her ample bosom on clear display over the top of the skintight Emergency Dessert Squad crop top she'd insisted on adding to Winnie's most recent supply order. "It's not the media's job to interview suspects. It's *yours*, Detective."

"I wouldn't consider Miss Worth a suspect," Detective Wyatt protested.

Winnie met Renee's widened eyes across the top of the detective's head and mentally pleaded with her friend to relax. Renee had enough on her plate with her own still-fresh divorce and the unfamiliar role of single motherhood that came with it. The last thing her friend needed was another person to worry about.

But it wasn't Renee who fought back. It was Bridget.

"And that, Thomas Robert Wyatt *the third*, is your second mistake." Bridget stamped her foot on the uncarpeted portion of the living room floor and thrust a finger in the direction of Winnie's uninvited guest. "Don't think I won't be on the phone with Thomas Robert Wyatt *the second* before you so much as touch the last cookie on that plate if you don't turn your ears on, young man, and get with the program."

Uh-oh.

Winnie pushed her chair back and started to stand, but dropped back down as the detective's face turned five shades of red. "M-my *second* mistake, Ms. O'Keefe?"

"That's right, son." Bridget's face softened a smidge but the intensity in her voice remained determined if not downright reproachful. "Your first mistake is being here — asking Winnie questions as if she's a viable suspect in the tragic death of this Melinda B. Tully person."

The detective started to reach for the last cookie but pulled his hand back when Bridget hit him with a death stare. Instead, he pushed his own chair back and cleared his throat. "She *is* a viable suspect, Ms. O'Keefe. She was the last one to see the victim alive."

"I've already told you three times, Detective, that I never saw Melinda. She wasn't back from class when we got to her room. We waited about fifteen minutes until Sam,

76

her RA, showed up."

"Who baked this" — he consulted his notes — "this *crisp,* Miss Johnson?"

"I did."

"Did Miss Worth help?"

Renee's answering snort was so loud and so sudden, Lovey darted off into the bedroom. "Help? Are you kidding me? That one brings new meaning to the word *lazy.*"

Alternating between a wary eye on Bridget and a knowing one on Winnie, the detective sat up tall. "Then if Miss Worth didn't help bake the murder weapon, how can she be a suspect?"

Winnie stopped herself, mid-nod, and swallowed. Hard. He had a point . . .

"Has the ME's report come in yet, Thomas?" Bridget snapped.

"No, but this crispy pie thing was found in the victim's mouth, and next to her body."

Bridget sauntered over to the detective's chair and yanked it backward with a strength Winnie didn't know the woman possessed. "Then these questions you're asking Winnie are premature. That young lady could have tripped and hit her head, she could have choked, or she could have had a hidden medical condition that no one knew about."

Detective Wyatt looked from Bridget to Winnie and back again with a quick visual pit stop on a still-seething Renee. "The toxicology report could be back as early as this weekend."

"Then come back then if it's the crisp." Bridget motioned the forty-something toward the door and then crossed her arms against her chest and waited. "And if it is, you best be certain you question Winnie's intern, too, or I'll be having a word with your father, young man."

When she was confident Detective Wyatt's unmarked car had vacated Serenity Lane, Winnie released her hold on the curtain panel and slumped against the wall. "I didn't think he was ever going to leave," she mumbled.

"Well, he did. And he won't be back unless he has something more concrete."

She abandoned her resting spot and made her way back to the table, her voice choked with a wide range of emotion, not the least of which was gratitude for the cotton-topped woman eyeing her closely. "Bridget, I don't know how to thank you for what you did. Your support means the world to me. It really does."

Slumping onto the table's lone bench seat,

she reached across the wooden surface and covered her elderly friend's hand with her own. "I don't know what to do with any of this. I really don't."

"You didn't kill her, did you, Winnie?"

She pulled her hand back in shock and hurt. "Of course I didn't, Bridget. How — how could you ask that?"

"It wasn't a question I needed you to answer, dear, but rather one asked as a way to remove your worries."

Winnie's gaze moved to the plate and the one cookie Detective Wyatt hadn't eaten. Knowing exactly what needed to be done, she grabbed hold of the plate, carried it across to the trash can, dumped the cookie inside, and waited for the sense of relief she needed.

But it didn't come.

Instead, she pulled the empty plate to her chest and did her best to blink away the tears forming in her eyes. "If it turns out my crisp is what killed her, Bridget, I'm done."

"If it's the crisp, dear, *Alicia* is the one who will be done, not you."

She squeezed her eyes against the fear-inspired reel beginning to play itself out in her head. "In terms of the Emergency Dessert Squad, it won't matter who did it,

Bridget. If it was a dessert from my business, no one will place an order ever again. Heck, no one has placed a call since the noon news and the anchor's *implied* cause of death. Can you imagine if it's confirmed and I had the killer working with me?"

The images in her head faded to reveal a specific face. "And if that happens, Bridget, not only am I without a job and a career, but Renee — who took an enormous leap of faith in signing on for the Dessert Squad in the first place — will be out of work. With a ten-year-old son to raise!"

"People love your desserts, dear. They love the clever names and the clever way in which you deliver them."

She mentally paused the reel long enough to really study her next-door neighbor. Short and stout, Bridget O'Keefe was a force to be reckoned with both in her role as a gossip columnist for the *Silver Lake Herald* and on her home turf of Serenity Lane. Despite the woman's propensity for bemoaning a long list of health issues — both real and imagined — she was sharp as a tack on the ways of the world. "Come on, Bridget, you know none of that will mean a hill of beans if that same business everyone thinks is so clever is tied to the murder of a college student!"

Before Bridget could comment, the reel began moving again, only this time, instead of Renee's face, it had moved on to a different one — one with the most beautiful blue-green eyes she'd ever seen. "I was just trying to help him, that's all."

"Help whom?"

"Jay. I just thought that if Alicia could get a real behind-the-scenes taste of an honest-to-goodness small business, and truly apply herself for the next three weeks, that it would help. But all I did was make things worse."

"If Alicia did this, *you* didn't make things worse, dear, *she* did," Bridget insisted.

"He just wanted the girl's grandmother to see her graduate. Now, if this really happened, all this dying woman is going to see is her granddaughter being locked up for murder. And why? Because I stuck my nose in where it didn't belong."

Bridget slowly rose to her feet and waddled her way around the table. When she reached Winnie's side, she cupped Winnie's face in between her hands and rested their foreheads against each other's. "If this happened — and Winnie, we know nothing concrete yet — you will be as much of a victim in all of this as Melinda. No one — not Renee and not Jay — will blame you for any of this. How could they?"

More than anything, she wanted to believe Bridget was right. Yet something about the whole situation made it impossible to do so. Maybe it was just all too close. Maybe she hadn't really given herself a chance to process the facts . . .

"Thank you, Bridget," she whispered. "Thank you for standing by me and believing in me."

"Anyone who knows you and loves you feels the same, dear. Of that I'm certain." Bridget stepped back, releasing her hold on Winnie's cheeks as she did. "I've seen the way that young man looks at you, Winnie. Nothing about any of this can change that."

"You really believe that?" Winnie lifted her gaze to Bridget's and held her breath in anticipation of an answer she desperately needed to hear.

Yet instead of words, Bridget simply recovered Winnie's phone from the center island, placed it inside Winnie's palm, and then waddled her way across the kitchen and over to the door.

"Wait! Where — where are you going?" Winnie stammered.

"Home."

"But why?"

"Because I'm tired and I'm hungry, that's why."

"I can make a — a roast! Or a stew, if you'd rather!"

A flash of something that looked a lot like hope ignited behind Bridget's bifocals, only to disappear with a fierce shake of her head. "Call him, Winnie. Let him console you and get you back on your feet. You'll be your old determined go-getter self again once you do."

CHAPTER 6

There was no denying the hush that fell across nearly every table and booth in Beans the moment Winnie stepped through the doorway. It was as if her entrance had been timed with some sort of mandatory no-talking ordinance put into place by Silver Lake officials. The whole thing had an eerie feeling about it, almost as if she'd been transported back to high school and that one particular moment in her junior year when she'd mistakenly wandered into the middle of a cheerleader meeting, wearing a shirt she'd borrowed from her mother.

In fact, the lip curl sported on more than a few of the faces staring back at her now was nearly identical to the one Betsy Rydale had sported mere seconds before the round of raucous laughter that had driven her back into the hallway seventeen years earlier.

She considered glancing over her shoulder in the event the uncomfortable silence was aimed at someone or something else, but what was the point? Silver Lake was a small town. News had a way of traveling around its restaurants, across its picket fences, and through its parks faster than the speed of light.

"Back here, Winnie!"

Slowly, she scanned the booths to her left, the line of patrons to her right, and the row of two-person tables along the far wall until she found the man who went with the voice. Then, mustering the most convincing smile she could find, she picked her way through the crowd and fairly collapsed into the empty chair across from Jay.

"So much for hoping people don't watch the local news," she mumbled just loud enough for Jay to hear.

His mouth inched upward but stopped well shy of an actual smile. Before she could dissect his response, he gestured toward the wall-mounted chalkboard and its colorful list of daily specials and regular menu items. "So what can I get you?"

"I — I'm okay. I know you have a limited window before you have to pick Caroline up from dance." She inched her fingers across the table and waited for him to intertwine them with his own, but he didn't. "I'm just glad you had some time. I could really use a — a friendly ear."

He pushed his chair back and stood. "I'm gonna get us both a hot chocolate. Sound good?"

She started to answer but he was across the room and merging in with the line before she knew what was happening. The bounce she managed to hold off in her thigh traveled to her opposite hand and she pressed it firmly against the tabletop.

Relax . . .

You're probably reading into something that isn't there . . .

Taking in a deep breath, Winnie allowed herself a recheck of the room. A few eyes still peeked over at her, but for the most part, the dull roar of noise that was as much a part of downtown Silver Lake's hip spot as the coffee it served was back and she was glad. Some of the faces she spotted around the café had been regulars at Delectable Delights; others were simply familiar in a normal small town way.

She glanced back toward the line. Jay was now at the register, placing his order, and she used the opportunity it gave her to drink him in. Yet as she did, she couldn't help noticing the slight slump to his normally confident posture and the way he seemed to be nervously fiddling with the napkin holder, his keys, and the coins in his hand.

Feeling her leg begin to bounce again, she forced herself to look away, to focus on something besides the dread she felt building in the pit of her stomach. She settled on the café itself.

Unlike its longtime predecessor, Silver Lake Coffee Shop, Beans oozed the sort of hip feeling her former landlord, Nick Batkas, was convinced Silver Lake needed. It was present in everything from the expansive (and colorful) chalkboard menu, to the high top tables with the bar-like stools. The walls were decorated with photographs of foreign cities and various travel memorabilia. Behind a glass partition bumped out from the back wall, customers could watch coffee beans being roasted. Overhead, music with a steady, almost headache-inducing beat wafted through the dull roar of background conversation.

"Your hot chocolate . . ."

She leaned back to allow him room to set down her oversized ceramic mug and smiled up at him. "Thanks, Jay."

"My pleasure." He lowered himself onto his own chair and busied himself with what seemed like an unnecessarily long sip of his drink. When he was done, he set the mug down and modulated his voice down to a level only she could hear. "Talk to me."

And just like that, the resolve that had accompanied her to the coffee shop disappeared, leaving in its place the same hopelessness she'd felt since Renee and company had arrived on her doorstep the previous night. "It's all blowing up in front of my eyes — the business, my livelihood, *Renee's* livelihood, my" — she scanned the room one more time — "*reputation.*

"I mean, one minute things were really beginning to look promising, like maybe Batkas did me a favor or something when he raised the rent on the bakery so high I had no other choice but to do something different. Word of mouth was really starting to drive business. And then . . . yesterday . . . or rather, *because* of yesterday . . . it's all changed."

His jaw noticeably tightened just before he took another pull from his mug. After what seemed like an eternity, he raked his hand through the light brown hair at the top of his head, the motion doing little to affect the hint of gray that peppered the area around his temples. "You mentioned on the phone that there was a cop at your house this afternoon?"

"Detective Wyatt — Thomas Wyatt."

The blue-green eyes that normally sparkled when they looked at her were dull at best as he leaned heavily against the back of his chair. "What did he say?"

"He seems to think my crisp had something to do with this Melinda girl's death. Which, of course, has him looking at me as the one who baked it." She wrapped her hand around the mug and willed the warmth of its ceramic sides to chase away the chill making its way through her body. "Everything that was used in the crisp was newly purchased and all expiration dates were checked. That's one of the things Renee does and one of the things I've always been borderline obsessive about checking myself — when Renee isn't looking, of course."

When Jay said nothing, she rushed to fill in the awkward silence. "But I don't get the sense they are looking at this as an accident. They seem to think this girl's death was deliberate. We just need to wait now and see if the medical examiner confirms that it was murder and, if so, how she was killed. I pray it wasn't my crisp, although based on what I saw when I walked in here just now, I'm not sure that will matter. The damage is already done."

She waited for him to speak, to try to lift her spirits or express his sympathy, but —

Bolting upright in her chair, she released her hold on her mug and splayed her hands atop the table. "Oh, Jay, I'm so sorry. I — I've been so wrapped up in everything that's going on as it pertains to *me,* that I failed to consider its impact on *you.* I'm so so sorry. Did you know Melinda well? Did you have her in one of your classes?"

"She wasn't in any of my classes, but I knew her." He checked his watch and then took another sip of his now nearly empty drink. "Everyone did — one way or the other."

"Meaning?" she prodded.

"If you're connected to Silver Lake College in any way, you know Melinda. The articles she wrote for the campus newspaper had a way of catching attention."

"In what way?"

He shrugged. "A few of our departments ended up getting recognized for classes they offer and faculty members who excel beyond the norm, because of Melinda's work."

Her curiosity piqued, she leaned forward, waiting for even the slightest reciprocating gesture from Jay. But it didn't come. "So she was good at what she did?"

"Very good. Some might even say *too* good."

"I don't understand."

"Melinda's forte was investigative journalism, hence the title of her monthly feature: *Caughtcha*. She got a charge out of uncovering stuff people didn't know — the juicier the stuff, the better. That young lady exposed a gambling ring among the college's maintenance staff when she was a freshman, a teacher in the English department who was employing a random grading technique during her sophomore year, and a little illegal recruiting on the part of the school's soccer coach at the end of her junior year."

Running the tip of her index finger around the rim of her mug, Winnie considered Jay's description, realizing it meshed with the one Alicia had given a little over twenty-four hours earlier.

Alicia . . .

She pulled her hand into her lap and tried to frame her next question in such a way as to avoid heaping any more stress on the man seated across from her than was absolutely necessary. Still, she needed answers. "H-have you spoken to Alicia today?"

"No. She's missing my class to work with you, remember?"

"She didn't come in today," Winnie said.

Jay drew back in his chair. "She didn't? Why not?"

She weighed her various responses and

91

went with the one twisting her gut most. "Well, if you happened to catch the noon newscast today, she's mourning Melinda. But if you heard what she had to say about Melinda right up until we delivered the girl's crisp, you might be a little skeptical of that reason."

"She didn't call? Didn't tell you why she wasn't coming in?"

Sensing his growing irritation, Winnie tried to soften things with a shrug. "It's okay. Today wasn't a normal day for any of us. I'm sure she'll be back tomorrow. Assuming, of course, that there even *is* a tomorrow for the Dessert Squad . . ."

She hadn't meant for her voice to crack on the last part of her sentence, but considering everything that had happened that day, and the cloud of uncertainty hanging over her company, it made sense. What didn't make sense, however, was the way Jay tapped the face of his watch and rose to his feet as if he hadn't noticed.

As if he didn't care . . .

"Well, I better head out. Caroline's class is ending in about ten minutes and I've got to get her right home. She has a test in biology tomorrow and needs her rest."

She opened her mouth to tease him about needing ten minutes to walk out the coffee shop's front door and up half a block to the dance studio, but something inside her made her stop.

A week earlier, he'd have reached for her hand and walked with her out to her car before heading into the studio to get his daughter.

A week earlier, he'd have caught the crack in her voice and refused to move from the table until he had done everything in his power to make her smile again.

Now all he did was drop his gaze to the floor, nod in her general direction, and then turn and make his way through the maze of coffee drinkers to the front door and the sidewalk beyond. She watched him disappear from view and then dropped her forehead into her palms, the tears she'd been fighting to hold back all day gathering with an intensity far stronger than she.

How could things go from being so wonderful to so awful in the blink of an eye? How could people in her own community think she was a kill —

Snapping her head up off her hands, she hit the mental rewind button on her brief time with Jay.

The dull eyes . . .

The inability to make eye contact . . .

The hint of nervousness . . .

The rush to leave . . .

She heard the gasp as it left her lips, even registered — on some level — the encore of stares trained on her face. But it didn't matter. Nothing mattered except the crushing reality that sent her running toward the door and the safety of Serenity Lane.

CHAPTER 7

There were times when Winnie wished the driveway couldn't be seen from Mr. Nelson's front window. Sure, she loved the man dearly, but he hadn't come by his nickname, Nosy Nelson, by accident.

If someone on Serenity Lane walked by and sneezed, Mr. Nelson knew it. Not because he heard the sneeze, but because he witnessed the sneeze. If a neighbor had a guest over, he not only knew the make and model (and year, in most cases) of the car they drove, but knew how long they stayed and what, if anything, they carried into or out of the house.

Unless, of course, he was napping, watching his favorite weather girl on the news, mooning after Renee, or playing chess with himself on the front porch. Then, and only then, was he not in the know.

In fact, Mr. Nelson's ability to know things the average person missed was a bone of contention between the man and their next-door neighbor (aka *Silver Lake Herald* Gossip Columnist), Bridget O'Keefe.

Sometimes, after a particularly long day at her now defunct bakery, Winnie had just wanted to collapse on her living room couch and read . . . or watch TV . . . or sleep. But Mr. Nelson was always waiting for her, checking to make sure she was okay and eager for a little conversation.

Tonight, though, she welcomed the sight of his face, peeking out around his living room curtain. She knew, from experience, that by the time she reached their shared interior foyer, he'd be caning his way over to his door. She also knew that she'd be on the second step when he'd invariably poke his head into the hall and say, "Winnie, is that you?"

More than anything, she needed Mr. Nelson's levelheadedness, even if it meant having to remind him to turn his hearing aid up. Maybe, just maybe, he could help turn her mood around. Short of that, maybe he'd dispense one of his hugs that always had a way of making the worst situations seem a little less awful.

She cut the engine, dropped the key into her purse, stepped out of the ambulance, and followed the flagstone walkway to the front porch. Rarely used during the long winter months, it became the go-to spot for Winnie and Mr. Nelson from the first sign of spring until the final days of fall. Here, she shared tidbits of her day with her friend, while he entertained her with jokes. If she wasn't quick on her feet and aware of her surroundings at all times, it was also the place he loved to stage his pranks — mindful of the chance for a greater audience than he'd have behind closed doors. When she read in one of the rockers, he challenged himself at the chessboard. And lately, the porch had housed more than a few brainstorming and tasting sessions for Winnie's new Dessert Squad.

Rarely a day went by when she didn't send up a prayer of thanks for renting this apartment, in this home, on this street, with this housemate — because really, she couldn't be any luckier (present situation with Melinda's murder and Jay's suspicions excluded, of course).

Two steps from the door, she changed course and made her way over to Mr. Nelson's open window, the thump of his cane on the other side of the screen confirming his proximity to where she would have been had she actually gone inside. "Mr. Nelson, can you meet me on the porch?"

she called.

The thumping paused and then picked up speed, prompting her to hightail it back to the door in order to hold it open for her elderly friend. "How was your evening with your young man, Winnie Girl?"

Once he was safely beyond the reach of the door, she closed it and wandered over to the front railing, her steps heavy, her heart still heavier. "I don't think he's too keen on the idea of being my young man anymore, Mr. Nelson."

The thump of his cane over her left shoulder ceased, and she turned to make sure he was okay. He, in turn, looked at her with such concern she knew it was only a matter of time before she was wiping her cheeks with the handkerchief he kept in the front left pocket of his flannel shirt.

"Come. Sit." Mr. Nelson lowered himself to the first of the two outdoor rockers and waited for Winnie to claim the other. When she did, he reached across the open divide between their respective armrests and covered her hand with his. "What happened, Winnie Girl?"

"He thinks I killed that girl yesterday."

Mr. Nelson's brows scrunched downward. "Distilled a girl? Is that some sort of new-fangled talk?"

"No." She tapped her ear and waited for her friend to turn up the volume on his hearing aid. When his hand returned to hers, she repeated her original words. "He thinks I killed that college girl yesterday."

His answering whistle was all she needed to know he was caught up. The flash of anger in his normally mischievous eyes let her know he wasn't happy. "Did he say that?"

"Not in so many words, no. But the whole time I was with him at the coffee shop he kept checking his watch like he wanted to be anywhere but there . . . with me. He wouldn't look me in the eye, he barely said a word, and he beat it out of there eight minutes sooner than he needed to in order to pick his daughter up from dance class."

"Maybe he was distracted by something else," Mr. Nelson suggested.

She tried to shrug, to act as if it didn't matter one way or the other, but once the tears started, they wouldn't stop. And with them came the verbal edition of the stream of consciousness that had accompanied her home from the coffee shop. "I know we've o-only known each other a short time b-b-but . . . me? A killer? I — I make desserts for a living . . . I blush when Renee curses . . . I —"

"Prove him wrong."

"It's not just him, Mr. Nelson." She smacked the back of her head against the top of the rocker and stared at the ceiling in an attempt to stop any more tears from running down her cheeks. "It's the — the whole town. You should have seen the reaction from everyone inside Beans when I walked in the door. All . . . conversation . . . ceased. Everyone stared. At me."

It was no use. The tears wouldn't stop. They just kept coming and coming, faster and faster. And then she felt it — a soft, linen-type object being shoved into her hand . . .

Lifting her head upright, she held Mr. Nelson's handkerchief against her face and let the fabric absorb as many of her tears as possible.

"Prove them *all* wrong, Winnie Girl — every last one of 'em."

"How? This whole . . . thing is . . . is going to . . . destroy the — the Dessert Squad," she said between breaths.

"Batkas essentially destroyed your bakery by raising your rent, didn't he?"

She nodded behind the handkerchief.

"You didn't give up then, did you? You rolled up your sleeves, put on your thinking cap, and now you've got *that*."

She lowered the handkerchief to her chin and followed the path of his finger to the ambulance parked in their driveway. "B-but this is . . . different. People think I — I killed someone . . . with my . . . with my baking!"

Hooking the same finger he'd used to point the way to the driveway, he slid it underneath her chin and guided her watery gaze in his direction. "You took the bull by the horns then, and you'll take the bull by the horns now."

"How?"

"Prove to everyone you didn't do it."

"How?" she asked again.

"By giving everyone the *right* person to point and stare at."

She tried to follow what he was saying, but her head was so full and her heart so heavy, that it was hard to focus. "I don't know who the right person is."

"Then figure it out."

Figure it out . . .

"You did that with Bart's killer," Mr. Nelson reminded. "Of course, I had to save you with my lightning-quick reflexes."

For the first time all evening, she smiled a genuine smile — one born of love for the wiry man seated by her side. "Your lightning-quick reflexes, huh?"

He lifted the end of his cane off the

ground and motioned it toward the door. "Now I want you to go inside, get those tears washed off your pretty face, and hop into bed. Everything is always a little easier to tackle in the daylight."

She wouldn't lie — the thought of slipping under the sheets and saying goodbye to such an awful day was more than a little appealing. Still, Mr. Nelson had exerted a lot of energy to get himself onto the porch . . .

"Let me see you inside before I do," she offered.

"I'm fine out here, Winnie Girl. There's somethin' about bein' out here that helps me plan my own horn grabbin'."

Standing, she held her hand out to her friend and waited for him to grab hold and lift himself off the rocker. But he didn't. "Mr. Nelson, I don't want you losing sleep worrying about my problems. You're right. I need to get to the bottom of what happened to Melinda B. Tully. But I can do it by myself."

"That ain't the horn grabbin' I'm plotting."

"Oh?"

"No siree. Mine is making sure that Mayor Rigsby and Councilmen Medders and Rawlings don't stand by, blindly letting that Batkas fella ruin our town."

Realizing he had no intention of standing, she dropped her hand to her side. "What's he up to now, Mr. Nelson?"

"He's taking work from our own residents."

"How?"

"I'm not sure. But it's happening. You know that intersection that's been needing attention for years now? The one on the way to the park?"

She nodded.

"A company from Batkas's town won the bid."

"Maybe his price was better," she suggested.

"Coming from an hour away? I doubt that. Something else is going on, I'm sure of it."

Lifting her fingers to her left temple, she tried to knead away the headache she felt forming — a by-product of all the crying, no doubt. But no matter how much she rubbed, the pain only intensified. "Nick isn't a nice guy, Mr. Nelson. Maybe you should stay out of it."

"That fella doesn't scare me, Winnie Girl. I was in the Navy, remember?"

She had to smile at the tidbit she'd been told and overheard virtually every day since moving in some two-plus years earlier. "I remember."

"Then you should know I'm not going to stand by and twiddle my thumbs while something crooked is going on. I helped elect the officials in this town and you can be sure I'll help vote them back out if they're not operating in the best interests of Silver Lake and its residents."

She wanted to ask more, but it would have to be later, when the pounding in her head was gone and she could think. "I'm here if you need my help."

"Same holds true on my end, Winnie Girl. You know that, right?"

"I do. And it's one of a bazillion reasons I adore you, Mr. Nelson." She leaned forward, whispered a kiss across his wrinkled forehead, and then turned and headed toward the door, stopping to look back at him one more time before she called it a night. "You sure you're okay out here? I mean, I could help you get inside and turn off the porch light before I head upstairs for the night."

"I'm just fine out here on my own. Now go on in and get some sleep. You need it."

"Thank you, Mr. Nelson."

"Make sure you give that cat of yours a big cuddle before you get in bed. Animals have a way of making everything better."

She half laughed, half sighed at the ridiculousness of the man's words. "Please. If I cuddled Lovey, she'd scratch my eyes out. You know that."

"Give her time, Winnie Girl. Give her time."

"If she's still hissing at me after six weeks, I'm pretty sure time isn't our issue, Mr. Nelson."

CHAPTER 8

Winnie pushed her notebook and pen across the kitchen table to Renee. "I came up with a couple of new dessert ideas while I was in the shower this morning."

"And?"

"And I want to try them out on you and see what you think. If you like them, we can add them to the list."

Renee took the pen, twirled it between her now-fuchsia-tipped fingers, and then deposited it back on the table. "The writing is on the wall, Winnie. It doesn't matter if we add ten more cute names to the menu or give away dessert for free, this whole thing with this college kid has destroyed us."

She felt the answering flip of her stomach but refused to give it any credence. "Don't you think that's a little premature to say?"

Renee spun her phone around, lit up the screen with a push of a button, and held it up for Winnie to see. "It's eleven o'clock,

Winnie. The phone hasn't rung with an order or an inquiry even once. I think that's telling us something, don't you think?"

"We've only been in business six weeks. We've had quiet mornings before." But even as she spoke, Winnie knew her words weren't meshing with reality. Sure, they'd had quiet mornings — in the beginning. But since word started getting out about what they did and how it worked, those quiet mornings had become a little less quiet.

"Winnie, I —"

She placed her palms on the table and pushed to a stand, her need to follow Mr. Nelson's line of thinking overpowering. "Look, Renee, there was nothing wrong with that crisp. I baked it right here in this kitchen the way I've baked every other order for the past six weeks. I am not going to roll over and let this destroy our business. I'm just not. I can't. And I won't."

Renee, too, stood, only instead of pacing around the table as Winnie was starting to do, she made a second stop at the coffee-maker with her now empty mug. "So what do you suggest?"

"We prove to everyone in this town that the Emergency Dessert Squad had nothing to do with Melinda B. Tully's death."

"And if the ME comes back with the crisp

as the cause of her death?" Renee slowly turned to face Winnie, her usually limitless amount of energy falling somewhere between subdued and nonexistent. "What then?"

"There's no way it can."

Renee looked down into her mug of black coffee and then back up at Winnie. "I have to ask you again, was Alicia ever alone with the crisp?"

"Meaning?"

"Did you break off to go to the restroom when you got to campus?"

"No."

"When that other girl — the RA — let you into the room, had you gone off in search of someone to help you?"

"No. She saw us and came over." She made another lap around the table and then stopped beside the notebook, keenly aware of the hope it represented. "Renee, please. Can I just tell you my dessert names? They're really kind of cute . . . and fun. We need that right now."

For a moment, she thought her friend was going to protest. But Renee reclaimed her spot at the table and flipped open the notebook. "Okay, lay them on me."

Winnie lapped back around to her own side of the table, yet remained standing.

"Black and Blue Cookies — for someone who has suffered a fall or gotten banged up in an accident of some sort."

"Black and *blue*?" Renee clarified even as she added the name to the list. "So I need to make sure we have blue food coloring in the pantry, yes?"

"We do. I checked when I got out of the shower." She pointed at the notebook and kept going. "A Grin and Bear (It) Claw for someone who is getting a little tired of their boss, or a family member who is driving them nuts."

Renee laughed. "And we'll put the *it* in parentheses, yes?"

"Exactly."

When it had been added to the list, Renee looked up. "Anything else?"

She gave in to the squeal she felt building and lowered herself back onto the bench. "This one is adorable. Ready?"

Renee waved the pen in front of Winnie and made a face. "Doesn't it look like I'm ready?"

"Kootchy-Kootchy-Koo Kuchen!"

"Kootchy-Kootchy-Koo Kuchen?" Renee repeated.

"You know, that thing people say when they're tickling someone? This will be for someone who needs a happy little lift. An edible tickle, so to speak."

"But what's a Kuchen?"

"It's essentially a German coffee cake, but you can add a variety of different things to it depending on a person's particular palate. I can do peach, apple, or even custard, if they want."

"Kootchy-Kootchy-Koo Kuchen," Renee said, adding it to the list. "I really don't know how you come up with this stuff."

She shrugged. "I don't know, either. It just kind of comes to me. Anyway, I say we make them so we can add pictures of them to the website."

Renee's smile disappeared as she met Winnie's gaze across the table. "Winnie, I'm —"

"Don't. Please. Can't we just be happy for a few more minutes?" When Renee said nothing, she continued, the boost she'd managed to get from sharing her latest round of dessert ideas quickly waning. "Alicia is just a kid, Renee."

"That doesn't mean she couldn't have done this. You heard her on Monday when I said the name of the person the order was for. She started running off at the mouth, telling us all the reasons she couldn't stand this girl. Yet, twenty-four hours later, she's publicly mourning the very same person as if they'd been best friends?" Renee book-marked the page of ideas with the pen and then closed the notebook. "C'mon, Winnie. That should be raising some red flags for you just like it is for me."

"But —"

"And to top it all off, she hasn't shown up for her internship duties here since this girl was killed."

"She's lazy, Renee. I knew this when I took her on."

To help a man who now thinks I'm a murderer . . .

She shook off the troubling reminder and forced herself to focus. Mr. Nelson was right. It was up to her to take the proverbial bull by the horns. And she would. She just didn't want her quest to lead to Alicia.

"Lazy, no doubt," Renee agreed. "But I think we need to consider another reason for her failure to show up here again."

"Another reason?"

"Guilt."

She drew back, confused. *"Guilt?"*

"For using your company to carry out her own agenda."

"Renee . . ."

"If the crisp killed Melinda, Alicia is the only possibility." Renee leaned forward against the table. "You know this, Winnie."

The truth was, she did. The part that didn't make any sense, though, was why she was fighting it so hard. After all, if Jay could think Winnie capable of hurting someone, she really shouldn't be afraid to think the same of his student . . .

Take the bull by the horns, Winnie Girl. Prove them wrong.

Reaching across the table, she swiped Renee's mug and took a fortifying sip. Then, returning the drink to its original spot before her friend protested, she got to her feet and resumed the pacing that always helped her think. "Okay, so Sam, the RA, heard us knocking on Melinda's door and she came out into the hall. I told her why we were there and that we had a delivery for Melinda. She said she couldn't let us in without permission from Melinda or Melinda's roommate, but we could leave it on *her* desk until either Melinda or the roommate returned."

"Wait. You left it with someone else?" Renee asked quickly.

"We didn't really have any other choice. Sam wasn't sure if Melinda would be back in ten minutes or an hour, and I couldn't justify wasting that kind of time."

Renee smacked her hand down on the table so hard the remaining coffee inside her mug swished up against the sides and threatened spillage. "Uh, hello? Winnie? Maybe this Sam girl did something to it?"

Winnie stopped pacing and waved off her friend's latest theory. "No. Sam was nice. Those two were definitely friends. In fact, I had to move a whole pile of Melinda's stuff — papers and pictures, mostly — off to the side of Sam's desk to even have a place to set the crisp down."

"But that wasn't Melinda's room, right?"

"No. Melinda's room was across the hall and down one. But from what Sam said, there was a whole bunch of tension between Melinda and her roommate as of late and so Melinda was using Sam's room as a sort of escape to do her homework and to hang out in when she wasn't working on a story for the campus paper or studying in the library."

Renee's eyes narrowed in on Winnie. "Tension with her roommate?"

"It happens. Especially at this time of year. These kids are crazed over finals, stressed over graduation, and scared about all those post-college unknowns." Winnie bypassed her tried-and-true pacing route in favor of the window and a sleeping Lovey. Without thinking, she reached out and ran her hand from the top of the cat's head all the way to her tail before Lovey wised up and realized the hand was attached to her full-time nemesis.

Hissss . . .

She yanked her hand back to her side and stepped over to the second window and the view it provided of Serenity Lane. The street was quiet as it usually was at this time of day with most of its elderly residents inside eating lunch. Soon, many would lie down for a short nap and then be outside again in droves — gossiping, gardening, and keeping watch over the comings and goings of their neighbors.

"So let me get this straight. You and Alicia, who we well know despised the victim, left the dessert in question in another girl's room and —"

Lifting her chin to the noon sun, Winnie tried to keep her answer void of the impatience she felt. "Sam didn't do anything to the crisp. I'm as certain of that as I am of the fact that *I* didn't."

"You're easy — you had no motive. But you don't know if this Sam person had one or not."

"I do know about Sam," she argued.

"How?"

"She had pictures of her grandparents all over her dorm room." Even with her back

114

to Renee, she could feel her friend's disdain. She turned and met it, head-on. "You can think I'm a freak if you want, but I'm confident she had nothing to do with what happened to Melinda. End of discussion."

Renee looked as if she was about to argue but thought better of it. Instead, she lifted her index finger into the air and pointed at Winnie. "Fine. But don't you tell me I can't wonder about Melinda's roommate. If the tension between them was so uncomfortable Melinda escaped to this Sam girl's room all the time, maybe the roommate did something to the crisp."

"How?"

"You just said that Sam offered to hold on to the crisp until either Melinda or the roommate returned to their room. Maybe the roommate got back before Melinda and stuck something inside it."

Slowly, Winnie returned to the table and the bench she'd left multiple times already that morning. "That would certainly open up the means with which to do it."

Renee began nodding before Winnie was even done speaking. "Exactly! And whatever caused the tension could, potentially, be the motive."

Was Renee right? Had they just put two and two together and come up with the culprit behind Melinda's death?

Take the bull by the horns, Winnie Girl. Prove them wrong.

Once again, she rose to her feet, only this time, instead of pacing, she grabbed her keys from their hook beside the door and jingled them in Renee's direction. "Call me if anything comes up. And in the meantime, get those new dessert names up on the website. We'll add the pictures later."

CHAPTER 9

She slowed for the traffic light near the center of Main Street and instinctively turned her head to the right, her focus narrowing in on the Corner Pocket Billiards Hall, which had, until two months earlier, been a bakery — *her* bakery.

In some ways it seemed like just yesterday she'd been whipping up desserts in the small back kitchen each morning, and chatting with her regular customers off and on throughout the day. Yet at other times, as it did at that moment, it seemed like forever since she'd packaged up a half-dozen specialty cupcakes and handed them to someone across the glass-fronted cabinet.

Things had been easier with the bakery. Customers came in and out all day long and —

The ring of her phone interrupted her thoughts and she returned her focus to the traffic light, which was now green, and the unmistakable exhaustion in her voice as she hit the speaker button. "Hello?"

"Hello, dear, it's me — Bridget. I apologize in advance if my voice sounds a bit strained, but I think I have a growth forming on my vocal chords."

She offered the appropriate sympathy she knew was required, and then did her best to suggest another, more likely, alternative to the medical doomsday scenario her friend frequented. "There are an awful lot of plants and trees blooming right now, Bridget. Perhaps it's your allergies . . ."

"No, I'm certain it's a growth." Bridget paused to let her dire diagnosis sink in and then moved on. "I'd ask if you heeded my advice yesterday and reached out to Jay, but Parker filled me in when I was heading out to the newspaper office this morning."

"I'm okay, Bridget." Then realizing whom she was talking to, she offered a more reality-based addendum. "Or I'm trying to be."

"Did you get any orders this morning?"

She slowed to a stop, waved a male pedestrian across the street, and then watched as he stepped onto the sidewalk and peered into the window of what had once been Silver Lake Pizza. "Um, Bridget? Do we know what's going into the space where

Tony and Lizzy's place used to be?"

"Another restaurant."

A honk from behind forced her to keep moving but her thoughts, her words, stayed rooted at the same spot. "Do you know what kind?"

"No idea, dear." Bridget stopped, muttered something unintelligible, and then added, "But whatever it is, I'm sure it will be something over the top. Because this new generation of let-my-device-do-everything-for-me-including-think wants to have an *experience* when they eat."

"I keep wondering when Batkas is going to take a good hard look at the demographic in this town and realize there's far more elderly than there are hipsters."

"He's preparing. For when we all die off."

"Bridget!"

"That, dear, is *his* quote, not mine. Though with this growth forming on my foot, he might not have to wait too long for me to go."

The notion of reminding her neighbor that the growth was in her throat, not her foot, ran through Winnie's head, but it stopped shy of her lips as it always did. Bridget was a hypochondriac for sure, but she was also a tremendous friend — one Winnie was lucky to have. Instead, she changed the subject entirely. "How's your next column coming along?"

The responding pause was back, only this time it lingered long enough that Winnie actually glanced down at the phone to make sure they were still connected. "Bridget? Are you still there?"

"I wanted to warn you about this weekend's paper, dear."

"Warn me?" she echoed.

"There will be a picture of your crisp in the first section — possibly on the front page."

She pulled off to the side of the road and shifted into park. "M-my crisp?"

"The blackberry one," Bridget clarified, although no clarification was needed. "I had a picture of it in my file."

"Why?"

"It was from that story I did on the bakery last year."

"No. I mean, why are you running the picture again this weekend?" she asked.

"Because it's the last thing Melinda Tully ingested before her death."

She threw her head back against the headrest and squeezed her eyes closed. "It's been confirmed then?"

"I'm sorry, dear."

"It's not your fault, Bridget." She heard

the wooden quality of her voice, but any effort to humanize it seemed too daunting.
Her life's passion had *killed* someone . . . "I
don't understand. How? When? *Why?* Why
my crisp?"

"That, dear, is what we need to find out."
We . . .
We . . .
God, she loved this woman . . .

"I — I'm trying to do that. Today — *now,*
as a matter of fact." Slowly, she opened her
eyes, her gaze settling on the sign, not more
than fifty feet ahead, that indicated the ap-
proaching turnoff for Silver Lake College.
"I thought I'd stop by Melinda's dorm and
see if I could talk to her roommate."

"May I go with you, dear? As a critical
member of the *Silver Lake Herald* team, I
am particularly skilled at interviewing people."

She started to decline, but thought better
of it. After all, two sets of ears were better
than one. Especially when one set came
with a more inconspicuous car . . .

Slipping the gearshift into Drive, Winnie
did a U-turn and headed back into the
center of town. "I just turned around. I'll
be in the parking lot in less than five minutes."

"I'll be ready. First, though, I need the

121

clever little name you used for the photo caption."

"Clever little name?"

"For your crisp — the one that killed that poor girl."

She swallowed back the bile that rose halfway up her throat and forced herself to answer if for no other reason than to put the subject behind them before they drove to campus together. "Fade to Black-Berry Crisp."

"How very apropos, dear."

They were halfway down the hall when Winnie noticed the discrepancy in their gaits. Hers was slow, maybe even reluctant. Bridget's was a bit quicker, as if there was a blue plate special in danger of ending.

She understood the reason for her own.

She didn't understand Bridget's.

Two doors shy of their destination, Bridget stopped so suddenly, Winnie nearly tripped. "Let me do the interrogating on this one, dear."

"Interrogating?"

"Yes. If something hinky is going on, I don't want you messing up our chances at getting to the bottom of things."

Ahhhh . . .

Now her friend's pace made sense . . .

"I'm not going to mess anything up." Winnie peeked around Bridget's broad frame at Melinda's wide-open door, and then dropped her voice to a near whisper. "Remember, Bridget, this is my livelihood that's hanging in the balance right now."

"Which is why you need to let me do the talking, dear. If this girl recognizes you, she might clam up."

"I never met the roommate," she reminded. "She wasn't here when I made my delivery."

Bridget waved at Winnie's words like one might wave at a bothersome gnat. "Don't argue, dear. I know what I'm doing."

Before Winnie could mount a stronger response, Bridget continued on her way, silently beckoning Winnie to follow.

"Bridget, I —"

Her friend reached the victim's open door and poked her head inside. "Hello? Is anyone here?"

A voice from the left side of the room replied just as Winnie slid into place behind Bridget. "Yeah, yeah, I'm here."

Bridget took a step forward and swung her head in the direction of the voice. "Nina?"

She was about to ask how Bridget knew the victim's roommate but refrained as her

123

gaze fell on the pair of paper stars affixed to the open door — the same personalized stars she'd used to verify Melinda's dorm room a little over forty-eight hours earlier.

A rustling off to their left brought her focus back in line with Bridget's just in time to see a tall blonde roll off the bottom bunk and stand. "Yeah, that's me." Winnie watched the girl's dark brown eyes scan their way up and down Bridget before moving on to Winnie, her too-thin shoulders visibly tensing as they did. "Melinda's folks are staying in town, I think . . ."

"We're not related to Melinda."

The reassurance was barely past Bridget's lips when the girl's upper body sagged with relief. "Phew. Good. I don't think I could stomach any more crying jags today."

"So you're holding up okay?" Bridget inched forward and then stopped. "I don't mean to press, but I've worked situations like this in the past and I know being here" — Bridget lifted her hands into the air and slowly turned in a circle — "during the aftermath of something like this has to be difficult. On so many levels."

Nina lowered herself onto the edge of her bed and shrugged. "Monday was just a blur of cops. Yesterday was even worse thanks to more cops *and* Melinda's parents."

"I bet they had a lot of questions for you."

"Did they ever." Nina scrunched up her face and alternated between a deep and almost squeaky-sounding voice. "Did you see her eat the dessert? Did Melinda say anything? Did she know some Winnie Johnson person? Did —"

"They asked if she knew m—"

Bridget's coughing fit drowned out Winnie's inquiry and brought Nina to her feet. "Oh . . . hey . . . are you okay? I might have a tissue or something . . ."

For a cough?

"Well, aren't you sweet." Bridget composed herself, shot a glare at Winnie, and then turned back to Nina, her smile bright. "Did you, dear?"

Nina blinked as if slapped. "Did I what?"

"See her eat the dessert?"

"Yeah. She ate it the way she ate everything — loudly."

"You *heard* her . . ." Bridget fairly purred.

"I tried not to, but some sounds you just can't block out no matter how hard you try." Nina lifted her feet onto her bed and leaned her upper body against the standard, run-of-the-mill dormitory headboard that Winnie remembered from her own college days. "I was trying to take a nap, but she made it difficult as always."

125

Winnie sagged against the wall. "So you didn't *see* her eating it?"

For the first time since the inaugural once-over when they first entered the room, Nina really looked at Winnie. "Trust me, the lip smacking was verification enough. And if it wasn't, the blue stain on her lips and tongue when she fell out of her chair ten minutes later sure as hell was."

"Were you here when your RA brought the dessert in for Melinda?" Bridget asked after sending another warning glare in Winnie's direction.

"I was here. Melinda wasn't."

She caught the slight rise of Bridget's left eyebrow and knew it mirrored her own.

"Oh?"

Again, Nina's attention was back on Bridget. "I got back from a meeting with my accounting advisor and Sam came in with the thing. She stuck it on Melinda's desk and left."

"Who is Sam?"

"The RA," Nina and Winnie said in unison. Then, turning back to Nina, Winnie took charge of the questions. "Were you alone in here when she dropped it off?"

"For a few minutes, yeah. But then my friend Nate showed up."

"Did he see the dessert?" She heard the

excitement in her voice and did her best to stifle it. At least until she and Bridget were back outside and trading notes . . .

Nina reached up to the underside of the upper bunk and started picking at something Winnie couldn't see from where she was standing. "I take it you've not met Nate Daniels. 'Cause if you had, you wouldn't need to ask that question."

"Oh?" Bridget repeated.

"He eats like a pig. Morning, noon, and night. Only now that he's not on the team anymore, he might want to slow it down a little. If he doesn't, he's gonna have an old man's pot belly by the time he's twenty-five."

Winnie halted Bridget's next potential question with her hand. "Did you two give it a little taste test?"

"A taste test? No. But I know I, for one, gave some thought to hurling it out the window." Nina dropped her hand back down to her unmade bed and tossed her legs over the edge of the bed once again. "Fortunately, as things ended up working out, my uncle called and told me he left a package for me over at the student center."

"I'm not following," Winnie said.

"I went to the student center to get my package."

Bridget nixed Winnie's muting hand gesture with a quick head-shake/teeth-clenched combination. "And your friend, Nate?"

"He went with me."

"Are you *sure*?"

Bridget's best glare had nothing on Nina's. "Uh, yeah. I'm sure. He thinks all packages at college should include junk food, so he was pretty disappointed to find that my uncle's didn't. Even so, he still ate half the contents before we stopped at the dining hall on the way back across campus."

"For . . ." Winnie prompted.

"For dinner, what else?"

She looked at Bridget for help but the woman was already on the case. "So you didn't come back here right away?"

"No."

"And when you *did* come back? What then?"

"The Rat was here . . . fawning over her damn pie."

"Crisp," Winnie corrected.

Nina's glare was back on Winnie. "Excuse me?"

It was too late to turn back now. She might as well play it out and see what happened . . . "The Rat was here," Winnie prompted. "Fawning over her damn *crisp.*"

Nina took in the clock on the wall above

Bridget's head and made a beeline for her desk and the stack of books precariously resting along its left edge. "Burned on the side or not, I could really care less. All I know is that I'm graduating in a little over two weeks and I no longer have to worry about spending the time I have left here dealing with the Rat. For the first time all year, I can talk on the phone or converse with my friends without worrying about what she's recording in that damn notebook of hers. And I can sleep!"

"Sleep?" Winnie echoed.

"The Rat *snored.* Every. Single. Night." Nina plucked a pen from a cup holder atop her desk and tossed it into the oversized tote bag now hooked over her shoulder. "I guess things really *do* have a way of working themselves out, huh?"

CHAPTER 10

They watched the elevator doors swish to a close at the end of the hallway and then turned and looked at each other.

"Well, that was interesting . . ."

"Not in the way it needed to be." Winnie fingered Melinda's star on the now closed door and did her best to block out the image of a girl she'd seen only on the local news. But try as she might, she couldn't stop mixing that image with one of her blackberry crisp . . . "Bridget, what am I going to do?"

"*We* are moving on, dear. To our next subject."

"Next subject?"

"Yes, the RA."

She pulled her finger back and dropped her hand to her side, turning to face her next-door neighbor as she did. "Sam didn't do this, Bridget. I'm confident about that."

"And maybe you're right. But that doesn't

130

mean she can't have information that might prove helpful." Bridget wrapped her hand around Winnie's and gave it a gentle tug. "C'mon, dear. Let's go get some more answers."

She wanted to protest, wanted to head toward the elevator and the parking lot out front, but she was too tired, too zapped, to argue. Instead, she merely pointed her friend toward the correct door on the other side of the hallway. "Sam's room is over there. Second one on the right. But maybe you should talk to her alone."

"Why on earth would I do that?" Bridget asked.

"For starters, Sam actually saw me on Monday. She might freak if I show up at her door now."

"We'll deal with that if and when it happens." Bridget exchanged her gentle, reassuring hold on Winnie's hand for one far more insistent, if not downright bossy, in the center of Winnie's back. "Now go . . ."

The eighty-year-old's push propelled Winnie down the hall and over to the correct door just as Sam stood beside her desk chair and froze. "It's . . . you — the one who delivered that dessert for Melinda on Monday."

Winnie eked out a noise that could pos-

131

sibly be interpreted as a yes, but to be sure, she added a nod.

"Winnie had nothing to do with that girl's death." Bridget nudged her way around Winnie and into Sam's room. "She wouldn't hurt a flea, let alone a college student, and I can say that with absolute conviction."

Sam opened her mouth to answer but closed it as Bridget pointed at a picture on her windowsill. "You know Betty Langley?"

"She's my great-grandmother."

"Betty and I go back a long way — to first grade, as a matter of fact." Bridget lingered her attention on the photograph for an extra second or two and then turned her attention back to Sam. "I'm Bridget. Bridget O'Keefe. I work at the *Silver Lake Herald* and I live next door to Winnie here."

At the sound of her name, Winnie stopped gawking and managed to nod one more time.

"I'm sorry about everything that's happened," Sam said, looking from Winnie to Bridget and back again. "All of this must be really awful for you right now."

Something about the young woman's sincerity moved Winnie to near tears and she squeezed her eyes shut for a brief moment. When she opened them, Sam was again focused on Bridget. "How can I help?"

"You can start by telling us about Winnie's crisp. We know you brought it to Melinda's room when the roommate returned."

Sam nodded along with Bridget's account. "I did. I wanted to hold on to it myself, but I had a meeting to go to before dinner and another immediately following dinner. I was afraid if I didn't drop it off in Melinda's room before I left, the dessert wouldn't still be fresh when I got back. So I took the chance and left it with Nina."

Something about the girl's last sentence sent a shiver up Winnie's spine. "Took a chance?"

"It's like I told you on Monday, when you tried to deliver the dessert. The two of them don't get along. It's why Melinda was working on her big investigative piece at my desk instead of her own."

"Investigative piece?" Bridget repeated.

"Melinda was a really good reporter — too good, in many ways."

Seizing on the limited information she'd gleaned from both Alicia and Jay, Winnie probed for more. "What do you mean by 'too good'?"

"She did such a good job that her facts were virtually indisputable."

"Meaning?"

She was surprised when it was Bridget's

voice that answered, rather than Sam's. "Meaning she made her fair share of enemies, didn't she?"

Sam nodded.

"Was Nina one of them?" Winnie asked quickly.

"I'm not sure. I know something was going on there, but what, exactly, I don't know. Melinda was always very tight-lipped about whatever she was working on until it came out in the paper. Said she didn't want to compromise the story, or go public with something that she hadn't quadruple-checked first."

Bridget sauntered over to the desk and the pile of notes haphazardly strewn across the top. "These are yours?" she asked Sam.

"No. I haven't used my desk in nearly a month thanks to whatever story Melinda was chasing for her *Caughtcha* column."

"Did that bother you?" Winnie asked. "I mean, an RA is just supposed to make sure people are following the rules. It's not your job to give up your desk for someone having roommate issues."

"You're right, it's not. But I liked Melinda." Sam wandered over to the desk and stood beside Bridget. "Anything she uncovered around campus was happening whether she wrote about it or not. She just called at-

134

tention to it so it could be stopped."

"I wish more people valued the work of a good journalist." Bridget lifted a few random pieces of paper off Sam's desk, examined them for a moment or two, and then returned them to their original spot. "And you have no idea what she was working on in here?"

"No," Sam said, shrugging. "I asked her once, but she said she had to make sure she had her facts straight before she could say anything."

"Did she say anything else? Like maybe who it involved?"

Sam considered Bridget's questions, but in the end, she offered yet another shrug. "I'm assuming it involved Nina on some level, but that's really just a guess. I suppose it's entirely possible that whatever was going on between them was simply the result of two completely different personalities being shoved together under one roof for entirely too long. It happens. Trust me."

"What's this?" Winnie and Sam both turned back to Bridget in time to see the elderly woman reach her hand over a digital camera to grab hold of a leather-bound notebook held shut by a rubber band. "Was this Melinda's?"

"It was. It was the notebook she carried

around when she was 'on the hunt,' as she liked to say."

Bridget fingered the top of the notebook and then held it out to Sam. "I have one almost exactly like this."

Unsure of what, if anything, she was supposed to say, Winnie remained silent and waited. Sam took the notebook from Bridget's outstretched hand and slowly ran her own along the edges of the colorful sticky notes sticking out from between various pages.

"This story Melinda was working on? It was important to her?" Bridget asked.

Sam pulled the book against her chest and nodded, her eyes pained. "It was. It's all she worked on the last few weeks."

"Then let me finish it for her. As a fellow journalist," Bridget coaxed. "If whatever Melinda was working on consumed her final days and weeks in the way that you say, it's the least we can do for her now."

"I — I don't know, Ms. O'Keefe. I don't know if that's my place."

"You were friends, weren't you?"

Sam nodded.

"She trusted you enough to work on this particular story in your room, didn't she?"

Again, Sam nodded.

"You believe this story meant a lot to her,

don't you?"

"I *know* it did. Melinda was a rule follower across the board. It ticked off some of the girls on this floor, but I appreciated it. Made my job easier in many ways because I knew she had my back. And while I don't know what, exactly, she was working on, she did say it was about the truth — about making sure things were right and fair before there was no going back."

"Making sure things are right and fair," Bridget repeated. "Those are certainly concepts *I* believe in . . ."

Winnie saw Sam's throat move with a swallow just before the girl's eyes dropped to the notebook clutched against her chest. "I believe in them, too. It's why I always liked Melinda no matter how many enemies she made along the way. Her heart was always in the right place."

"Then let's help Melinda finish whatever she started — in the name of making sure things are right and fair."

"In the name of making sure things are right and fair," Sam whispered. Then lifting her gaze to Bridget's, she handed the notebook back to the elderly woman. "For Melinda."

Winnie looked across the center console at

Bridget and smiled. There was no getting around the fact that Bridget O'Keefe was gifted at getting what she wanted.

"Wow. You're good," she finally said as the elderly woman steered them off campus. "*Really* good."

"Why, thank you, dear." At the stop sign, Bridget turned left and headed toward the center of town.

Winnie pulled her attention off the driver and fixed it on the notebook now resting atop her lap. "So you're really going to write this girl's story for her?"

"Not the story she intended, necessarily, but hopefully the only one that matters."

She flicked the tip of her index finger across the blue, green, and yellow papers sticking out from the side of the notebook. "The only one that matters?"

"That's right." The car slowed as Bridget piloted them into the parking lot behind the *Silver Lake Herald* office building and pulled to a stop next to Winnie's ambulance. "You're going to the council meeting with Parker and me tonight, yes?"

Oops . . .

"I, uh —"

"Don't tell me you forgot, dear."

"No. I didn't forget."

Liar, liar, pants on fire . . .

138

"Take Melinda's notebook home with you and I'll get it from you later — after the meeting."

Winnie looked from Bridget to the notebook and back again. "Don't you want to take it into work with you? So you can write her story for the paper?"

"Once I know you're cleared, dear, *then* I'll write her story."

CHAPTER 11

The meeting room in Silver Lake Town Hall was what you would expect in a small town — folding chairs for the residents, cushioned chairs for the mayor and council members, and a table along the back wall that was filled to capacity with baked goods. A stack of one-page agendas was positioned on a smaller table just inside the doorway.

Winnie took a moment to look around as they waited for the meeting to start. To her left were a handful of business owners like herself who'd been forced to close up shop due to the rising cost of rent along Main Street. They all had the same grim set to their mouths, the same balled fists on their laps. The chairs to her right were occupied by a half-dozen or so unfamiliar faces — all smiling, all happily swapping stories with one another.

"I have half a mind to whack that fella over the head with my cane," Mr. Nelson grumbled loud enough to turn a head or two in his direction.

Winnie followed her housemate's gaze toward the front of the room and the average-sized man now seated in the front row with a large poster at his feet. Even from the back, with nothing more than a thick crop of dark hair and broad shoulders to go on, she knew she was looking at the very reason she was sitting there in the first place.

"Think I could plead senility and get away with it?"

She rested her hand atop Mr. Nelson's fist and gave it a quick pat. "Maybe, but let's try the more civilized route first, shall we?"

"A *boot* works, too, Winnie Girl. Though that's better suited for somethin' other than his head . . ."

Wordlessly, Bridget widened the gap between her and Mr. Nelson by two seats, leaving Winnie to decipher his latest hearing issue on her own.

Boot?
Boot?
Ahhh . . .

She lifted her index finger to her ear and tapped it once. When Mr. Nelson adjusted the volume on his hearing aid, she repeated

141

her answer. "I said, let's try the more civilized *route* first, Mr. Nelson. Route . . . not boot —"

"Winnie!"

She craned her head around Mr. Nelson to find Bridget making a number of gestures in Winnie's direction — none of which she could decipher. Before she could ask for a verbal interpretation, though, Bridget reclaimed her original chair next to Mr. Nelson and pressed a small compact mirror into Winnie's hand.

"What's this for?" Winnie whispered.

"For you," Bridget whispered back. "He's coming!"

"He? He who?"

Again, Bridget resorted to hand gestures, though this time Winnie was able to make out the one about her hair and a tube of lipstick . . .

Lipstick?

Movement to Winnie's right brought Bridget's motions to a stop and a knowing smile to Mr. Nelson's mouth. Slowly, Winnie turned to her right and the breathtakingly gorgeous man now seated in the next chair.

"Had I known you were going to be at this meeting, Winnie, I wouldn't have spent so much time dreading the ride over here."

There was no two ways about it, Greg Stevens (aka Master Sergeant Hottie to virtually every female in Silver Lake) was, well, *hot*. His eyes (which Winnie likened to the exact color of chocolate melting in the double boiler) saw no one but the person in front of him. His toned (read: muscular and oh so fine) body spoke to the way he spent his time between calls at the Silver Lake Ambulance Corps. And his hair, cut close at the sides and well shy of his ears, made it easy to fantasize about what he must have looked like during his days in the military.

Beyond all of that, he was simply a nice guy — a nice guy that had been more than a little interested in Winnie when they first met. But despite a push or two (read: hard shove) from both Bridget and Renee, Winnie hadn't shared that interest. She'd been content with her baking and her friends on Serenity Lane.

That is, until she met Jay Morgan.

Jay . . .

Shaking the name and the man from her thoughts, Winnie returned Greg's smile. "I take it you come to these often?"

"Every month."

Mr. Nelson leaned in front of Winnie and shook the paramedic's hand. "That's a good thing, young man, because if those suits up there don't turn on their ears and open their eyes, your lifesaving skills might be needed this evening."

"That's good to know, Mr. Nelson." Greg's eyes crackled with amusement just before they narrowed in on Winnie's once again. "So how have you been? How's the Dessert Squad going?"

She waited for her current reality to roll across his face, but it didn't come. "I . . . uh —"

This time, when Mr. Nelson leaned in front of her, his bony elbow dug into her thigh. "Winnie's business is at a little bit of a standstill at the moment."

Greg's left eyebrow shot up. "Oh?"

"Seems folks might be a little skittish about her desserts right now."

Greg's confusion only grew, making it all but certain he'd somehow missed the news about Melinda B. Tully. Or at the very least, her purported connection to the victim. But before she could find just the right place to dive in with the details, Bridget leaned into Mr. Nelson, further increasing his weight on Winnie's thigh.

"Her blackberry crisp appears to have been the murder weapon in a young woman's death." Bridget scanned their surroundings and then lowered her voice an octave. "But don't you worry, we're going to get to the bottom of this. One way or the other."

Greg looked from Bridget, to Mr. Nelson, and finally back to Winnie. "Is this a joke?"

"I don't know how you missed this," Winnie said quietly. "It's been all over the news for two days."

"I've been out of town since last Friday. At my sister's place. I literally drove into town just now."

"Then welcome back." She stuck her hand out for him to shake, and when he did, she added, "If this doesn't get cleared up, maybe you can buy my ambulance after all."

He held her hand a second longer than necessary and then slowly released it back to her lap. "I don't want your ambulance anymore. It's not meant to be restored, it's meant to deliver desserts."

"I hope you're right." It was all she could think to say, but that didn't make it any less true.

"What's Jay say about all this?" he asked.

Bridget sniffed in disgust, thus blowing her I'm-not-eavesdropping-but-I-am cover. Mr. Nelson retracted his elbow and squeezed the top of his cane. Winnie merely looked at the floor.

"No . . . Don't tell me he's buying into

this," Greg hissed.

She nibbled her lower lip and tried to think of the best answer she could give — one that would keep the tears at bay until she was back home and safely tucked away in her bed. Alone. "The victim was a student at the college."

Greg reared back with such force, his folding chair scraped the floor and cast a momentary hush over the crowd. "I don't care if the victim was a family member. He has to know you better than this."

"Good evening, everyone. I'd like to welcome you to our monthly Silver Lake Town Council meeting and get things moving along. If you didn't grab an agenda on your way in, raise your hand and Lorna will see that you get one."

Despite Mayor Rigsby's boisterous introduction, Winnie could still feel Greg's eyes trained on the side of her face. There was no denying it. Greg's absolute faith in her innocence was touching. Needed, even. And she was grateful.

She looked back at him and tried to smile. "I'm going to get through this, Greg," she whispered. "Bridget, Mr. Nelson, and Renee are doing everything they can to help me."

"And so will I. You can count on that."

"The first item up for discussion this

evening is the ongoing efforts by Nick Batkas to put Silver Lake on the map."

Mr. Nelson steadied his left hand on the
top of his cane and raised his right into the
air.

"Yes, Parker, would you like to speak?"
Mayor Rigsby asked.

"You're darn tootin' I would." Scooting
forward on her seat, Winnie helped the man
onto his feet and braced herself for the
storm he'd been waiting to unleash on the
town board for weeks. "First, Silver Lake is
already on the map. Folks have been coming to our town for years. Some of us live
here year-round and have for more years
than any of you at that table have been alive.
Some, like them folks who have them man-
sions along the lake, have chosen to make
this town a much-needed getaway from an
otherwise busy life down there in Cincinnati. You catch that, Mayor? Councilman
Medders? Councilman Rawlings? And" —
Mr. Nelson's voice noticeably hardened —
"*Mr. Batkas?* A getaway. If folks wanted
Vegas, they'd move to Vegas."

Tim Rawlings, seated two spots over from
the mayor, planted his elbows on the table
and tried, unsuccessfully, to cover his smile
with his fisted hands. Winnie felt Mr. Nelson
stiffen in response.

Before either could speak, though, a chorus of agreement rang up among the displaced business owners to Winnie's left. One by one their verbal assents gave way to clapping and, eventually, standing.

She swung her gaze back to the front table just in time to catch Councilman Rawlings's patronizing smile tighten and then disappear altogether. Mayor Rigsby tried to remain impassive, but he, too, wore the faintest hint of irritation. Corey Medders, the councilman seated between the two, stared out at the crowd, clearly unsure of what to make of their reaction.

The object of Mr. Nelson's ire raised his hand from his seat in the front row. "Mayor? May I address this?"

"Sure thing, Nick. Have at it."

Winnie's former landlord rose to his feet, retrieved the poster from its spot beside his chair, and crossed to the podium. Lorna, the mayor's secretary, suddenly appeared at his side with an easel.

Once the poster — which Winnie could now see was an artist's rendering of Main Street — was situated on the easel, Nick cleared his throat and looked out over the crowd, which had taken their seats the moment he stood. "No one is trying to turn Silver Lake into Vegas. Vegas is Vegas."

"And Silver Lake is Silver Lake," Mr. Nelson shot back.

The mayor held up his hands for silence. "Parker, you had your say. Now it's time for Nick to have his."

Mr. Nelson sat taller in his chair and waited. Winnie's former Main Street colleagues did the same.

Again, Nick cleared his throat. Winnie wondered, briefly, if the man was nervous, but the oversized ego that was Nick Batkas's essence reared its head and showed her otherwise.

"Have you ever had stale bread, Mr. Nelson?"

"I have, indeed."

"And?" Nick prodded.

"It's for the birds." Rocking back on his chair for just a moment, Mr. Nelson allowed himself a moment to enjoy his unexpected joke. "Ha! It's for the birds . . . get it?"

Tim Rawlings's smug smile was back, only this time it was on Nick Batkas's face. "It is, isn't it? That's because fresh is better. It tastes better, looks better, and sells better." Clearly confident in whatever direction he was taking, Nick stepped out from behind the podium. "In fact, if you went to a store that continually sold stale bread, you'd stop buying it there, wouldn't you?"

Uh-oh . . .

Heads nodded to Winnie's left and right.

"That's what Silver Lake had become, Mr. Nelson. A piece of stale bread that no one was interested in buying."

The heads to her left froze. The heads to her right nodded harder.

Winnie swallowed.

"Slowly, though, that's starting to change. And that's because I'm getting fresh bread back on the shelf. Fresh bread that people *want* to eat."

When Mr. Nelson said nothing, Winnie raised her hand.

Nick pointed at her. "Yes, Miss Johnson?"

"As you know, Mr. Batkas, I was a business owner on Main Street up until six weeks ago. I didn't go out of business because of a lack of customers as you're implying here. I was forced to close down because you raised the rent to a level that was way out of line."

Stepping behind the podium once again, he whipped out a pen from his pocket and brandished it at the poster-topped easel. "For a town with stale bread, perhaps. But for a town with fresh bread, no."

"We were doing just fine!" Chip Granderson, owner of the now defunct Silver Lake Coffee Shop, fired off from somewhere behind Winnie. "But this isn't about folks like my wife and me . . . or Winnie . . . or Tony and Lizzy back here. It's about you, Nick, you and your desire to make more money."

Smugness turned to a laugh as Nick glanced over his shoulder at the mayor and council members. "Chip says *money* like it's a bad thing, doesn't he?"

"When the pursuit of it compromises what we've all come to value in this town, then yes, it *is* a bad thing," Mr. Nelson shot back as he struggled up and onto his feet once again.

The laughter stopped. "I'm getting the sense you have a personal agenda here, Parker." Nick leaned forward on the podium, his eyes narrowed on Winnie.

Interesting . . .

"I've lived in this town for nearly forty years. You bet it's personal."

Nick cocked his head to the side, furrowing his brow as he did. "See, now I'm wondering if this is more about the woman sitting next to you than it is about anything I'm doing."

"You mean her?" Mr. Nelson jerked his head in Bridget's direction so hard, he almost toppled over. "She's lived here even longer than I have, so of course it's about her, too."

"I was referring to your other side."

Winnie stood beside her friend and quieted his response with a hand on his forearm. "He's talking about me, Mr. Nelson."

"And your former bakery," Nick interjected. "Though from a business standpoint, that new idea of yours held such promise . . . until, you know, this week."

The meaning behind the man's latest volley landed like blows to her face and gut, causing her to stumble backward into her chair. She heard the hush that swept across the room but only for a moment.

A scraping sound to her right was followed by a voice — Greg's voice.

"This is not the time, nor the place, Mr. Batkas. So I suggest you get back on topic or you can count on being named in a slander suit."

"Okay, okay, let's get back to the issue at hand." Mayor Rigsby came out from behind the table, set his hand on Nick's shoulder, and whispered something in the man's ear. When he was done, he looked out at first Greg, and then the rest of the crowd. "It's time to get to specific issues or we'll move on with the agenda."

"There are rumors going around about outside companies — from as far as an hour away — taking work from our own people. Like that intersection out by the park — why isn't Silver Lake Paving doing the work?" Chip asked.

"Maybe because someone else came in with a lower bid," Nick replied.

Mr. Nelson slid his cane out from behind the row of empty chairs in front of them and pointed its tip at the man behind the podium. "Someone who just happens to have ties to you, Batkas!"

A second hush fell over the crowd, giving Winnie a chance to catch her breath and shake off the roar in her head in time to hear Mayor Rigsby take control of the conversation. "What are you implying, Parker?"

"We should be looking out for our own. Not yankin' their legs out from under them."

"My top priority is, and always has been, serving the residents of this community."

"That's certainly what *you* and" — Mr. Nelson slowly moved the tip of his cane in line with the council members still seated at the table — "*each one of you* were elected to do. But these last few months, it seems the only one getting served around here is the man at the podium."

"All bids for all projects are sealed, Parker. Always have been, always will be." Mayor Rigsby parted company with the side of the podium and took a moment to look around at the crowd, his angst over the direction the meeting had taken palpable. "I love this town and its people every bit as much as all of you. I, too, would prefer to see jobs go to our own residents. But even more than that, I don't want to see anyone paying higher taxes than necessary."

A few heads nodded around the room and she looked at Mr. Nelson to gauge his feelings. What her elderly friend was thinking was anyone's guess. Whom he was glaring at, though, was as plain as the once-broken nose on his face.

"Mr. Nelson," she whispered. "It's time to sit down. You've had your say."

After several long beats of silence, he swung his attention onto the mayor. "I think I speak for many of us in this audience when I say, Silver Lake is perfect the way it is . . . or rather, was. There ain't nothin' wrong with a place bein' quiet. Ain't nothin' wrong with that at all."

Chapter 12

It was nearly ten o'clock when she lowered her shoulder bag to the ground and leaned back against the door, completely spent.

"Lovey? Are you here?" She turned her head to the right, half expecting to see the outline of a sleeping mound in the center of the otherwise darkened armchair, but there was nothing. "Lovey?"

Holding her finger to her lips, she paused and listened. Straight ahead and to her left, she heard the soft hum of the refrigerator. To the right of that, she heard the tick tock of the wall clock Mr. Nelson had given her as a Christmas gift shortly after she moved to Silver Lake — its hands fashioned out of measuring spoons, its center point a baker's hat.

A cold chill moved up her spine and propelled her away from the door and toward the light switch that had been fool-ishly positioned on the kitchen wall rather than next to the door. Even more foolish was the okay she'd given Renee to put a potted tree on the door side of the switch . . .

Slowly, she made her way around the plant until she found the light.

Hissss . . .

She gave her eyes a moment to adjust to the light and then looked in the direction of the greeting. There, on the far wall, nestled inside the windowsill hammock, not more than six feet from where Winnie had started, was a clearly irritated Lovey. "I'm sorry, Your Highness, did I wake you?"

Without waiting for an answer, she tossed her keys onto the table and eyed the phone she'd deliberately left behind for her evening with Mr. Nelson and Bridget. It was funny how things could change on a dime, even if she didn't feel like laughing.

Three days earlier, she wouldn't have dreamed of leaving her apartment without her phone in hand. To do so, would have put her in jeopardy of missing an order. But now, post-Melinda, she'd left the phone behind in an effort to preserve her sanity. If she didn't have her phone, she couldn't know it wasn't ringing . . .

"What are you doing at the window?" she asked as she crept closer to the table.

"That's your late morning, and sometimes early afternoon spot, silly."

At the table's edge, she glanced at the cat (yup, still blinking, still irritated). "So? Are you going to tell me if any calls came in or do I have to check and see myself?"

Lovey blinked and lowered her head back down to her paws.

"Gee, thanks for the help." Winnie sank onto the bench, pulled the phone in front of her, and pushed the top button.

Three missed calls.

Inhaling sharply, she lifted the phone from the table and tapped into the missed call log. As was the case with her phone, the most recent call was listed at the top.

Sergeant Hottie.

"Word of advice, Lovey. Never leave your phone unattended in Renee's presence," she mumbled as she scrolled down to the next name.

Renee the Beautiful.

She savored her first laugh in hours and scrolled down to the final missed call.

Jay.

"He called?" Then, realizing whom she was talking to, she clicked the phone's main button and stared down at the voice mail icon.

2.

She couldn't help it — she squealed. And once again, Lovey rewarded her with a tired hiss.

"Oh, put a sock in it, will you?" She tapped the icon and held the phone to her ear, her hand trembling ever so slightly.

"Hey, Winnie." She closed her eyes at the sound of Greg's voice and willed herself to listen to his message all the way through. "It was great to see you tonight. It's been too long, quite frankly. I'm really sorry about what that Batkas guy said about your tie to that college student's death. I know you've been dealing with this stuff since it happened, but I want you to know it really irked me. I know you had nothing to do with what happened to this girl and I'm not going to sit idly by while people imply you did. It's not —"

She pressed Save before he could continue and allowed herself a moment to breathe. Yes, she needed to hear those words, needed to lose herself in the comfort they provided, but at that moment, she needed to hear them from someone else even more . . .

Stealing herself for the powerful impact she knew Jay's voice would have on her heart, she counted to three in her head, and pressed Play.

"Hey, girlfriend. It's me. Renee. Or as I

programmed into your phone while you were out gallivanting around town this morning, Renee the Beautiful. It has a nice ring, doesn't it?"

She tried to listen to what her friend was saying, but it was hard. She'd been so sure the second voice mail had come from Jay . . .

Why didn't he leave a message?

And then, just as quickly as the question had formed in her thoughts, an answer came on its heels.

Because he hadn't meant to call . . .

"Anyway, I added those new dessert names to the website like you asked."

Focus, Winnie . . .

Focus.

"While I was on there, I went ahead and took off the one you had me add after . . . um . . . Monday's delivery." Renee's voice disappeared from Winnie's ear momentarily, only to return a second or two later. "I didn't want to give the creeps at Channel Five any more ammunition than they seem to already have against you."

She knew Renee was trying to help. She really did. But at that moment, she just couldn't stomach any more. It was time to shut out everything — the not-so-subtle and oh-so-public barb from Nick, Mr. Nelson's too quiet demeanor on the way home from the town meeting, the missed call from Jay that had obviously been a mistake, and the pending demise of her dream.

Like it or not, those realities would be waiting for her the moment she opened her eyes in the morning. Tonight, she just wanted to pretend they didn't exist.

Or try to anyway.

She shifted the phone's ringer to silent, flicked off the overhead light, and made her way across the darkened kitchen, muttering softly as she bumped into the wall while feeling around for her shoulder bag. At the window, she stopped and peered down at the dark mound that was Lovey. "I'm taking the bed tonight, madam."

Hiss . . .

Too tired to roll her eyes, Winnie merely walked around the corner and into her room, the sight of her bed, centered along the back wall, the welcome refuge she'd been seeking all day. A quick stop in the bathroom to brush her teeth and wash her face was all that stood between her and the covers she desperately wanted to pull over her head — both literally and metaphorically.

Yet once she was finally ready to climb into bed, she knew sleep wasn't going to come easily. Too much was still swirling around in her head — Mr. Nelson, Nick Batkas, the visit with Melinda's roommate, Jay . . .

No.

Determined to maintain control over her mood, Winnie reached for the paperback mystery novel on her nightstand and opened it to the bookmarked page. Two chapters in, though, she realized she wasn't absorbing any of what she was reading and exchanged the book for her shoulder bag and the word search book it contained.

She dipped her hand inside the cavernous bag and stopped when she felt something unfamiliar. Peeking in, she spied Melinda's notebook.

"Ugh. I was supposed to give this to Bridget this evening . . ."

A quick glance at the clock confirmed it was too late to call and admit her mistake. Still, she pulled the book from her bag and set it on the nightstand to help her remember to bring it next door in the morning.

Returning her focus to her bag, she found and retrieved the word search book she'd been seeking and settled against her pillow with her favorite pen. Two puzzles later, her thoughts still scattered, she tossed the book onto the nightstand and watched it slip across the top of Melinda's notebook and off the other side.

Without really thinking, she pulled the notebook onto her lap, rescued the word search book from its precarious spot on the edge of the table, and sat up against the headboard. She looked down at the colorful sticky notes poking out around the edges of the dead girl's book and pulled off the rubber band tasked with holding it closed.

"What were you writing about your last few days, Melinda?" she mumbled.

The soft pitter-patter of feet across the hardwood floor pulled her attention off the book long enough to acknowledge Lovey's entrance. "If you think I'm giving up my bed for you tonight, *cat,* you're wrong. This is my bed, in my apartment. I'm happy to share these things with you, but you're not pushing me out. That stuff stops. Now."

Lovey stopped next to the bed and peered up at Winnie, eyes wide and disapproving.

"Don't look at me like that, Lovey. I'm not in the mood."

Rearing back on her haunches, Lovey jumped onto the bed and stopped.

Winnie suspected the shock she saw in Lovey's eyes was mirrored in her own. Yet just as Winnie didn't move, neither did Lovey.

"Yes?" she finally said while simultaneously bracing herself for the hiss she knew would come.

Lovey, of course, did not disappoint.

Hiss . . .

But this time, instead of being hurled in her direction, Lovey's standard response to all things Winnie seemed tired, almost robotic.

O-kay . . .

"Do you want to sleep up here with me, little one?"

Lovey paused, threw a glance in Winnie's direction, and then turned herself around in a circle before dropping onto the blanket. Afraid to move, let alone breathe, Winnie stared down at the cat.

"Well," she whispered, "wonders never cease, do they?" She reached out, stroked the top of the animal's head, and retracted her hand with lightning-quick speed at the far less tired hiss she earned in response.

"Whoa. Okay. I won't push it."

Lovey gave her one final death glare and then lowered her chin onto her paws.

"Well, alrighty then . . ." Winnie flipped open the cover of Melinda's notebook and took in the uneven, almost illegible writing that graced the first page. Bringing the book closer to the light, she tried to make out a few of the words, only to realize what she was looking at were names. Six of them.

Doug Cummings — or was it Lummings . . .

Pete Blyss . . .

Art Joel . . .

Alicia Worth . . .

Interesting . . .

Nate Daniels . . .

Nina . . .

Nina? As in Melinda's roommate?

The question had barely assembled itself in her thoughts when she began to nod. Nina was the only one listed that didn't include a last name. That spoke to a different level of familiarity.

"Lovey, I have a feeling we're about to find out why Nina and Melinda weren't getting along . . ."

If Lovey cared, it didn't show. Instead, the feline simply flicked her ear and covered her now closed eyes with her left paw. On a different day, Winnie might have tried to snap a picture of the cat's close proximity in the likely event it never happened again, but at that moment, all she could really think about was turning the page.

Scrawled across the next double page was another name. Below that were two questions — both underlined and starred multiple times:

164

Dave Wright.

Who is he?

Why Silver Lake?

With all thoughts of sleep gone, Winnie turned the page again to find a slip of paper, folded into a square, wedged into the center seam. Intrigued, she pulled it out, unfolded it to its full size, and smoothed it down across the top of the notebook.

The paper was thin, almost receipt-like, with penciled notations down the center. The writing was neater than what she'd seen in the actual notebook, leading her to deduce it was written by someone other than Melinda.

5 English Lit — Marrow.

3 European History — Griffin.

Below that, in slightly darker pencil, were equations:

5 × \$250 = \$1,250.

3 × \$300 = \$900.

Total: \$2,150.

20 percent = \$430.

Nate: \$322.50.

Me: \$107.50.

Interesting, yes. But considering Winnie had no idea what she was looking at, it was nothing more than gibberish. Still, if she was a betting person, she'd say the person who'd jotted this slip of notes was female.

165

Beyond that, though, nothing stood out except —

She flipped back to the previous page and scanned the list of names.

Nate Daniels.

Was Nate the same person referred to on the slip of paper?

Considering the relatively uncommon name, she suspected it was the same person. But "me"? Who was that?

Again she looked at the list of names, stopping on the last one.

Nina.

The only female name on the whole list.

Hmmm . . .

Tucking the slip back into the book's seam, Winnie turned to the next page, Melinda's larger, sloppier writing taking center stage once again.

Nate, himself? Or a middleman?

If a middleman, for whom?

Why?

~ Greed?

~ Retaliation?

~ Because he can?

There was no getting around the fact that much of what Winnie was reading went completely over her head. She didn't know Nate, didn't know any of the other names, except Nina's. Maybe Nina had written the

166

calculations on the slip of paper wedged inside the previous page, but even if she had, what did it mean?

Shifting Melinda's notebook off her lap and onto the bed, Winnie pulled her shoulder bag onto the mattress and fished out her own notebook. Slowly, she turned her way past one grocery list after the other, the ingredients noted on each page instantly conjuring up the dessert they'd come together to create.

There was the One Smart Cookie she'd made for the little girl two streets over who'd won her class spelling bee . . .

There were the All Out of Dough-nuts she'd made for the teenage boy who spent the money he'd been painstakingly saving from his lawn-cutting jobs on a used car . . .

There was the Never Give Up-side Down Cake for the woman on Clover Street who'd gotten yet another rejection on the manuscript she'd been trying to sell for over a year . . .

Each dessert represented a much-needed pick-me-up or dose of encouragement for someone. The spelling bee winner had danced in place when Winnie arrived at her door with the cookie-topped stretcher. The teenage boy had laughed and placed his dad in a playful headlock for the edible joke.

And the writer had hugged her husband (and then Winnie) and promised she wouldn't give up — ever.

And it had been that way with every rescue she'd made. No matter what was going on with the person she was asked to rescue, her desserts were always met with a smile. She couldn't ask for a better job than that.

Prove them wrong . . .

How she was going to heed Mr. Nelson's advice, she wasn't sure. But her gut was telling her Melinda's notes were a good place to start. She could reminisce about her desserts and her clients later. When Melinda's real killer was behind bars.

She kept flipping until she came to a blank page, retrieved her word search pen from the nightstand, and began jotting down her own questions.

Why did Melinda have Nina's (?) paper tucked in her notebook?

Did Nina know Melinda had it?

What does it mean?

She was contemplating her next question when Jay's voice appeared in her thoughts.

Melinda's forte was investigative journalism . . . She got a charge out of uncovering stuff people didn't know . . .

Just the memory of Jay's voice threatened

to derail her attention from the task at hand, but she resisted. After all, when it came to the people she intended to prove wrong, Jay Morgan was at the top of the list.

CHAPTER 13

In hindsight, Winnie could see how maybe the way she'd grabbed Renee by the arm and propelled her into the living room and onto the couch could be construed as slightly pushy, but in the moment, she'd just been so anxious to try her theory out on a two-legged being, she hadn't really been thinking clearly.

Yet now that Renee was staring at Winnie like the crazed (read: sleep-deprived) woman she was, Winnie opted to take a breath and allow Renee to do the same. "Um, I — uh could make you some toast or something if you're hungry?"

Renee smoothed her too short skirt over her thighs and peered up at Winnie. "You accost me at the door, push me onto this couch, and ask me if I want toast?"

"Sorry about that," she said, backing against the ottoman on the other side of the hooked rug and dropping down onto its cushiony top. "I guess I got a little ahead of myself."

"Meaning?"

"There's just a lot I want to tell you and I thought you were going to be here twenty minutes ago." The first part was true, of course. The second part, not so much. Renee was never on time for work, and Winnie, of all people, knew that better than anyone. "So . . . about that toast?"

"Nah. I made pancakes for Ty this morning before school and I might have eaten one or two."

Winnie laughed. "Might have?"

"Okay, so I ate three." Renee rubbed at the waning imprint of Winnie's fingers on her arm and then extended her legs straight out from the couch. "So? What do you think?"

"I think three pancakes are fine, Renee. Really."

Renee shook her head and pointed at the sunshine yellow stilettos she moved from side to side. "I'm talking about my shoes. Aren't they gorgeous? I found them at Rothman's Department Store —"

"Lovey slept with me last night!" Winnie drew back, surprised at her words. Yes, she'd been waiting to share details of her night since Renee walked through the door, but

Lovey hadn't been one of those details . . .

"I told you she'd come around." Renee took one last admiring look at her new shoes and then slowly lowered them back down to the floor. "You just needed to stop hissing at her all the time."

"*I* needed to stop hissing at *her*?"

"You say that like we haven't discussed this before . . ."

"And I've taken issue with it every time you've said it." Winnie stopped, planted her hands on her thighs, and stared across the room at her friend. "I think I might have found a motive last night."

"It's not rocket science, Winnie. Cats like cuddling up next to a warm body." Renee cocked her head in thought, only to straighten it up with a sly smile. "Then again, who doesn't?"

She saw Renee's mouth moving in real time, even heard everything she was saying as she was saying it, but it took a moment or two to fully grasp the response that bore absolutely no resemblance to the one she'd been imagining since about four o'clock that morning.

Pushing off the ottoman, Winnie stood and wandered over to the television stand, her thoughts ricocheting between the limited information she'd pieced together in lieu of sleep and how best to get Renee up to speed. She opted for the direct approach. "I'm not talking about Lovey's motive for sleeping with me, Renee. I'm talking about a potential motive for killing Melinda."

Renee's focus left her shoes once and for all and came to rest, squarely, on Winnie. "I'm listening . . ."

Now that she had Renee's undivided attention, she wasn't exactly sure where to start.

"Winnie?"

Start at the beginning . . .

Armed with the immediate benefit of a deep, fortifying breath, Winnie jumped in feet first. "Remember what Alicia said on Monday? About Melinda snooping around, listening to private conversations, and writing about people in the campus newspaper?"

"Yeah, I guess. Sorta."

"From what Jay said on Tuesday night, it sounds as if Melinda broke a big story every year she was at Silver Lake College. One year it was some sort of gambling thing with the maintenance staff. Another year it was something with a teacher — a grading scam, I think. And another year it involved the athletic department and something about their recruiting techniques."

173

Renee picked a speck of something off her skirt and waited for Winnie to continue. When Winnie didn't, she made a face. "I'm waiting."

"Oh. I was waiting for you," she said.

"For what?"

"To say something to indicate you're following along."

Running a hand through her pixie-style haircut, Renee rolled her eyes with nearly award-winning theatrics. "I'm following. Go on . . ."

"I need coffee. Do you need coffee?" Without waiting for a response, Winnie crossed the hooked rug lengthwise and headed straight for the kitchen, the adrenaline that had kept her eyes open all night now responsible for the warp drive speed at which she walked. "And how about that toast?"

"Stop right there!"

Winnie stopped a few feet shy of the stove and turned around to face her friend. "What?"

"Talk before coffee."

"Come again?" Winnie whacked the side of her head with an open palm and then stared at Renee. "I realize I haven't slept in something like twenty-eight hours at this point, but I could swear you just said, 'Talk

174

before coffee.' "

"Because I did." Renee scooted forward on the couch and then rose onto her new shoes. "Now, freeze *right there* and tell me what you found out about Melinda."

She met Renee at the table and they both took a seat, Renee waiting for more information, and Winnie wishing she had something solid to provide. "I'm not sure what she was onto, exactly, but I think it involved a handful of students — one of which was her roommate, and another that was her roommate's friend."

"Did you find this out yesterday when you went to the college?" Renee asked.

"Bridget managed to talk Sam into letting her borrow Melinda's notebook, only Bridget gave it to me to hold and I forgot to give it back to her after the town meeting last night."

Renee's hand shot up between them. "First, who's Sam?"

"The RA on Melinda's floor."

"Okay, I knew that. And secondly, you took Bridget with you when you went to the college?"

It was impossible to miss the hint of hurt in Renee's voice, and Winnie rushed to stamp it out before it overpowered the subject at hand. "Bridget asked to go. And honestly, I'm glad she did. Her nose for journalism actually came in handy. Without her, I wouldn't have Melinda's notebook and I wouldn't have spent all of last night running through it with a fine-tooth comb."

Renee looked as if she wanted to call foul, but in the end, she simply looked down at her now-yellow fingernails and shrugged. "So Bridget helped you uncover this possible motive?"

"Bridget doesn't know any of this. I haven't seen her yet today."

The hint of hurt faded to something a lot closer to glee before Renee interlaced her fingers and brought them up to her chin. "What did Melinda dig up this time?"

"I'm not sure exactly. But I think I have enough that I can start asking questions."

Renee's cat green eyes narrowed in on Winnie's face. "What kind of questions?"

"What was Melinda onto? Who did it affect? Who knew what she was working on? And was it something that might have made someone want to kill her?" Winnie leaned to the side and grabbed the notepad she'd placed at the end of the table earlier that morning. "Then depending on those answers, I have more questions all ready to go in here."

Renee looked from Winnie to the notepad

and back again. "Okay, but a few minutes ago you said something about Melinda's roommate. Is there a reason she's on your radar right now?"

"The roommate's name is one of six written in Melinda's notebook. Another is your favorite person, Alicia, and another is Nina's friend."

"Nina is the roommate, yes?"

Winnie nodded.

"What did this notebook say exactly?" Renee asked.

"Right now, it's just about a few lists, questions Melinda herself had, and some sort of money notations. But I think, with a little snooping around of my own, those things might start to make more sense — help to color in the picture a little better."

Renee paused a moment and then lowered her hands back down to the table. "Do you have any sort of gut feeling at this point?"

"I do. But I could be way off base." Winnie swung her legs over the side of the bench and stood. "I'll be right back."

Less than a minute later she was back, Melinda's notebook in her hand, and Lovey at her feet.

"Good morning, Lovey." Renee dropped her hand in line with her ankles and scratched Lovey behind the ears, earning herself a thank-you purr in the process. "I'm glad she's warming up to you, Winnie."

"I'm not sure if last night was about warming up to me, or a case of Lovey making sure I know the bed is still hers even if I'm in it." She reclaimed her seat, set the notebook on the table, and spun it around for Renee to see. "Watch."

When she was sure her friend's attention was on the table rather than the cat, Winnie opened the book to the page responsible for her gut feeling and slowly unfolded the second slip of paper she'd come across during the night.

Art Joel — Griffin. Due April 12. Delivered April 10.

$300 pod.

Renee looked up as Winnie's finger reached the bottom. "What is this?"

"It's some sort of bookkeeping record."

"From . . ."

"I think it belongs to Melinda's roommate, Nina. The writing is the same as a slip of paper I found back here." Winnie held their current spot in the notebook with one hand and used the other hand to turn back to an earlier page and the first folded note she'd found. "Pod, in this case, obviously means paid on delivery. My hunch is that Art Joel-Griffin is a student at the college, but it's just a hunch."

Renee pointed at the folded slip of paper wedged into the earlier section Winnie held open with her hand. "What's this one say?"

"You can open it if you want, but it's just more bookkeeping stuff."

"If this is Melinda's notebook, why are bookkeeping notes from her roommate inside it?" Renee unfolded the other slip of paper and held it next to the first one.

"I think Melinda took them. And I think it's this stuff that probably alienated the two girls from one another."

Leaning forward, Renee's gaze slipped down the newly unfolded page, with Winnie's in hot pursuit. Though in all fairness, Winnie had the contents and their order memorized at this point.

5 English Lit — Marrow.
3 European History — Griffin.
5 × \$250 = \$1,250.
3 × \$300 = \$900.
Total: \$2,150.
20 percent = 430.
Nate: \$322.50.
Me: \$107.50.

"Oh. Wait. There's that name again. So this Art Joel-Griffin person takes European History, yes?"

"It looks that way." Winnie gestured her

chin toward the napkin holder in the middle of the table. "Can you grab one of those and put it where my left hand is?"

"Why? You don't enjoy being a human bookmark?" Renee waited Winnie out for a moment and then did as she'd been asked. "So now what?"

Winnie flipped the page over onto the napkin and sat back, her thoughts taking her on an imaginary tour guided by her mouth. "I go back to the school and ask more questions. Only now, instead of just asking questions about the blackberry crisp and who may or may not have had access to it, I can ask other stuff — stuff I hope will eventually tie back to the crisp and who really killed Melinda."

"Who are you going to ask?"

She pushed Melinda's notebook out of the way and tugged her own into its place. With a practiced hand, she flipped past the grocery lists and went straight to the pages of notes she'd made during the night. "I think I'll start with Sam first. See if she knows any of the names Melinda mentions. If she does, I'll see what she can tell me about each one. Then I'll track them down and talk to them myself. See if something one of them says will help make sense of" — she waved at Melinda's book and the separate notation papers — "this stuff."

"Maybe one of them can tell you if the person who wrote this is *paying* a hundred and seven dollars or *receiving* a hundred and seven dollars. And if they're receiving it, why are they getting *a quarter* of what this Nate guy is getting?"

CHAPTER 14

Winnie was almost disappointed when the pair of girls passed her on the steps leading to Bryant Hall. Sure, she'd been waiting for an opportunity to enter the building for far longer than she'd imagined, but the wait had begun to yield a few unexpected opportunities. In fact, for the first time all week, she was actually getting to enjoy the picture-perfect spring weather from a vantage point other than Lovey's window. And not only did the sun feel good against her skin, but it was also lulling her off to the sleep she desperately needed . . .

Wiping the hint of drool from the corners of her mouth, she shook herself into full consciousness and leapt to her feet in time to grab the door just before it clicked shut behind the girls. She was all for the safety that came with swipe-card access until it meant she couldn't get into a building on her own.

For the third time in four days, she headed straight for the lone elevator in the center of the building and rode it up to Melinda's floor.

Melinda's old floor . . .

The floor once inhabited by the late Melinda . . .

She was actually grateful when the elevator door slid open and brought her inane mental blabbering to an end. This was why she baked — to lose herself in something productive and creative rather than her own head.

More than anything, she wanted to bake again. To take orders, match them with just the right recipe, and use them to put a smile on someone else's face. It's all she'd ever wanted to do in life. Trying to navigate her world without that was more than she could comprehend.

Then again, she could never have imagined one of her desserts being tied to a person's death, either.

She pushed the thought from her head long enough to take a deep breath and pass the lone remaining star on Melinda's closed door. She didn't really need to look back for verification of which star was missing, but still she did.

Sure enough, the only name now on the

door was Nina's.

That was fast . . .

Then again, was it? Would she, as a college senior, have wanted her dead roommate's name on the door?

Yes.

In memoriam.

Feeling an odd chill beginning to form at the base of her spine, Winnie continued down the hall, the sight of Sam's door a welcome one.

"Sam?" She knocked on the open door and smiled when the girl inside turned in her direction. "Do you have a minute?"

The casual ease the resident assistant had displayed the first day was gone, in its place the same apprehension with which she'd greeted Winnie and Bridget yesterday. "I suppose."

Winnie hesitated at the door. "Is everything okay?"

"Do you have Melinda's notebook?"

She patted the side of her shoulder bag and stepped into the girl's room. "That's why I'm here. I want to ask you a few questions about some of the things she wrote in here. See if any of what she wrote makes sense to you."

"I — I shouldn't have given that to you and your friend. I gave my word to Melinda

184

I wouldn't show it to anyone." Sam shifted nervously from foot to foot, her gaze darting from Winnie to the door and back again. "I'd like it back now, please."

It was a request she hadn't been prepared to hear, and one she was even less prepared to handle. Which meant she had to think fast, had to convince Sam that letting Winnie hang on to the notebook benefited Melinda.

"Sam, I know you don't know me from a hole in the wall. I also know Melinda was your friend. But I know I didn't kill her." She reached into her bag and pulled out the notebook. "That said, I think it's possible that the person who did is mentioned in this book."

The girl's eyes widened as if she'd been slapped. "You do? *Who?*"

"I don't know all the players Melinda mentioned in here but I'm hoping you can help me with that."

"Players?" Sam echoed.

Winnie looked down at the rubber band she'd slipped back into place around the book and then back up at the girl standing not more than three feet away. "You said yesterday that Melinda was working on a story for the paper. Something she didn't want anyone to know about until she had all the facts, right?"

Sam nodded but said nothing.

"I don't understand everything I read in here last night, but something was definitely up. And my guess is that the something she was onto contributed to her death."

"You mean someone killed her for *revenge?*"

It was the same question she herself had entertained during the night, the same question that had yielded the answer responsible for her being there, in Sam's room, for the second time in as many days. "Melinda hadn't yet gone public with whatever she'd uncovered so I'm guessing revenge wouldn't be the motive."

"Then I'm not sure what you're saying," Sam said, her voice strained.

Winnie held the notebook between them and gave it a little shake. "I think there's a chance that someone in here may have killed Melinda to keep her quiet."

"Keep her —" Sam stopped, swallowed, and started again. "Keep her quiet?"

"That's the only thing that makes sense." She took a deep breath and crossed her fingers underneath the notebook. "I think Melinda's notes could lead us to the person who did this if we put our heads together and follow its trail of breadcrumbs."

"May — maybe we should give it to the police. Let — let them handle it."

It was a valid point for someone whose livelihood wasn't hanging in the balance . . .

"Sam, I have to ask you to trust me on this. Just give me a few days. See if we can figure out what Melinda was onto first."

"But that's what the police are supposed to do," Sam argued.

"In time, maybe the Silver Lake Police could figure it out, but I don't have the kind of time I suspect they'll take. My business is literally imploding right now. People aren't placing orders because the media is more than happy to keep mentioning me in relation to Melinda's death. It's juicy and it's fun. For them. But I can't afford to let a connection between Melinda's death and my desserts linger out there. If it does, it won't matter what the cops uncover a few weeks from now. I'll already be convicted in people's minds."

And then, because she was desperate, she threw in one more plea. "Please, Sam. *Please.* Baking is my life. I'd be lost without it."

She could see the protest raging in Sam's eyes, but in the end, the girl shrugged and offered her desk chair to Winnie. "I've got about ten minutes before I have to head out to my next class."

It took everything in her power not to squeal and throw her arms around Sam, but she resisted. Instead, she sat down, pulled off the rubber band, opened the dead girl's notebook, and began rattling off names.

"Do the names *Doug Cummings, Pete Blyss,* and/or *Art Joel-Griffin* mean anything to you?" she asked.

Sam leaned against the wall next to her bed and let loose a tiny grin. "That's Lummings on Doug. And yeah, they all go here. Only it's Art Joel, not Art Joel-Griffin, or whatever you just said."

Fishing her hand back into her shoulder bag, Winnie removed her own notebook and opened it atop Melinda's. Then reaching back into her bag, she plucked out a pen and made the necessary correction to her notes.

"Do you happen to know what their tie is to Melinda's roommate? Are they close friends?"

Sam's eyebrows rose in unison with each other. "Close friends? I don't think so. Doug plays in the pep band here on campus. Not the brightest bulb in the box, but a nice enough guy."

"And Pete Blyss?" Winnie prompted with

her pen poised and ready to make more notes.

"I'm not as familiar with him, but I know he's a super big partier."

Winnie wrote that down next to Pete's name and then looked back up at Sam. "Anything else on him?"

"Unlike Doug, who at least tries when it comes to academics, Pete could care less. He's not here to learn, he's here to socialize and drink."

She added that tidbit and then placed the pair of notebooks on Sam's desk for better support. "How about the last name? Art Joel? And you're sure there isn't a hyphen at the end of that?"

Pushing off the wall with her foot, Sam crossed to her backpack and began placing books inside. "I'm positive there's no hyphen. And yes, I know Art. In fact, I dated him for a while my sophomore year. Biggest. Mistake. Of. My. Life."

"Oh?"

"Turned out to be a total jerk." Sam grabbed a pen off her desk, tossed it into a smaller pocket on the front of her backpack, and then zipped closed both sections. "The guy was always looking for a way around everything — he had unlimited swipes in the dining hall, yet was always carrying food

189

out. Half of it he ended up tossing anyway. He's the guy you see complaining at a restaurant, or a store, or wherever, because he knows that if he complains to just the right person, he'll get something for free. Yet he comes from money. Big money, as a matter of fact."

"And you didn't see that at first?"

"I was blinded by the fact that my friends thought he was hot and he was interested in me. Took me all of about a week to realize there was nothing below the surface — not a personality, not a heart, not a brain." Leaving her backpack on the floor, Sam stood and checked the time on the desk clock. "Live and learn, you know? Anyway, I've only got about five more minutes . . ."

Winnie scanned the list of names in Melinda's notebook, tapping her finger on the second to last one. "Nate Daniels. That's Nina's friend, yes?"

There was no missing Sam's eye roll. What exactly it meant, though, was another story.

Winnie returned to her own notebook and the page she'd set aside for Nate and Nina. "Not a fan, I take it?" she prodded.

"You ever meet a person who blames everyone around him for his own shortcomings?" At Winnie's nod, Sam continued. "Nate was on the soccer team until last spring. One of the stars, actually. He was even on a full ride. Turns out, though, that he managed to pull one over on the coach when he was being recruited."

"What do you mean by 'pull one over'?"

"He faked his grades so they'd pay for his tuition."

"And his high school didn't know?"

"According to Melinda, Nate's mom worked at the high school."

Winnie's head snapped up. "According to *Melinda*?"

Sam peeked at the clock again and returned to her backpack. Reaching down, she grabbed hold of the straps and hoisted it onto her left shoulder. "Yeah. Melinda is the one that exposed the truth. She's why Nate got kicked off the soccer team."

Unsure of what to say over the dull roar in her head, Winnie took a moment to process the information. "Did he have to pay back his first three years of tuition?"

"You'd think so, wouldn't you?" Sam snorted and slowly made her way toward her door. "There was some song and dance that Nate, too, had been a victim in this. How, I'll never understand, but that's the way it went. He did, however, have to pay for this year."

She noted that in her book and then asked

one last question. "Do you have any idea why Nina may have been keeping some sort of money tally related to school fees?"

Sam stopped just inside the open doorway and shrugged. "No clue. Except she is an accounting major, so maybe it's something to do with that."

"Maybe." Winnie gathered the notebooks into her arm and stood, her desire for another ten minutes with Sam making it difficult to leave. "Thanks for answering my questions, Sam. I'm not sure what all of this means just yet, but I intend to find out."

Doubling back, Sam returned to the desk and retrieved a bright green lanyard from its resting spot beside a lamp. At the bottom of the lanyard and attached with a clip, was a small key and a plastic card with a swipe strip across the back. "Can't forget this." Then, making her way back to the door, the girl started to speak, stopped, and then started again. "Winnie, I get that you're trying to help and I get the why. I really do. But I need you to understand that Melinda was my friend."

"I get that." And she did. She just didn't get why Sam was reminding her of that fact.

"I can only give you a few days with that notebook. After that, if you haven't gotten anywhere, I'll need you to give it back to me so I can show it to the police."

She wanted to argue, to plead for as much time as she needed, but to do so would be unfair. To Winnie, Melinda was just an image. To Sam, Melinda was so much more.

"I understand."

Sam stepped into the hall and then turned back to Winnie. "Do me a favor, okay? Pull my door shut when you leave?"

"Don't you want me to leave with you?"

"That notebook is only some of the stuff Melinda left on my desk. Most of it is junk — candy wrappers and silly doodles I just can't make myself throw away yet. But there's other stuff, too." Winnie followed Sam's tour guide style narration back to the desk and its pile of clutter. "There's a memory stick over there somewhere that she was always popping in and out of her computer whenever she was in here, and that camera over there is hers, too. Oh, and when she wasn't on her computer, she was making notes — in her notebook, on sticky notes, across envelopes, you name it. Go through it. Maybe something will help."

She switched the notebooks to her other arm and studied Sam closely. "You're sure it's okay? For me to stay here without you?"

"Yeah. It's okay."

"How will I know if something is Melinda's or yours?" she asked.

"If it's on the desk, it's Melinda's. I use my bed and the floor around it." Sam tapped the wall next to the door and then hooked her thumb over her shoulder. "Good luck, Winnie."

CHAPTER 15

Winnie leaned against the picnic table and lifted her face to the late afternoon sun, guilt be damned. Yes, she should have turned right out of the campus parking lot and headed back to the house, but when she was faced with that option, one lone word had made its way past her lips.

Why?

Why, indeed.

Customers weren't calling.

Jay wasn't calling.

And if things didn't turn around soon, she'd be forced to fire —

Her phone vibrated against the table's wooden slats and jarred her back to the present. Reaching over her shoulder, she felt around until she found the phone and brought it to her ear. "Hello?"

"Hey, it's me. You still out at the college?"

She contemplated the benefit of a non-committal grunt, but in the end, she answered truthfully. "I'm actually at Silver Lake Park."

"What's going on over there?" Renee asked.

"Nothing."

"Okay . . . So, um, why are you there?"

"That's why." Extending her legs out as far as they would go, Winnie toed at a rock on the ground until she pushed it out of reach completely. "Because there's nothing going on."

She could almost hear Renee's wheels turning right up until the moment she started talking again. "There's nothing going on here, either, Winnie."

"I know." Lifting her elbows onto the table behind her, she took in the empty playground, the empty walking trails, and the lake in the distance. "But the nothing *here* is a little easier to take."

"You do realize you've lost me, don't you?"

"The nothing *here* is about sitting on this picnic table bench and looking out at the lake. The nothing *there* is about a phone that isn't ringing, and . . ." She grabbed the end of her ponytail with her free hand and pulled it in front of her shoulder. "It's killing me that no one is calling. It's killing me that I'm not baking. And it's killing me that

196

I'm going to have to let you go if something doesn't turn around really, really fast."

A brief but distinct kissing sound in her ear gave way to Renee's voice once again. "Lovey keeps wandering over to the door like she's lost, you know. I think she's missing you."

"I doubt that."

"I take it things didn't go well with the dead girl's RA?" Renee asked.

Winnie flicked the tip of her hair against the side of her cheek and then let it fall back down her back as she stood. "Things actually went okay. She was able to tell me who everyone was and a little bit about each person, too."

"That's good. Anything that ties them all together?"

"Other than the fact that they're less than stellar students? No." She dug her hand into her front left pocket and extracted the peppermint candy she'd hijacked from her purse en route to the park. "Oh. And that Art Joel guy? There's no hyphen and no Griffin."

"Then who's Griffin? And what does he or she have to do with European history?"

Winnie unwrapped the candy, popped it in her mouth, and stared out at the lake. Renee's question was akin to a glass of cold water to the face. She didn't need to jog back across the gravel parking lot to the ambulance for Melinda's notebook. The slip of paper with the monetary notations was seared into her brain thanks to the hours she'd spent studying it instead of sleeping.

3 European History — Griffin.

The first few times she'd seen it, she'd been so busy trying to figure out the ensuing math, she hadn't really paid attention. And then, later, when she'd discovered the second slip of paper and the name appeared again, she'd mistakenly read the dash as a hyphen.

Art Joel — Griffin. Due April 12. Delivered April 10.

$300 pod.

"Maybe the dash was related to the part that came after it with the due date and the delivery date. Maybe whatever was delivered went from one to the other."

Renee exhaled in Winnie's ear. "Right. And one of them got three hundred bucks for whatever it was."

"Three hundred bucks," she repeated. Slowly, she made her way past the playground, across the trail, and down to the water's edge, her feet propelled as much by the questions firing away in her head as any intentional choice on her part. "I'm kicking myself for not putting this together while I was in Sam's room. If I had, I could have asked her."

"So call and ask her now."

"I don't have her number."

"You could always ask someone else connected with the college . . ."

She opened her mouth to ask who, but closed it as the intention behind Renee's suggestion took root in her head. "You can't be serious, Renee."

"Why not? This is a reason to call him."

"What, and have him hang up on me?" She followed the shoreline halfway around the lake with her eyes and then turned away as the corner of the home Jay shared with his daughter came into view. "Please. What's the point?"

"C'mon, Winnie, you really think he'd hang up on you?" Renee challenged. "Because I don't. That guy is crazy about —"

"Four days ago, I'd have said no. But four days ago, he didn't think I was capable of murder." Winnie blinked away the tears spawned by Renee's gasp and, instead, unleashed the kind of laugh that was part wounded, part psychotic. "What? I didn't tell you?"

"No, you didn't tell me . . ."

"Ahhh, sorry, I guess it slipped my mind."

She took one last look at the lake and then slowly turned back in the direction from which she'd come. "Yeah, Jay thinks I murdered Melinda."

Renee's tone turned icy. "He *said* that?"

"He didn't have to." Halfway to the picnic table, she changed direction and wandered over to the trio of swings in the center of a heavily mulched play area. "It was written all over his face when I met him at Beans on Tuesday night."

"You can't tell something like that just by someone's face!"

Winnie lowered herself onto the flimsy rubber seat and rested her cheek against the chain tethered to the metal upright above her head. "If that's all there was, I might have to agree, but it wasn't. He wouldn't make eye contact, he had little to say, and he got out of there as fast as he could."

"All things that could be explained by other stuff," Renee mused. "Maybe he wasn't feeling good. Maybe all the stuff he was stressed about over the weekend is still weighing on him. And maybe he had to go because of something with his kid."

"Caroline was in dance class next door. He left ten minutes before her class ended."

"Did he walk you out?"

"Nope." Ever so gently, she pushed off

the ground with her foot only to realize that without both hands on the chains, she was in for a cockeyed ride. "Renee, he thinks I killed this girl. I know it."

"You *think* it, Winnie. You don't *know* it. And let's face it, you've been under an enormous amount of stress since Monday night. Maybe your radar was off."

Was Renee right? Had she projected her own fears onto Jay?

"Call him, Winnie. Ask him who this Griffin person is. And maybe, if you do, you'll realize you're wrong about him."

"And if I'm not?" she asked.

"Then you know for sure, and I can move him from my good-guy list to my jerk-guy list," Renee said.

"Okay." She toed herself to a stop but remained seated on the swing. "I'll do it later. When I get home. In the meantime, why don't you set the phone to forward all calls to my cell and head home yourself. Maybe you can catch the end of Ty's soccer practice."

"I'll do that if you call him as soon as we hang up."

"Why? What difference does it make?"

"You need to know what's going on with him for your own sanity." Renee hesitated, but only for a moment. "*And* we need to figure out what happened to Melinda asap because you need to bake again, Winnie. It's who you are. So call him. Now."

Before she could mount a worthy protest, Renee was gone and Winnie was alone with her thoughts.

Was Renee right? Should she call?

Yes, Jay would be a good source for information on a student named Griffen. And yes, she was craving the sound of his voice in her ear. But what if he hung up when he realized she was on the phone? What if, when prodded, he confirmed her fears and admitted he believed she was a murderer?

I didn't kill Melinda.

Winnie looked out over the lake, tightening her hold on the chains as she did. "I didn't kill Melinda," she said aloud. "If Jay believes otherwise, that's his issue, not mine."

Her mind made up, she hopped off the swing and scrolled through her contacts until she reached Jay's name. Then, fortifying herself with one deep, elongated breath, she hit the Call button and brought the phone to her ear.

One ring . . .

Two rings . . .

Three —

"Hello?"

Closing her eyes, she imagined him sitting in his office, the phone pressed against his cheek, his blue-green eyes crackling with a purely innate sense of happiness. She swallowed and then made herself speak. "Hi Jay. It's me. Winnie."

The beat of silence that met her greeting told her everything she needed to know. The fact that it was also everything she didn't *want* to know was beside the point. The only difference this time was the emotion it stirred inside.

At Beans, she'd been devastated by the reality that Jay Morgan had his doubts about her character. Now, less than forty-eight hours later, the same realization made her angry — *teeth-clenching* angry.

For a moment, she actually considered tearing into him, listing every single reason her name should never have been tied to Melinda's death. But in the end, she moved on to the reason for her call.

"I was hoping you could answer a single question for me. If you can, great. If you can't, no big deal, I'll find out what I need another way." She started toward the parking lot and the Dessert Squad, her gait one of purpose if not anger. "Do you know of a student at the college by the last name of Griffin? Probably connected in some way

203

with the history department?"

"History?" Jay repeated.

Winnie nodded only to realize the error of her ways. "Early European history, to be exact."

"Carl Griffin *teaches* Early European. Could that be who you're talking about?"

"Oh. Wow." She floundered around for a moment, trying to process Jay's words. A teacher? She hadn't seen that one coming. "Are — are you sure?"

"Yup."

"But Art Joel is a student, yes?"

"A senior, yes. Why are you asking?"

Why indeed . . .

Unsure of where exactly she was going with the meaningless threads she'd managed to string together in her head, Winnie took a stab at tying them together. "Would you happen to know if he is a student in this Carl Griffin's class?"

"I can't say for sure, but I know that Early European History is one of the core classes students tend to wait until the last minute to take."

She swirled his words around in her head and then spit them out in the form of a different question. "So it's not necessarily a class that history majors take?"

"As freshmen or sophomores, yes. As

seniors, no."

"Tough class?" she asked.

"For the majors, probably not. For the last-minute core fulfillers, yes."

Hmmm . . .

"So, how's Caroline?" she asked, shifting gears.

"Fine."

Fine . . .

A week or two earlier, he'd have elaborated, telling her about his daughter's classes, grades, friends, and any disagreements they were having. In light of what Winnie now suspected where Jay was concerned, his curt "fine" fit perfectly.

She stopped when she reached the ambulance, transferred the phone to her other ear, and yanked open the driver's side door. The ache in her heart matched the burning sensation in her eyes but she refused to fall prey to either.

Not now. Not here.

"Um, hey . . . uh . . . how's work going? Any . . . new dessert ideas?"

Dropping into position behind the steering wheel, Winnie leaned her head against the seatback. "At the moment, there is no work and no need for new dessert ideas."

The ensuing silence lingered. Only instead of being awkward, it merely motivated

Winnie to move on with her investigation, her day, her life. She didn't kill Melinda; it was that simple. If Jay believed otherwise, he wasn't worth any more of her time.

"I have to go now." She shifted forward in her seat and slipped the key into the ignition. "Good-bye, Jay."

Chapter 16

Acting tough and being tough were two very different things if the drive home from the park was any indication. The urge to press Redial had bubbled to the surface as she turned onto the main road, as she approached the first of three traffic lights tasked with getting her across town, and as she turned onto Serenity Lane.

She'd been so sure she'd know Mr. Right the moment they met, and up until the last few days, she was sure he was Jay. But now that her world had tipped on its axis and he had run the other way, she had to face the fact that she'd been wrong — about Jay and her ability to spot Mr. Right.

Letting up on the gas pedal, Winnie allowed herself a moment to soak up her surroundings — the older yet meticulously maintained homes, the freshly weeded flower beds, the smattering of front porches and their accompanying rocking chairs, the relative peace and quiet of the dinner hour, and the sense of peace it stirred inside her soul.

This was where she needed to be.

This was where she'd find her footing once again.

Inhaling deeply, Winnie pulled into the driveway and shifted the ambulance into Park. It was time to put Jay out of her mind. All that mattered now was finding out who killed Melinda B. Tully and why. With that behind her, she could focus once again on growing the Emergency Dessert Squad.

Unfortunately, the second she stepped onto the driveway and spied Lovey looking back at her from one of the second-floor windows, she felt her resolve dissipating behind a surge of self-pity.

"You ready?"

She spun around so fast, her purse slipped off her arm and spilled out across the driveway.

"Oh. Hey. I didn't mean to startle you. Let me help you with that." Master Sergeant Hottie (aka Greg) placed his three grocery bags on the ground and then bent down to gather up the handful of items that were now scattered around Winnie's feet — the soft pink lipstick she never wore, the miniature package of tissues she'd utilized within

208

moments of ending her call with Jay, the last of the red and white striped peppermint candies Mr. Nelson had insisted she take after their weekly pizza date, and her phone. When he had everything back in her purse, he stood and handed it to Winnie. "Here you go."

She looked from Greg to her purse and back again, her heart rate finally returning to normal. "I'm sorry I jumped like that. I guess I just didn't hear you." Gesturing toward the grocery bags he reclaimed, she did her best to shake off her dour mood. "So what's in the bags?"

"I wasn't sure what you might want to make, so I kind of went a little nuts in the baking aisle. I had no idea just how many different kinds of chocolate there were to choose from, or how many different baking ingredients there really are." He grinned at her over the top of the bags. "I can only imagine how excited *you* must get in there."

"It's kind of like Christmas morning for me, actually." She savored the momentary lift to her spirits and rose up on her tiptoes to peer into the first bag. "Vanilla, flour, sugar, brown sugar . . . white chocolate baking squares. That's a good start."

Greg beamed proudly. "Why, thank you."

"So what are you planning on making

exactly?"

His smile faltered as he met her gaze. "I was kind of hoping you'd be able to come up with something based on what's in these bags."

"*I* could, sure. In fact, truth be told, that's my favorite way to bake."

"Then we're all set."

"All set?" she echoed. "For what?"

He drew back, all signs of his smile gone. "You didn't get my message?"

She started to shake her head but stopped as she rewound back to the previous evening and the message Greg had left on her voice mail — a message she'd cut short in the hope that the second voice mail might be from Jay. "I'm sorry, Greg. Things have been a little nutty and I guess I —"

"No, I should have double checked with you before I went hog wild at the grocery store like I did." Taking a step backward, he motioned his chin in the direction of the black two-door sedan parked in front of the house. "Maybe we can do this some other time."

Her curiosity aroused, she stopped his full turn with her hand. "What did your message say?"

"I don't know, it was probably dumb."

"I doubt that. But hold on." She reached

inside her bag, fished out her phone, and pressed the voice mail icon. With a click of a few buttons, Greg's voice filled her ear.

"Hey, Winnie. It was great to see you tonight. It's been too long, quite frankly. I'm really sorry about what that Batkas guy said about your tie to that college student's death. I know you've been dealing with this stuff since it happened, but I want you to know it really irked me. I know you had nothing to do with what happened to this girl and I'm not going to sit idly by while people imply you did. It's not right and it's not fair."

She mouthed a thank-you at the man standing in front of her and then jammed her hand against her opposite ear in an effort to make out the rest of his message over the distant whir of a lawn mower. "Anyway, I think you need a pick-me-up. I'd suggest a movie or even a walk, only I suspect you would benefit from something else entirely. So, if you don't call and tell me to back off, I'll be at your house tomorrow for a little in-home therapy session." He paused and then added, "We're going to figure this out, Winnie. You have my word on that."

When the message ended, she looked up and swallowed. "*We're* going to figure this out?"

"That's right."

"But why?" she asked. "This really isn't your problem."

"You're special, Winnie. Anyone who knows you thinks that."

"If only that were true," she rasped.

"Let me amend then. Anyone who knows you and has a brain in their head thinks that." Greg jiggled the bags a second time. "But right now, I think you need a distraction."

Finally it all made sense — the smile, the grocery bags, their contents, all of it. What didn't make sense was how she could still be so crushed over Jay. Shaking the immediate image of the college professor from her thoughts, she took hold of one of the grocery bags and allowed its contents to work their inevitable magic. "You're going to *help* me bake, aren't you?"

"If you don't mind walking me through every single step like a two-year-old, then yeah, that was kind of what I was hoping." Greg's earlier smile returned to his face with such ease Winnie could only imagine the countless females who would be swooning if they were in her shoes at that very moment.

Her thoughts raced ahead to all the possibilities — the white chocolate pastry puffs, the miniature Boston crème cupcakes, the cinnamon pinwheels, the —

"So what do you say?"

She peeked into the bags again and let loose the squeal she could no longer hold back. "I say you're on."

She could feel his eyes studying her as she mixed the crushed graham crackers with the melted butter and then pressed the concoction into the bottom of the baking pan. Oddly, it didn't make her feel uncomfortable.

"You really love this, don't you?" he asked from his spot on the other side of the island.

"It's that obvious, huh?" she joked. At his answering nod, she moved on to the butter that needed to be creamed. "It's been like this since I was a little girl. I guess knowing that something I made could put a smile on someone's face kind of hooked me."

He set his forearms on the counter and leaned forward. "And the smile on *your* face?"

"That's the cherry on top. No pun intended." She set the mixer aside long enough to add the required amount of white and brown sugar. "Trust me, I know how blessed I am to be able to make a living doing what I love."

"It *is* pretty cool, isn't it?" He plucked a chocolate chip from a small bowl in the center of the island and popped it into his mouth. "I guess we're fortunate in that way."

"What you do is on a completely different level. You help people. I just make them something to eat."

He reached for another chip, but stopped just shy of his target. "We're both helping, Winnie. And we're both doing what we love."

"Your job matters. Mine is something people could do without." In a separate bowl, she combined flour, baking soda, and salt and added that to the butter mixture. "And if I can't figure out what happened to this Melinda girl, they will."

The second the words were out, she wished she could recall them. Greg was right — she needed light and fun. The subject of Melinda Tully wasn't either of those things.

"We already know you didn't do it, so that part is already figured out. We just need to make sure the rest of Silver Lake knows it, too." His shoulders noticeably drooped when she took charge of the chip bowl and poured them into the mixture. "I have to confess, my mom's nickname for me growing up was Chip Monster."

"Chip Monster?"

"As in *chocolate* chips."

She tried to focus on his banter, but every time she did, her thoughts took her right back to reality. "How can you be so sure I didn't do it? I mean, you haven't known me all that long."

"I don't need to. Look at you. Look at the way you live."

"Meaning?"

"I'm not entirely sure a new car could have gotten a bigger smile than the one I saw when you looked into the bags out on the driveway. I just don't think the kind of person capable of murdering a college kid would get excited over a bottle of vanilla and a few bags of chips." He leaned forward again, only this time, he did it to gain a better view of the mixture inside her bowl. "And then there's your choice of residence. Instead of renting an apartment on the other side of town like other single people our age, you pick a street where the median age is what? Seventy-five?"

Shrugging, she added the required amount of marshmallows to the mix and then spooned it over the waiting graham crust. "Something like that, I suppose."

"You like it here, right?"

"I love it here. Mr. Nelson, Bridget, Cornelia Wright, Peggy Landon, Jed and Gladys Mavery, and even Harold down the street . . . they've become like family to me. I feel safe here. Happy. Centered."

He watched her spread the mixture atop the graham cracker crust and then came around the counter to stand a little closer. "I've always wondered, but I've never asked. So now I'm asking. Why old people?"

"Because, time and time again, they accept me as I am. And it's been that way since I was a kid." She rested the mixing spoon against the side of the bowl and carried the pan to the oven. Once it was safely inside and the timer was set for ten minutes, she turned to face Greg. "My parents and I moved when I was in fourth grade. To a town where everyone had known each other since they were born. The last thing any of those kids needed was a new friend."

Reaching around her, he ran his finger along the top edge of the bowl and then shoved it inside his mouth. "Go on."

She contemplated a host of responses to his thievery, but settled on a dramatic shake of her finger. "*Anyway,* I felt so out of place I couldn't wait for the school day to be over. But even when it was, it wasn't any different. I still had to walk home alone. I still had no one to play with when my homework was done. Then, one day, I decided to take a different way home and I passed an older man named Mr. McCormick. He waved at me and asked me what subject I liked best in school. The next day, I decided to walk that same way . . . and there he was again. Only this time, he waved me over to see a table he was making with his own hands. Soon, I was walking home that way *every* day. Before I knew it, I wasn't so lonely anymore. Mr. McCormick and his wife and their neighbors became my friends. They asked about my day, shared stories about their own childhoods, and made me feel like I mattered."

"But you're an adult now." Greg walked to the sink, rinsed off his finger, and then sauntered back to the island.

"And my elderly friends still make me feel like I matter." She poured a handful of miniature chocolate bars onto the counter and began to unwrap them. When she had the pieces she needed, she put them into a separate bowl and popped them into the freezer. "When something goes right, Mr. Nelson and Bridget are right there, ready to celebrate with me. And when something goes wrong, they're at my side, encouraging me until I'm back on my feet or feeling better about things. I can't imagine my life without them."

He glanced over his shoulder in the direction of the oven timer and then leaned his back into the counter. "Isn't the constant heartbreak hard, though?"

"Heartbreak?"

"When they die."

And just like that, the fortress she'd erected around her emotions collapsed and the tears she'd managed to keep at bay thus far began their descent down her cheeks. "I've lost some of them, sure. It's life. There's always going to be loss regardless of age."

Pushing off the counter, Greg wrapped his arms around Winnie and pulled her close. For several minutes they simply stood there as he rubbed her back and she gave in to the tears that were as much about her current predicament as anything else. When she'd had her cry, she stepped back and hooked her thumb over her shoulder. "The timer is going to go off in about thirty seconds. Can you grab a small handful of marshmallows from that bag over there while I get the pan out of the oven?"

They met back at the center island, where she placed the partially cooked bar in front of him. "Now scatter the marshmallows across the top and I'll put it back in the oven for another ten minutes."

"What about the chocolate pieces you put in the freezer?" he asked as he released the marshmallows from his fist and onto the top of the still-cooking bar.

"Those go on the second we pull it out of the oven for good." When the last marshmallow was in place, she carried the pan back to the oven and again set the timer for ten minutes. "I'm sorry for falling apart like I just did. I don't usually do that."

"It gave me an excuse to hug you, didn't it?"

Feeling her cheeks begin to warm, she busied herself at the sink with the dirty mixing bowl and measuring cups. It was easier that way. "I — I guess I've just got a lot on my plate right now with this girl's death, and all the fingers being pointed at me and my Emergency Dessert Squad."

"We're gonna figure this out, Winnie. I promise."

"I wish everyone shared your conviction as to my culpability in this whole thing." There was no denying the tremor to her voice or the way Greg closed the gap between them in response.

Reaching around her, he flicked off the faucet, pulled her hands from the soapy water, and slowly turned her until they were facing each other. "Jay Morgan is a fool, Winnie — a fool for thinking you could have anything to do with this girl's death, and a fool for leaving the door wide open."

"Leaving the door wide open?" she echoed.

"For me."

CHAPTER 17

She followed Lovey down the stairs, their collective feet guided by the rhythmic creek of Mr. Nelson's rocker and the melodic lilt of Bridget's voice. When they reached the bottom step, she paused just inside the screen door and allowed herself a moment to breathe in the normalcy that was a spring evening on Serenity Lane.

Here, everything was as it should be. Cornelia Wright was taking her sheltie, Con Man, for his last walk of the evening, and Harold Jenkins was following behind on his motorized scooter trying to pretend as if he'd chosen that exact moment to get a little fresh air. Farther down the road, Peggy Landon, the road's centurion matriarch, was sweeping any unwanted remnants of the day from her front porch before turning in for the night.

"You going to keep standing there like that

or are you going to come out here and join us?"

Smiling, Winnie stepped out onto the porch, her mental ten-count only reaching five before Bridget's indignant response filled the air.

"How is it that you've not acknowledged a word I've said over the past thirty minutes, Parker, yet you can hear Winnie standing inside the doorway, silent as a church mouse?"

Mr. Nelson's mouth drooped with feigned surprise. "You've been talking, Bridget?"

Winnie gave in to the laughter she sorely needed and then bent around the side of her next-door neighbor's chair and planted a kiss atop the elderly woman's head. "Ignore him, Bridget. The volume on his hearing aid is turned all the way up. He's been listening."

A mischievous smile flitted its way across Mr. Nelson's mouth as he craned his head upward for a kiss, too. "Stop blowing my cover, Winnie Girl."

Clicking her tongue against her dentures, Bridget invited an all-too-eager Lovey onto her lap. Once the cat was settled and purring, the eighty-year-old gave Winnie a thorough once-over complete with a dramatic sidelong glance in Mr. Nelson's direction.

"Uh-oh," Winnie said as she took up shop against the front rail. "What did I do now?"

"We were sitting out here when he left, dear."

"He?"

And then she knew.

But before she could explain, Bridget continued on, her wrinkled and age-spotted hand slowly making its way down Lovey's back. "I almost fell out of my chair when I saw Master Sergeant Hottie step onto this porch."

"That's if you believe she didn't already know he was here when she waddled across the yard an hour or so ago." Mr. Nelson reached up, adjusted something in his ear, and then rested his head against the back of his rocker.

"Are you implying I was snooping out my window, Parker?" Bridget stopped petting Lovey long enough to point an accusatory finger at her counterpart. "And I do not waddle."

Mr. Nelson cocked his head, scrunching his eyebrows as he did. "What was that, Bridget? I didn't catch that."

Winnie tried to stifle her laughter, but if the glare she earned from Bridget was any indication, she'd been grossly unsuccessful.

Oops.

Anxious to head off the next world war, Winnie tackled Bridget's curiosity once and for all. "Greg and I were baking. It was fun."

"Faking?" Mr. Nelson repeated. "Faking what?"

Winnie tapped her finger to her ear and waited for her housemate to engage his volume feature once again. When he did, she repeated her original statement.

"Does Master Sergeant Hottie *bake,* dear?" Bridget asked between lip licks.

"Can we just call him *Greg,* please? This whole Master Sergeant Hottie thing is a little too weird, you know?"

Bridget's hand finally resumed petting duty. "I find it to be a very accurate moniker quite frankly. He *is* one very fine man, Winnie."

One very fine man?

Determined to gain control of the conversation, Winnie pushed off the railing and made her way over to the vacant rocker on Mr. Nelson's right. "Anyway, he knows I've been going through a lot these last few days, and he thought a baking session might cheer me up. And he was right. It was fun."

Mr. Nelson leaned forward and slowly looked around the porch. "I don't see any baked goods 'round here. What did you make?"

"A S'more bar. And I let Greg take it with him. I figured the guys at the ambulance district would enjoy a special treat during the overnight shift."

"Drats." Shifting back into his seat, Mr. Nelson peered up at the porch ceiling. "Now what do you call that for the Dessert Squad again, Winnie Girl? Worry No S'more Cake?"

"Worry No S'more Bar." She slouched into the rocker and stared out at the massive pin oak in the front yard. "But it doesn't really matter. It's just a plain old S'more bar now."

She didn't need to look at either of her companions to know they were exchanging glances. About her. And on any other given day and regarding any other topic, she'd rush to tell them not to worry, that she had things under control. But it wasn't any other day and she didn't have things under control.

Not by a long shot.

"You didn't kill that girl," Bridget declared.

Mr. Nelson stopped rocking long enough to put his heart and soul into his nod.

A few days earlier, their steadfast belief in

her innocence had meant everything. Now, she saw it for what it was — a nice touch, but sorely inadequate. "I know that, Bridget. You know that. Mr. Nelson knows that. Renee knows that. Greg knows that. But my customers don't know that."

Lovey's head popped up and she gazed at Winnie through the slats of Bridget's wicker armrest. For once, there was no glower, no animosity. And then, before she realized what was happening, the cat left the elderly woman's lap and came to sit on the floor next to Winnie.

"Looks like Lovey, here, knows you're innocent, too." Mr. Nelson slowed his rocking a smidge and focused his attention on Winnie. "I saw you leave this afternoon. That wasn't for a delivery?"

"I wish." Realizing she was mumbling, she elevated the volume of her voice so as to be heard by her friends. "No, I went to the college to talk to Melinda's RA again."

"Did you learn anything, dear?"

She thought back to everything she'd learned that day. All of it, while interesting, didn't deliver a suspect to her door. "I don't know."

"What do you mean, you don't know?"

"I asked Sam about the names Melinda had written in her notebook." Twisting to

226

the side, Winnie hiked her leg onto the rocker and used her body to move the chair. Lovey remained by her side, lazily taking in the yard and the porch. "Other than identifying them all as seniors and not the greatest students, there wasn't much to learn."

"Were they *friends* with Melinda?" Bridget asked.

"It didn't sound that way. From what I gather, Melinda was a good student — a serious student. The people she mentioned on one of those slips of paper I found wedged into her notebook weren't."

She thought back to her brief conversation with Jay and did her best to share only the parts that mattered. Anything beyond that and she might not be able to keep her emotions in check. "One of the names on the list, though, belonged to a teacher at the school. A history teacher, to be exact."

"What's his name, dear?"

"Griffin. Carl Griffin."

Bridget paused and then shook her head. "I don't recognize that one."

"His name showed up on a bookkeeping sheet of some sort. On that same sheet there was a student's name and the amount of three hundred dollars. Next to the amount, 'pod' was noted."

"Paid on delivery." Bridget slowly rose to

her feet, wandered over to the small table near the center of the porch, and plucked a plate of fresh fruit from its surface. "I stopped at Medders' Fruit and Farm Stand on my way home from the newspaper office this afternoon. Cindy said the strawberries were extra delicious and she was right, wasn't she, Parker?"

"Tasted like regular strawberries to me," Mr. Nelson groused.

Bridget made her way back across the porch with the plate of strawberries in her hand. When she reached Winnie, she held out the plate. "Ignore him, he's being grouchy. They're delicious."

"Are you being grouchy, Mr. Nelson?"

"Yes. He is." Bridget moved on to her own chair. "But once I tell him she has a Bradford Pear for sale that would fit very nicely in the side yard, he'll change his tune."

Mr. Nelson sat up tall. "Medder has a Bradford Pear?"

Bridget helped herself to a strawberry but stopped shy of eating it so she could flash a knowing grin in Winnie's direction. "See?"

"What else does he have up there?"

"*She* has fresh fruit, baby trees of just about every variety, and a greenhouse filled with all kinds of interesting and unusual plants — flowering and otherwise." Bridget took a bite and worked the fruit around in her mouth before finally swallowing it. "Corey helps her, of course, but I get the sense Cindy is the one with the green thumb."

Winnie tried to pay attention to the conversation going on around her, but it was hard. Her thoughts were at the college with Sam, and back on the phone call with Jay.

Jay . . .

Shaking the handsome business professor from her thoughts, she dropped her foot back down to the ground and gestured toward the screen door. "If I went upstairs and got Melinda's notebook, could I show you the sheets? You know, in case you spot something I've missed?"

At Bridget's nod, Winnie pointed down at Lovey. "I'll be right back, Your Highness. Don't disappear."

Less than five minutes later, she was back on the porch and swapping Melinda's notebook for Bridget's plate of strawberries. Then bending down, she used her free hand to open the book to the first page, and her finger to guide Bridget's eyes down the hastily scrawled list of names.

"Doug Cummings, Pete Blyss, Art Joel, Alicia Worth, Nate Daniels, and Nina,"

Bridget read aloud. When she was done, she looked up at Winnie. "Alica Worth . . . is that the girl you had working with you when you made that delivery to the college?"

"Yes."

"Nina? Is that Melinda's Nina?"

"I believe it is, yes."

"And is this Nate the same Nate that Nina told us about? The one who showed up at Melinda and Nina's room within moments of Sam dropping off your pie?"

She marveled at the elderly woman's memory, but rather than comment on it, she simply nodded.

"What do you know about the others?" Bridget asked.

"Well, Doug's last name is actually Lummings . . . that's an L, not a C. I made the same mistake. Other than that, it's what I told you earlier — they're all seniors and less than stellar students.

"Now, read that." Winnie flipped to the next page and the slip of paper wedged inside the seam. "See what you think when you do."

Bridget removed the slip of paper, unfolded it atop the notebook, and gazed down at the names and numbers Winnie had all but memorized.

5 English Lit — Marrow.

3 European History — Griffin.
5 × \$250 = \$1,250.
3 times; \$300 = \$900.
Total: \$2,150.
20 percent = 430.
Nate: \$322.50.
Me: \$107.50.

When she reached the bottom, Bridget flipped it over, saw that there was nothing written on the back, and then turned it right side up once again. "Melinda didn't write this. The penmanship is completely different."

"I think Nina wrote it."

Bridget looked down at the slip of paper again, her lips forming words Winnie couldn't hear.

"Bridget?"

"You said earlier that this Griffin is a teacher, yes?"

She swallowed back the urge to mention Jay and, instead, stuck to the only answer that really mattered. "That's right. He's part of the history department at the college."

"Hence the European history notation beside his name." Bridget's finger, crooked with arthritis, ran up the slip of paper to the top. "Therefore, I think it's safe to assume Marrow is a teacher at the college, as well. In the *English* department."

"I hadn't thought of that, but you're right, that makes sense." And it did. There was no denying the fact that Bridget was sharp. "Now look at this . . ."

Winnie flipped ahead to the next slip of paper wedged into the center seam and unfolded it beside the first. Before she could say anything, Bridget began spouting initial observations. "The writing on both of these papers is the same. So if Nina wrote the first, she wrote this one, as well."

"That's what I'm think —"

"They're cheating!" Bridget declared.

Winnie grabbed hold of Bridget's armrest and stared at the woman. "Excuse me?"

"They're cheating."

"But —"

"Look." Bridget guided Winnie's eyes down the second slip of paper . . .

Art Joel — Griffin. Due April 12. Delivered April 10.

$300 pod.

"Something was due in this Carl Griffin's history class on April the twelfth. This student, Art Joel, turned it in on April tenth." Bridget's finger hopped over to the first slip of paper and made its way slowly up to the top. "My guess is that these teachers are taking bribes in exchange for grades and Melinda found out."

Feeling the porch begin to spin around her, Winnie tightened her grip on Bridget's chair and made herself take a slow, deliberate breath. "Bribes?"

"Sure." Bridget waved the first slip of paper in the air and then turned back to the first page in the notebook. "And these six names, right here, represent the students doing the bribing."

Considering what Sam had told her about the lack of academic interest for the named students, it actually made sense. Still, she took a moment to digest and dissect Bridget's theory.

"Okay, so let's say you're right and Melinda uncovered this," Winnie mused. "Her murderer could be any one of those students."

"Or teachers," Mr. Nelson pointed out. "Six weeks ago, I'd have never said such a thing. But there's not a one of us on this porch who doesn't know better now."

Bridget refolded the slips of paper, worked them into their appropriate pages, and then handed the notebook to Winnie. "I can see a student going unnoticed in a dormitory, but not a teacher."

"I don't understand." Winnie tucked the notebook under her arm and handed the strawberry plate back to Bridget. "What does the dorm have to do with — wait. My crisp. They had to have access to my crisp."

Mr. Nelson stopped rocking and looked up at Winnie. "You never told me what you called your crisp."

Looking back, the name had seemed so clever for someone whose college career was drawing to a close. The fact that Melinda loved blackberries had made it all the more perfect. Yet now, knowing what she knew, it was hard not to see the name as foreshadowing.

"Fade to Black-Berry Crisp," Bridget said, rising to her feet. "Can you imagine?"

If Mr. Nelson was bothered by the name in relation to Melinda's demise, it didn't show. Instead, he positioned his cane slightly forward of his rocker and helped himself to a stand. "I guess, if nothing else, you have an alternate career option if this nonsense continues to affect the Dessert Squad."

"Oh?"

"Sure." He caned his way over to Winnie's side, leaned forward, and planted a sweet kiss on her cheek. "You could be a psychic."

CHAPTER 18

Winnie hated that the simple ring of a phone could make her run, but considering their predicament, she supposed it made sense. Still, Lovey wasn't pleased when her food dish went sailing across the floor, compliments of Winnie's foot.

"Shhhh," Renee hissed as she covered the phone and glared.

Mouthing an apology, Winnie scurried across the kitchen, retrieved Lovey's food bowl from its landing spot, and returned it to its rightful place alongside the bright blue water dish. As she went, she couldn't help noticing Renee's pen gliding across the order pad . . .

Slowly, she tiptoed her way over to the table for a peek. Sure enough, they had an order — the first order in days.

"We'll have that to them by lunchtime." Renee clicked off the phone and squealed. "We did it! We have an order!"

She lifted her arms to join the celebration but yanked them back down just as quickly. "And you think this is a real order? Not just a prank?"

"Master Sergeant Hottie is real, isn't he?" Renee ripped the order from the pad and handed it to Winnie. "He wants the Butt Kickin' Shoe Fly Pie delivered to Stan and Chuck over at the district building in time for lunch. He says they need it."

"So this is a pity order," Winnie mumbled.

"Maybe it is, maybe it isn't. But does it really matter?"

She skimmed her way down the order form, stopping as she reached Greg's credit card information. "I don't want Greg going broke trying to keep me in business. It's not right."

"It's sweet."

"It's not right." Placing the form back down on the table, Winnie took hold of the phone. "I appreciate what he's doing but I can't accept this order."

Renee smacked her purple-tipped fingers down on the table and then pointed one of them back up at Winnie. "You can and you will. He requested a service, he paid for that service, and we'll deliver that service because that's what we do, Winnie. Maybe this is a pity order, maybe it's not. Maybe he sees Jay's stupidity as his chance to make a move, maybe he doesn't. It doesn't matter either way. What matters is that ambulance" — Renee hooked her thumb in the direction of the door — "out there in the driveway will be driving down the streets of Silver Lake with a rescue dessert for a customer in the back. *That's* what matters here. *That's* the counteracting image the people in this town need to see right now. And, Winnie, we're going to give it to them."

She looked from the phone to Renee and back again. Renee was right. An order was an order. Especially now . . .

Exchanging the phone for the order form, she carried it over to the counter, the thrill that always accompanied a baking project beginning to rear its head. "Okay, let's do this."

Renee tossed her stiletto-capped legs over the bench and clacked her way to the pantry. "Fire away."

She took a moment to breathe and then began listing off ingredients in rapid-fire succession. "Baking soda, flour, shortening, dark molasses, and that's — no, wait. We need brown sugar, too. And, of course, we have to bake a crust."

"This is so exciting," Renee said between squeals. "We're coming back, Winnie, we're coming back."

"This doesn't even qualify as a *baby step* yet, Renee." She knew she sounded pessimistic, but it was reality — a reality she'd been grappling with ever since the local news first plastered her face and her Dessert Squad on the Tuesday midday newscast. "Let's just enjoy this moment for what it is, okay?"

It was hard, but Winnie did her best not to focus on the pedestrians who turned and stared as she piloted the Dessert Squad through the center of town. She tried to pretend, for the first block or two, that the reaction was still one of intrigue and amusement as it had been the first few weeks she'd been in business. But even the most gifted imagination couldn't ignore the lack of smiles and the occasional fist shake.

"Seems we're not as popular as we once were, Your Highness." She stole a peek at the brown and white striped tabby in the passenger seat and was surprised to find the animal looking back at her with the faintest hint of . . . *affection*?

Pulling her right hand from the steering wheel, she reached across the seat to pet Lovey, but aborted the attempt as affection turned to agitation.

Hissss . . .

"Well, alrighty then." She returned her hand to the wheel and her attention to the faces of the people they passed.

One irrefutable glarer . . .

One pointer . . .

One — no, two headshakers . . .

Oooh, and a back turner . . .

"Go on ahead," she mumbled. "Buy into the lies if you must. But soon, you'll realize you made a mistake. Every last one of you. And then just try to get a rescue dessert." She turned at the stop sign and drove west for two blocks. "Then again, who am I kidding? I'll need every order I can fill."

She let up on the gas as their destination came into view and slowly eased the Dessert Squad to a stop at the curb. "Okay, this is it. And you" — she pointed at Lovey — "will stay right here, understood?"

Hissss . . .

"Great. We're back to square one, I see." She shifted the Dessert Squad into Park, cut the engine, and dropped the keys into her rescue bag. Then, reaching across Lovey, she rolled the window down a crack. "I'll be back in ten minutes — tops. You also need to know that as soon as these spring days are over, you won't be coming on calls. It'll be too hot."

Straightening up, Winnie opened the driver's side door and stepped out, Lovey at her heels. "Lovey!"

In a flash, the cat was around the back of the rig and had disappeared behind the back tire. "Ugh. Ugh. Ugh!"

After several unsuccessful attempts to retrieve the animal, Winnie gave up and removed the pie-topped stretcher from the ambulance instead. Ten steps later, she was walking through the front door and into the Silver Lake Ambulance Corps. A familiar bald man looked up from behind a half wall separating the lobby area from the building's inner workings and smiled. "Hey! I know you. You're Greg's . . ."

"Friend," she supplied.

The man's answering smile warmed her cheeks so fast and so furiously, she really didn't need the framed mirror behind his desk to know she was embarrassed. The mirror simply provided verification.

Desperate to keep things from spiraling out of control, she let go of the stretcher and held out her hand. "How are you, Stan? It's been a while."

"I'm good." He elongated his neck so he could see over the half wall and pointed at the pie. "Is that what I think it is?"

"Before I answer that, is Chuck here?"

240

Bypassing the intercom system on the desk in front of him, Stan yelled, "Chuck, get up here. You've got a delivery to share with me."

Stan lowered his voice back down to a normal level and then pointed at the pie again. "He *is* going to share that. He has no choice."

A door behind Stan swung open and Chuck Rogers stepped out, his red hair mussed, his eyes drooping. "Can't a guy get a little sleep around —" The EMT stopped, midstep, his eyes widening as they came to rest on Winnie. "Hey there, Winnie. What's up?"

She moved back into place beside the stretcher and slid her fingers underneath the plate. "Chuck and Stan, you may only be halfway through your shift, but someone believes you need this Butt Kickin' Shoe Fly Pie."

Stan's round face grew still wider with the help of a near face-splitting smile. "Who's doing the kicking?"

"Greg," Winnie and Chuck said in unison.

"I'm not above being used, especially when it involves something that looks like *that.*" Stan leaned across the half wall and took the pie from Winnie. "Love the logo on the doily, by the way. Very cool."

"Thanks. We do that for all our desserts." She looked from Stan to Chuck and back again as the first part of Stan's sentence hit home. "You're not above being *used*?"

"Yeah, by Greg, so he can score points with —" He doubled over as Chuck's elbow dug into his side. "Hey! Watch it! You almost made me drop the pie . . ."

"You could stand to miss dessert," Chuck joked before turning his attention back on Winnie. "Don't mind him. He's . . . well . . . *Stan.* Anyway, the pie looks awesome, and as soon as I shake off the effects of my nap, I'll be trying it for sure."

Meow . . .

Stan threw himself back in his rolling chair and looked down. "Did you hear that?"

She started to speak but stopped as Chuck shook her off. "Hear what?" he asked.

Meow . . .

"That!"

"Nope. I don't hear anything. Do you hear anything, Winnie?"

Before she could respond, Lovey jumped down from the narrow piece of metal between the stretcher's legs and wound her body along the front side of the half wall.

"That's a — that's a cat," Stan sputtered.

Lunging forward, Winnie plucked Lovey

242

off the ground and held her tight. "A misbehaving one, yes. I'm sorry. I know she's not supposed to be in here."

Stan stood and came around the wall, reaching for Lovey as he did. "Can I hold her?"

Chuck's left eyebrow shot upward. "You're a cat lover, Stan?"

"Maybe I am. Maybe I'm not." Stan pulled Lovey into his arms and began to stroke her head. "Well, aren't you a pretty one? And boy, can you purr . . ."

Sticking her tongue out at Lovey, Winnie hiked her rescue bag onto the top of the stretcher and fished out the plates, napkins, and forks Renee had packed. She handed them to Chuck and then reached for the cat. "It's time to go, Your Highness."

"Wait. How are you holding up?" Chuck asked. "Greg told me about the effect that girl's murder has had on you."

"I'm doing okay." It wasn't the truth, but at this moment, he was her customer. As she started to reach for Lovey again, a thought struck. "Are you the one who got the call when Melinda was found?"

Chuck's answer came via a slow nod.

"Did you see my crisp, by any chance?" she asked.

Again, he nodded. Only this time, instead

of dropping his gaze to the floor, he held hers, the worry she saw there sending an unmistakable shiver of dread down her spine.

CHAPTER 19

A quick call to Renee as they were pulling away from the curb yielded the answer Winnie suspected: no more calls, no more orders. She tried not to let it bother her, but it was impossible. One delivery did not a business make.

"It'll be okay, Winnie."

She hated the way she sighed in response. She really did. None of this was Renee's fault. None of it. "Hey, while I'm out, is there anything I can pick up for you? Something for you and Ty to eat for dinner maybe?"

"Nope. Ty has a soccer game in Hastings this evening so we're going to do fast food when it's over." Renee dropped her voice to a near whisper. "Don't tell that to any of the supermoms from the team, okay? They'd tar and feather me if they heard I was taking my son for a hamburger and French fries."

"I won't tell. And neither will Lovey."

"*Lovey?*" Renee repeated.

"Yep."

"Oh no."

"Oh yes."

"At least tell me she waited in the car while you delivered the pie . . ."

"I would if I could, but I can't." Winnie steered around a parcel truck and headed in the general direction of home, Renee's sudden fit of giggles grating on her last nerve. "You realize this isn't funny, yes? That the health department could shut us down if they found out Lovey was going on calls."

The laughter ceased momentarily, only to start up again just as quickly. "Lovey doesn't touch the — wait! I know . . ."

Instinctively, Winnie checked the rearview mirror and both side mirrors. "What?"

"Your offer a minute ago. Could you really pick something up for me?"

"I offered, didn't I?"

She could almost hear Renee's eye roll over the phone and chose to ignore it just as she did whenever they were in a room together. Soon enough, her friend got to the point. "I just now remembered that it's Ty's day to bring a snack for the team."

"You want me to bake something?" Winnie

asked, perking up.

"Can't be homemade."

"It can't be homemade?"

"Don't ask," Renee groaned.

"O-kay . . . You want me to stop at the market and pick up some pretzels or something?"

"If it were up to me, yes. But the super-moms want" — Renee's voice took on a nasally quality — "healthy foods."

"You mean like fruit?"

"Of course, because that's what ten-year-old boys want most, don't you know?"

It was her turn to laugh, and laugh she did. "These moms had no idea what was coming when Ty joined the team, did they?"

"So I don't wear sweats and ponytails. Sue me."

At the next stoplight, Winnie flicked on her left turn signal and headed toward the road that meandered along the southern end of the lake. "I'll get some fruit and I'll be back at the house in less than thirty minutes."

"You're an angel, Winnie, thanks."

She clicked off the speaker button and set the phone on the seat next to Lovey. "Quick detour, Your Highness. We've got some fruit to pick up."

As they came to the lake, she rolled down

her window and reveled in the rush of fresh air that filled the front cabin. Somehow, even during the most trying of times, the warmth of the late spring sun against her skin had a way of lifting her spirits. And even if it only lasted until she turned onto the gravel driveway leading to Councilman Medders's farm, she'd take it.

Halfway around the lake, she turned left again, the Dessert Squad's tires kicking up a cloud of dust as they left pavement and headed toward the wooden fruit stand in the distance. When she reached the stand, she pulled into a makeshift parking lot to her right and let the car idle while she stepped out.

A woman's voice greeted her from somewhere just out of view. "Welcome to Medders' Fruit and Farm Stand. I'll be with you in just a moment."

"No rush." Winnie peeked back at Lovey through the partially opened window and then navigated her way across the gravel to the stand and its baskets upon baskets of fruits and vegetables. Everywhere she looked, strawberries, apricots, broccoli, cherries, zucchini, and asparagus called to her with their perfect hues. "Oh. Wow."

"Beautiful, aren't they?" A petite brunette popped up from behind the makeshift counter, her welcoming smile freezing midway across her face. "Oh. I — uh . . . you're Winnie, aren't you?"

For a moment, she was caught off guard by the woman's obvious discomfort, but it didn't last. Winnie was, after all, the talk of Silver Lake. She considered trying to clear her name, to explain her side of the story, but in the end, she simply nodded. "That's right. And you're Councilman Medders's wife, Cindy, yes?"

The woman nodded.

"It's nice to meet you." Winnie directed the woman's focus to the basket of strawberries. "I'm a little surprised the strawberries look so good this early in the season. Don't they usually peak around the middle of June around here?"

"They do. But we grow them in our greenhouses, too, which allow us to have an earlier crop than normal."

"I'd like enough to feed a soccer team of ten-year-olds, please. And I'll take some apricots, too."

Maybe it was the distraction of filling an order, maybe it was the realization that Winnie intended to leave after she made her purchase, but either way, Cindy's posture softened as she went about the task of filling a container and weighing its contents.

When the container was full, she addressed Winnie again. "Do you think this is enough on the strawberries?"

Winnie gave the container a once-over and smiled. "It looks perfect. Now maybe half that amount with the apricots."

"You got it."

While she waited, Winnie stepped back and took the fruit and vegetable baskets in as a whole once again. "Everything looks so good, you just want to eat it all."

The woman smiled her first real smile as she weighed the apricots and rang up Winnie's order on the register. "An elderly couple stopped by earlier today and said it was pretty as a picture."

"And did they take one?" Winnie reached into her purse for her wallet and counted the correct amount of money onto the counter.

"Take what?"

"A picture."

Cindy deposited the assorted bills and coins into the correct holders in the drawer and then pushed it shut. "I told them they could, but they didn't have a camera."

"That's too bad." Winnie stacked the containers on top of one another and then balanced them in her arms for the walk back to the car. "I'm sure they would have enjoyed documenting . . ." The words died on her lips as she found herself back in Sam's dorm room, gathering up the various belongings Melinda had left behind.

Sticky notes . . .

Doodled pictures . . .

A memory stick . . .

And a —

"A digital camera!" she blurted out.

"I'm sorry?"

Uh-oh . . .

Tightening her hold on the stack of containers, Winnie turned toward the Dessert Squad and Lovey. "I better go. There's a team of hungry soccer players waiting on this food."

"I went to school with Cindy Medders, only back then she was Cindy Phelps." Renee popped a strawberry into her mouth and crossed her ankles atop the ottoman. "She was nice enough, I guess, but if I'm remembering right, she was always a little overly skittish. I wouldn't put too much stock in her reaction when she saw you."

"I would." Shifting her body toward the left side of the couch, Winnie continued clicking through Melinda's pictures, one at a time. The first few she came to were from some sort of ceremony. Clearly, by what she

251

was seeing, Melinda had won an award. The banner stretched across the wall behind the girl led Winnie to believe it had been related to writing. "Her smile literally slid off her face the second she realized who I was."

Renee helped herself to yet another strawberry and shrugged. "Even if you're right, do you really care?"

She pinned her friend across the top of the camera. "Yes. And if you don't stop eating those strawberries, the supermoms are going to be gunning for your head at tonight's game."

"The horrors." With an air of defiance, Renee took one more strawberry and then snapped the container closed. "What I *should* do is bring a case of chocolate bars and *really* freak them out." Renee's laughter filled the space between them at the thought. "Can you *imagine*?"

Grunting, Winnie flipped ahead to the next series of pictures — some dorm room shots, some outdoor shots, and some food shots. She skipped ahead again and sat up tall. There, seated at a familiar-looking circular table among other familiar-looking circular tables, was Nina. Next to her was a young man Winnie guessed to be about the same age as Nina. On the other side of the table was a man Winnie had never seen before.

Slightly overweight . . .

Roughly fifty, fifty-five years old . . .

Salt and pepper hair on the sides, a run of the mill ball cap on top . . .

A coffee cup in his left hand . . .

With the help of the camera's zoom feature, she narrowed in on the coffee cup, the table's familiarity suddenly making sense. "They're at Beans," she said aloud. Panning outward once again, she confirmed the location by the slate gray walls, the white Christmas lights strung along the edge of the ceiling, and a handful of Silver Lake's more familiar faces at nearby tables.

Renee patted her lap for a passing Lovey and was rewarded for her efforts almost instantly. "Who's at Beans?"

"Nina, for sure. Possibly her friend, Nate. And a gentleman I'm guessing to be in his fifties, give or take a few years." She moved the image around just enough to take in the table and then panned back out to look at the trio of faces.

Nina looked a little . . . nervous.

The young man next to her looked eager, maybe even pleased.

And the older man wore an expression that was best described as matter of fact.

Like he had no real feelings one way or the other about sharing coffee with Nina and her friend.

Nina's father perhaps?

Or maybe the father of the boy *with* Nina?

There was no way to know at that moment.

"Is it a selfie?" Renee pulled the strawberry box closer to her chair and then pushed it away. "Nope. Not going to do it."

"No, Melinda was obviously taking it."

"Are they looking at the camera?" Renee asked.

Winnie took in the faces, their stance, the path of their eyes. "Not at all. In fact, if I had to guess, I'd say they didn't even know their picture was being taken."

"And the next picture?"

"Good question." Winnie hit the next button, only to find herself looking at a much younger Melinda on what was surely her first day at Silver Lake College. "Nothing. The Beans picture is the last one on here."

"Interesting . . ." Renee leaned over the armrest of the chair and pulled a magazine from the holder beside the end table. Holding it up, she pointed at the celebrity on the front cover. "Wouldn't you love to be followed around all day long by someone with air brush capabilities?"

The last one . . .

She clicked back to the picture in question and studied it more closely. And that's when she spotted the papers atop a folder in front of the man. Zooming in again, she moved the viewfinder around until she could read the largest font.

Evidence of the Bronze Age in Denmark

Art Joel

Mr. Carl Griffin

Confused, she panned back again, this time noting the man's wrist and the likelihood that he was pushing the paper toward Nina and her friend. Panning left, she studied Nina and her companion. Nina's hand was wrapped tightly around her still-full coffee mug. Her friend's mug was empty and set to the side. In his hand was —

She zoomed in again and gasped. "He's holding money! A big wad of it!"

Renee lowered the magazine onto Lovey and made a face. "Who's holding money?"

"The boy who's with Nina. The one I think is Nate."

"Okay . . ."

"And the man they're with has a stack of papers. One of which is some sort of history paper!"

Renee pushed the magazine off to the side

and scooted forward so fast, Lovey nearly fell off her lap. "Can you see anything else?"

Again, Winnie zoomed in, shifting the picture to the left and the right. "Wait . . . I think I can make out part of another paper. It's not a clear shot like the history paper, but it's cocked to the side enough to . . . ."

Her head snapped up from behind the camera and she stared at her friend. "Renee, it's an English paper. For Doug Lummings."

"And Marrow is the teacher?" Renee asked.

She took in the screen one more time, the zoom feature allowing her to make out the last five letters of a name just below Doug's — *arrow.* "I can't see the first letter of the name to be absolutely certain, but if I was a betting person, I'd say it is."

Renee lifted Lovey up off her lap, whispered something in the feline's ear, and then placed her down on the ground. "Where is Melinda's notebook?"

"In my bedroom. On the nightstand."

"I'll be right back." Renee's shoes clattered across the living room, through the kitchen, and into the bedroom, only to repeat the same sound variations in reverse order on the way back. This time, though, instead of sitting in Lovey's favorite chair,

Renee opted to sit on the couch with Winnie. "Can I see?"

Winnie handed the camera to Renee and pointed her way around the table in question. "That one there is Nina. That one, I think, is Nate. As for the man, I have no idea who he is at all." She hit the zoom button and pulled the image in tight to the papers on the table. "See? There it is. The history paper with Art Joel's name on it . . . on top of an English literature one that's slightly askew."

"Yeah, I see it."

Reaching across Renee, Winnie shifted the image to the right and pointed at the money inside the male student's fist. "And there's the cash I was talking about . . ."

Renee zoomed in still closer. "Whoa. I think those are all hundreds."

"I think so, too," Winnie mused. "Which makes me think Bridget might be right."

"About?"

"Melinda having uncovered some sort of cheating scandal at the school." Winnie studied the picture while revisiting the previous evening's conversation on the front porch. "Bridget thinks teachers were being bribed to give grades that weren't earned."

"Interesting possibility . . ."

"Which leaves us with a number of possibilities in the who-killed-Melinda saga." Winnie rubbed at the faintest twinge of a headache she felt brewing behind her right temple and contemplated whether she should take something and head it off, or wait and see if it progressed.

"I think I'm gonna get some —"

"Hold the phone a minute." Renee fairly shoved the camera into Winnie's lap, flipped open Melinda's notebook, and quickly thumbed her way to the first of the two folded slips of paper. With rapid fingers, the single mom unfolded the paper and smoothed it out across her lap. "I don't think this is about bribery at all."

Winnie slumped against the couch. "You don't?"

"Nope. I think these kids are buying papers."

"Buying papers?" she echoed as, once again, she focused on the image displayed on the back of Melinda's camera. "But wouldn't they do that from another student? This guy is old enough to be their father."

"Buying papers from other students on campus is risky. I mean, think about it, Winnie. The chance of getting caught is high. Some teachers really read those papers and remember them from year to year. Especially the really good papers that would

258

be most attractive to cheaters." Renee directed Winnie's attention to the unidentified man. "My guess is this guy has nothing to do with Silver Lake College."

Winnie took a moment to digest everything Renee was saying and compare it to the picture and the computations on the note. "Wait a minute. This makes sense now. 'Five English Lit — Marrow,' could mean five papers were purchased for his class. And three were purchased for Griffin's European history class."

As she spoke, she got more and more excited. Suddenly the notes that had made no sense the first dozen times she'd scoured them were taking on a whole new meaning. "The price breakdown refers to the amount paid per paper."

"Paid or *charged.*"

She looked from Renee to the paper and back again, her train of thought stymied temporarily by the sudden clarification. "What are you saying?"

"Well, look at this ledger of sorts. Doesn't it seem to be written from the standpoint of the person doing the charging, not the person paying?" Renee tapped the first equation with her finger. "The way I see it, why would a student care if anyone else was buying a paper? Yet this seems to be record-

259

ing the total number of English lit papers purchased."

Winnie gently pushed Renee's finger out of the way so she, too, could take in the totality of the paper. "So you're thinking each English lit paper is two hundred and fifty bucks, and each European history paper is three hundred bucks?"

"Makes sense to me."

"Okay, so then what's with this breakdown beneath the total?" she asked as much for her own benefit as Renee's.

"I'm not —"

"Wait! I got it! Whoever is selling these papers" — she guided their collective attention back to the image on the back of the camera — "which is probably this guy, is getting eighty percent of the total. Nate and Nina get twenty percent."

"You mean like a broker would?" Renee asked.

"Exactly. They're getting a cut of every paper this guy sells!"

"If that's true, why is Nina only getting twenty-five percent of the cut while this Nate kid gets seventy-five percent?"

It was a good question, with an answer Winnie could only guess at. "Maybe Nina's role is smaller. Maybe Nate is actually the one that makes the deal and Nina just . . . I don't know."

"Hangs on to the money maybe?"

Hangs on to the money . . .

"That's it!" Winnie yelled as she jumped off the couch, camera in hand. "Nina is an accounting major! She's the bookkeeper for this whole debacle! And it's slips like the one on your lap that probably aroused Melinda's suspicion."

Oh yes. It all made sense now.

Lots and lots of sense . . .

"So whoever killed Melinda knew she was onto them."

"Exactly!"

"But why?"

Buoyed by their newly gleaned knowledge, Winnie paced her way back and forth across her tiny living room, Lovey's eyes following her with a mixture of disdain and curiosity. "Because graduation was at stake for the students and perhaps jail time for the man selling the papers!"

"Okay . . . but the fact still remains that whoever killed her had to have access to your blackberry crisp."

She stopped pacing and stared at her friend. "You're right. Which means our suspect list has been narrowed to three — Nate Daniels, Alicia Worth, and Nina. All had motive, all had means."

"My money is on Alicia."

"Okay, but you can't discount the fact that Nina and Nate were making money on this venture." Winnie stopped beside the mantel and helped herself to the one lone miniature chocolate egg that remained from the previous month's holiday. "Greed can be a mighty powerful motive, you know."

"So can revenge," Renee reminded her before joining Winnie beside the now empty candy bowl. "Any word from Alicia this week as to where she's been or why she hasn't come back? Did she get hired by someone in Hollywood after her exquisite acting debut on Channel Five's noon news the other day?"

"She hasn't checked in, and she hasn't returned either of the calls I left."

"Have you asked Jay about her?"

"No. But I already know she was in jeopardy of failing *his* class. That's why I took her on in the first place."

Renee refolded the slip of paper and tucked it back into the notebook. "Maybe Jay's class was the least of her worries."

CHAPTER 20

It didn't matter how hectic (or pathetically un-hectic) her work week had been, or how many sleepless nights she'd endured for a variety of reasons, Winnie's Friday night pizza dates with Bridget and Mr. Nelson held something special for all of them.

For Bridget, the weekly dinner was all about maintaining a tradition.

For Winnie, it was about resetting her internal compass to what really mattered in life.

And for Mr. Nelson, it was about that first bite of sausage and pepperoni pizza. Or so he pretended . . .

But regardless of their individual motivations for being there, they were on the same page when it came to the locale shift that had been foisted on them several months earlier.

"If I've said it once, I've said it a thousand times . . . Mario's pizza is good but it isn't

Tony's."

Bridget, who loved to argue with Winnie's housemate whenever possible, nodded in complete agreement. "That's because Tony and Lizzy only used the highest-quality flour and they added the yeast to the flour instead of the water."

Like the weekly dinner itself, the bemoaning of Silver Lake Pizza's demise had become normal. And just as she did every week since the town's staple closed in late winter, Winnie stopped eating long enough to concur.

"First it was pizza, then it was your place, Winnie Girl, and soon it will be the very backbone of Silver Lake." Mr. Nelson took a bite of his pizza slice and chewed with greater intensity than normal. "You mark my words, something is going on in this town and it's not in the best interests of anyone but that Batkas fella."

Winnie tried to appear interested, to even offer a few well-timed groans intended to let her friends know she was listening, but her thoughts were wandering in a million different directions and all at the same time.

"Seems Mabel Nethers's boy, Jake, put in a bid on that new playground the council approved last month." Bridget cut the tip off her pizza slice and then pierced it with her fork. "It was more than competitive and even included a few extras — like a surface of shredded tires for safety reasons. Everyone thought he was a shoe-in for the project."

Mr. Nelson lowered his pizza slice to his plate. "He didn't get it, did he?"

"It went to a construction company in Hastings." Bridget paused her forkful of pizza just shy of her mouth and narrowed her eyes on Mr. Nelson. "N.B. Construction, to be exact."

"N.B. Construction," Mr. Nelson repeated. "I've not heard of them."

"You've heard of their president."

"I have?"

"I'll give the two of you a little hint. Those initials stand for this person's name." Bridget popped the pizza bite into her mouth and waited, her bifocal-enlarged eyes ricocheting between Mr. Nelson and Winnie.

Shaking herself back into the conversation, Winnie forced herself to concentrate if only for a moment. "What were those initials again?"

"N.B."

"Oh. That's easy. Nick Batkas."

"Nick Batkas?" Mr. Nelson thundered just before his hand hit the top of the linen-draped table and sent his unused fork and knife crashing to the floor. "He owns a *construction company* now?"

"According to my research, he has for a while, but it just now seems to be taking off." Bridget smiled at the waiter who scooped up their tablemate's cutlery and returned with a clean set in a matter of moments.

"Thanks to the Silver Lake tax payers, no doubt." Mr. Nelson pushed his plate into the center of the table and shook his head. "I'm telling you, something smells mighty bad around here."

Bite by bite Winnie worked her way through her slice of pizza, only to stop as she became aware of a rare silence from her tablemates. The silence, she quickly noted, was accompanied by an assortment of gestures in her direction. "What? Do I have pizza on my face?"

"You look pensive, dear." Like a crossing guard intent on getting a gaggle of kids across the street, Bridget held her hand up in front of Mr. Nelson. "We're all done talking about your former landlord for the evening."

Winnie tugged her napkin off her lap and wiped her chin just in case. "I'm sorry. I'm not meaning to be uncommunicative. I guess I'm just a little preoccupied."

"I saw you go out on a call this morning," Mr. Nelson said as he pulled his plate back to his spot and dove into his pizza once again.

Bridget's knife froze atop her pizza. "You had a call?"

If things were different, she might have called Bridget on her unbridled surprise. But they weren't, so she didn't. Instead, she filled in the details with a healthy dose of reality. "Greg ordered a treat for the guys at the ambulance corps. Which means it was a pity order and therefore doesn't really count."

"He paid for the dessert, didn't he?" Mr. Nelson asked as he plucked a particularly large piece of sausage off his pizza and popped it straight into his mouth.

"He did."

"Then it counts."

Bridget laid her fork down beside her half-eaten piece of pizza and propped her chin atop her fisted hands. "So Master Sergeant Hottie is sweet *and* thoughtful, I see."

Uh-oh . . .

She took one more bite of her own slice and addressed the elephant in the room. "*Greg* is a nice guy. He really is. But he's a friend, and nothing more."

"I think he'd love to be more if you'd let him," Bridget practically sang. "You should have seen the smile on his face when he left your apartment yesterday evening. He really cares about you, dear."

"I know." And she did. She just didn't care about him in that way. A flash of color caught the corner of her eye and she turned to look out the large plate glass window Mr. Nelson had insisted they sit near. A group of high school girls meandered past the restaurant, some talking, others listening, virtually all smiling.

Except for one . . .

Lifting her hand up off the table, Winnie waved at the face so like Jay's — the same blue-green eyes, the same perfect nose, the same possibility to power the world with her smile if she only would.

For the briefest of moments she sensed a hesitation in response, but just as Winnie's breath hitched in anticipation, the girl moved on.

"I don't know why that young girl has such an issue with you," Bridget pronounced. "I've never seen you be anything but wonderful to her."

She felt the familiar weight of despair on her shoulders and did her best to counteract it with as lighthearted a sigh as she could muster. "It doesn't really matter now, does it? Caroline didn't want to share her father and now she doesn't have to."

Mr. Nelson inched his hand across the table until it was on top of Winnie's. "You were good for that young fella. One day she'll realize that having her father be truly happy benefits her, too."

"Maybe she will, maybe she won't." Winnie tried to get excited about her remaining pizza but any pull it once had was gone, stolen by the appetite-killing reality that was her life at the moment. "Either way, it has nothing to do with me any longer. It's over. Jay thinks I killed Melinda."

"You're going to prove him wrong, Winnie Girl."

"Of course I am. But I could never be with someone who could think that of me." Unable to eat any more, Winnie pushed her own plate to the side and took a long sip from her water glass. "Since we're on the topic of Melinda, I think Renee and I have found the motive."

Bridget's ears virtually perked beneath her snow-white hair. "Bribing the teachers. And you got that from me, remember?"

"Actually, we've tweaked that a little, thanks to the last picture Melinda took with her camera." She took another sip of water and then helped herself to the final pepperoni on her cast-off pizza slice. "We think that four out of the six names on that paper I showed you last night were buying term papers for specific classes. And the other two names — specifically Nina and Nate — were involved in the brokering of those papers from an outside source."

"Doesn't anyone know how to do things honestly anymore?" Mr. Nelson groused. "Whatever happened to the concept of *earning* something through hard work and good old-fashioned integrity?"

"Sounds to me like you have far more than motive now, dear." Bridget looked to her left and then her right before leaning forward and dropping her voice to a whisper. "You have suspects, too. Lots of them."

Winnie thought back to her conversation with Renee and the list they'd made over a late afternoon round of soda. "We have three. Alicia, Nina, and Nate."

"What about the other three on that initial list of names? And what about the person you think Nina and Nate were brokering the papers for? That's seven — *seven* — people who had reason to want to keep Melinda's story from ever seeing the light of day."

It was the same rationale she and Renee

had gone over again and again as they talked through the various possibilities before Ty's soccer game. But in the end, she had to agree with the verdict they'd reached. It was, after all, the only answer that fit. "It has to be someone who had access to my crisp. Like Alicia via the Dessert Squad, or Nina via her shared room with Melinda, or Nate via his friendship with Nina. They're the only ones who had motive *and* means."

"That you *know* of, dear."

"It all comes back to my blackberry crisp," Winnie reminded them. "My Fade to Black-Berry Crisp."

Mr. Nelson squeezed her hand then pulled his own back across the table to his plate and the last bite or two of his pizza. "You might want to think about taking that one off the menu, Winnie Girl."

"If I still *have* a menu by the time this whole nightmare is over, Mr. Nelson, I can assure you there won't be a blackberry *anything.*"

CHAPTER 21

"See that one over there? The one that's practically doing splits on the sidelines every time her son gets within three feet of the ball? That's Bitsy Bit."

Winnie swatted a fly from the vicinity of her hot dog and made a face at Renee across the top bleacher. "Stop. Her name isn't Bitsy Bit."

"Yes it is. Watch . . ." Renee adjusted the upper edge of her halter top to provide an optimal view of her ample cleavage and then tickled her fingers across the shoulder of the handsome thirty-something father seated one bleacher below. "Seth? Can you tell my friend, here, what her" — retrieving her hand long enough to point at the woman on the sidelines, Renee batted her longer-than-normal eyelashes — "name is, please?"

The man tried valiantly to avert his eyes from Renee's assets, but in the end, it was of little use. "Bitsy. Bitsy Bit."

"And that one over there?" Winnie followed Renee's finger toward a brunette clapping and jumping not far from Bitsy.

"That's Buffy."

Renee's seductive tickle morphed into a patronizing pat before returning to her own hot dog. "I'm telling you, Winnie, soccer moms are a breed unto their own."

"I thought Ty's game was last night," she said, moving on to the kettle chips Renee had insisted they split.

"It was. This is a different game." Renee ran her now pink-tipped fingers through her hair and then helped herself to a chip, too. "Thanks for coming today, by the way. It makes Bob's presence a wee bit easier to ignore."

Bob.

Renee's ex-husband.

Scanning the crowd at the mention of the two-timing weasel's name, Winnie found him sitting in a chair clapping for . . . *Bitsy Bit?* She cast a sidelong glance in Renee's direction to see if she noticed, but Renee's sights were on her son as he maneuvered the soccer ball down the field and into the goal.

"Woo hoo!!! Way to go, Ty!! That's what it's all about! Woot! Woot!"

Winnie, too, stood and cheered the boy's

accomplishment. When Renee started a wave, Winnie sent it right back. "Bitsy Bit has nothing on us," she declared under her breath, just loud enough for Renee to hear.

"You mean besides the attention of my ex-husband?" Renee lowered herself back to the bench and hijacked another chip.

"So you *did* notice . . ."

"I did. For all of about half a second. Any longer and I would have missed Ty's goal."

She sat beside her friend and draped an arm across the woman's shoulder. "You are amazing, you know that? I mean, I know you're still hurting over the divorce, but what you just said is so perfect. You dwell on the negative, you miss the positive."

"Something you teach me all the time," Renee said, ducking the side of her head against Winnie's shoulder.

Winnie dropped her arm back to her side and studied Renee closely. "*I* teach *you* that all the time? How?"

Renee pointed at Winnie's remaining hot dog. "You gonna finish that?"

"Yes." She picked up the hot dog carton, took a bite, and circled her finger between them. "Don't change the subject . . ."

"Look at the way you handled the demise of Delectable Delights. One day you're turning over the closed sign for the very last time, and the very next day you're coming up with plans for the Emergency Dessert Squad." Renee reached out, broke off a bite-sized piece of Winnie's hot dog, and popped it in her mouth. "Jay turns into an idiot almost overnight, and you're cozying up to Master Sergeant Hottie in your kitchen barely twenty-four hours later."

She considered throwing the last of her hot dog at her friend, but went with a more civilized eye roll instead. "I was not cozying up with Greg. We were baking. That's —"

"And here you are, smiling and having a good time with me despite all the looks and whispers." Renee watched Ty's team converge on the sideline for a break and then turned her attention fully on Winnie. "I'm not sure I could handle it as cavalierly as you are."

"Looks and whispers?" Winnie repeated. "What looks and whispers?" She followed Renee's gaze to her left and the group of women pointing and whispering in her direction. To her right, more of the same. Confused, she looked down at her shirt to see if she'd dripped any ketchup. Nothing. Next, she grabbed her phone, hit the camera button, and studied herself on the screen. Nothing.

Taking in the group on the left once again,

Winnie noted the way one woman kept looking behind the bleachers and then back at her friends, her hands moving as she spoke.

"What the . . ." And then she knew. The parking lot was behind the bleachers. And she'd parked the Dessert Squad in that lot. People weren't whispering about her because of ketchup or some sort of defect in her appearance. They were talking about her because of the continued news coverage involving both Winnie and Melinda.

She swallowed hard and made herself look back at the field.

"Ah geez, Winnie, I thought you knew."

She shook off her friend's pity and tried to seek solace in the knowledge that she was innocent. But still, it was hard. "I'll be fine, Renee. I didn't do it. That's all that matters."

"Um, hey, the strawberries and apricots were such a huge hit with the kids last night, Bitsy Bit stole the idea — and the source — for her snack slot today. So good job, Win."

"I hope you didn't tell the moms that I'm the one who actually picked them up out at the fruit stand," she mumbled as she swept her gaze along the sideline, picking out Ty among the throng of boys now circling the cheerleading mother and the now familiar

276

Medders' Fruit and Farm Stand travel container.

Renee shrugged. "What difference would it make either way?"

"The difference would be Ty's soccer buddies not being allowed to eat the snack for fear I poisoned it or something."

"We're getting close to the truth, Winnie. You know this. We've got the why and the how. All we need now is the who. And once we've got that, we're going to make sure everyone in this entire town knows what really happened."

Noting the Medders' Fruit and Farm Stand sign in her rearview mirror, Winnie let off the gas enough to allow for the U-turn that came next. It wasn't so much that she had a pressing need for fruit at that moment, because she didn't. Quite frankly, a vat of melted chocolate and a spoon held far more appeal given her post-soccer game mood, but giving in to that would be akin to giving up, something she refused to do even under the worst of circumstances.

Turning left at the fading but still visible sign, Winnie drove down the same gravel driveway she'd traveled the previous day. At the end, instead of turning right into the crowded parking lot, she parked under a large oak tree off to the left. She tried to tell herself that decision had nothing to do with people seeing what car she stepped out of, but she knew better. She'd never enjoyed being the center of attention — her desserts maybe, but her? No.

She stepped from the ambulance, slid the keys into the front pocket of her shorts, and headed toward the chalkboard tent sign a few feet away. An arrow at the top pointed her toward a greenhouse and a sale on flowering plants. An arrow near the bottom pointed her toward the wooden stand and its line of customers eager to purchase a variety of fresh fruit.

Yes, she wanted to buy a container of strawberries so she could whip up a treat for Mr. Nelson and Bridget, but the thought of bringing them each a flowering plant as a surprise held its own appeal. Any momentary hesitation she encountered while looking at the sign disappeared as she settled on the best option. After all, why couldn't she surprise them with a plant *and* make them a treat, too?

Her mind made up, she turned in the direction of the greenhouse and ventured up the short hill that would bring her to its doorstep. She could tell, by looking through the glass walls, that there were a handful of people inside, some smelling plants, some checking prices, and others talking animatedly to their spouse or friend. If any of them had heard of Winnie's purported connection to Melinda B. Tully's murder, it wasn't on their radar at that moment.

The prospect of wandering among the flowers and plants without accompanied stares and whispers was as alluring as the potpourri of scents beckoning her inside. An invitation she was more than happy to accept.

Inside, she walked up and down the shelf-lined aisles, sniffing, touching, and reading the name of each plant as she passed. Some plants had flowers, some berries, and some just had leaves. But all looked lush and healthy.

"That's a thimbleberry you're looking at, young lady."

Winnie glanced over her shoulder to find an elderly man, in his mid-eighties, studying the plant from beneath the bill of his Silver Lake Seniors hat. She smiled at him. "I don't think I've ever heard of a thimbleberry," she replied, pointing to the fruit spawned by the plant. "I thought it was a raspberry."

"That's a common mistake. But it's a thimbleberry all right. My father used to grow them beside the stream that ran along our property. Said they were good for erosion control."

"And the fruit? Is it as good as a raspberry?" she asked, captivated.

"They're rather bland if you ask me, but my mother often used them to make jams and jellies and they were always delicious in that form."

She turned to face the man and held out her hand. "I'm Winnie. It's a pleasure to meet you."

"And I'm Raymond," he said, closing his hand around hers. "The pleasure is mine." He gestured back to the plant and then shrugged sheepishly. "My daughter is always telling me I shouldn't be so chatty. That sometimes people want time alone. But when I come here, I can't help myself."

"I'm glad you said something. If you hadn't, I'd be thinking this was a raspberry." Sensing the man's sudden hesitation, she linked her arm inside his and slowly walked to the next plant. Again, it was one she didn't recognize. "What about this one? Any idea what this fruit is?"

Ray brightened immediately, his knowledge of plants obviously a great source of pride. "That's a pawpaw and it tastes like a cross between a banana and a mango."

Winnie studied the small yellow-green fruit and waited for more. Ray did not disappoint. "Underneath the skin is a soft orange flesh with a creamy, custard-like consistency and a sweet flavor. My father often referred to it by its common nickname, custard apple. My mother, on the other hand, jokingly referred to it as the poor man's banana."

"As a person who loves to experiment with different tastes when I bake, I'm more than a little intrigued . . ." She took one last look and then guided him to the next plant, the answering spring in Ray's step impossible to miss. "Oooh, this looks interesting. What is this?"

"That is an infant hazelnut tree. It'll have to be transplanted outdoors soon, though I doubt it will take here. Ohio doesn't offer the right climate."

From somewhere outside the greenhouse, she heard someone calling the man's name and she did her best to hide her disappointment. She liked Ray — liked his company and his knowledge. Just as the elderly people in her childhood hadn't cared that she was the new kid, Ray didn't care what car she'd gotten out of or what she did for a living. He was simply thrilled to have a captive audience.

She looked down the remaining stretch of aisle and the various colorful fruit and plants and felt the tension of the day finally dissipating. "Ray, I've enjoyed this. I really have. Thank you."

CHAPTER 22

Winnie added a dollop of whipped cream to the top of each parfait glass and smiled down at her latest creation.

The image for the recipe had come to her as it often did, in a flash, while holding a particular ingredient. In this case, it had been a container of blueberries. Next thing she knew, she'd been running through the grocery store snatching up the rest of the ingredients she needed — heavy cream and white chocolate baking squares.

"You do realize I'm an old man on the backside of life, don't you, Winnie Girl?" Mr. Nelson joked from his spot at the kitchen table. "Take much longer and I might not be here anymore."

She felt her smile falter at the image Mr. Nelson painted and did her best to shrug it away.

"And you wonder why you never got married, Parker," Bridget sniffed.

Before Mr. Nelson could come back with a response, Winnie grabbed hold of the tray and gave in to the giggle of anticipation that always preceded the unveiling of a new dessert. "Are you two ready for something truly sinful?"

At their chorus of assent, she turned and made her way around the center island and over to the table. "I present to you my White Chocolate Mousse Blueberry Parfaits."

She heard Bridget's audible intake of air and reveled in the positive reinforcement she knew it to be. But it was her housemate's odd expression that gave her pause. "Mr. Nelson? Is everything okay? Do you not like blueberries?"

"Of course he likes blueberries. Don't you remember how he ate an entire blueberry pie by himself a few weeks ago?"

"It was your Don't Be Blue-Berry Pie," Mr. Nelson said by way of agreement. "You made it for me because —"

"Because Renee was out sick for a few days and he missed ogling her from his front window as she came and went to work each day," Bridget interjected. "Don't you remember?"

"That's right. I do now." She placed a parfait glass and spoon in front of Bridget, another in front of Mr. Nelson, and the last at her own spot. "Try it. I think you're go-ing to love it."

Mr. Nelson swiped his finger through the whipped cream and inserted it into his mouth. "The topping is good . . ."

"Trust me, that's only the beginning."

Swapping his finger for the spoon, he shoveled up some of the blueberries and the mousse and raised it into the air between them. "But the name needs work."

"I get that it's a little wordy, but it's what they are."

"It needs a better rescue name." He popped the parfait into his mouth and moaned as he closed his lips around it.

Bridget nodded and followed suit, her own moan of pleasure accompanied by closed eyes and ample lip-licking. "Oh, Winnie, this is . . . wonderful. So creamy, so delicious, so . . ." Bridget dove her spoon into her parfait glass once again and happily depos-ited her efforts into her mouth. "Mmmm . . ."

"I know!" Mr. Nelson said around his third bite. "How about, Don't Be Blue-Berry White Chocolate Mousse Parfait!"

"That's already taken, Parker. For her pie," Bridget reminded him. "Maybe some-thing around a bruise — like Black and

Blue-Berry White Chocolate Mousse Parfaits."

Mr. Nelson pointed his spoon at Bridget. "That could work."

Winnie ran her finger down the outside of the parfait glass — blueberries, mousse, blueberries, mousse, each layer registering on some level. "I appreciate your efforts, you two, I really do, but the name is fine the way it is."

"Winnie, dear, you know that part of the appeal of the Dessert Squad is finding a dessert that goes with whatever ailment — either physical or mental — that the recipient is dealing with."

She pulled her hand into her lap and shrugged. "I know that, Bridget. But right now I need to just enjoy baking for baking. Thinking about the Dessert Squad right now isn't doing me any good.

"Winnie, I —"

Mr. Nelson waved Bridget off with his spoon and then pushed his empty parfait glass into the center of the table. "So what else would you like to talk about, Winnie Girl?"

She started to shrug, but stopped as a safe topic moved into the foreground of her thoughts. "I think I met one of your friends this afternoon."

"Oh?"

"I met him while I was out at Medders' Farm and — oh my gosh, I forgot! I have another surprise for both of you." She set down her spoon, pushed back from the table, and headed across the kitchen. When she reached the tiny hallway that led to her bedroom, she stopped dead in her tracks. "Lovey! No!"

"What's she doing, Winnie Girl?"

"She's — shoo, Lovey! Shoo!" Winnie bent down, plucked the two small pots off the ground, and carried them back out into the kitchen. "Well, these were *supposed* to be plants for your gardens."

"Oh, Winnie, I've been wanting to add a new lilac to the border between our homes." Bridget took the pot Winnie held in her direction and placed it beside her on the wooden bench. "Thank you, dear."

"I'll put mine next to yours, and we'll have two." Mr. Nelson gazed down at the slightly munched plant and then back up at Winnie. "Lovey didn't do any harm."

"But why is she eating plants when she has food in her bowl?" she asked.

"Because she can." Bridget clicked her tongue against the inside of her teeth, and like clockwork, Lovey came running to her side. "Hello, sweet girl, how are you this evening?"

"Sweet girl? She just tried to eat your plant." Winnie felt Mr. Nelson studying her and turned in his direction. "Tell her, Mr. Nelson. Tell her not to reinforce Lovey's bad behavior."

"So you met Ray," he prompted instead.

At the mention of the elderly man who'd helped turn her day around, she sat back down at the table. "I did. How did you know?"

"If you were at the farm, it had to have been Ray. He's a retired horticulturist."

She helped herself to her first bite of the parfait — the creamy richness and combination of flavors exploding inside her mouth. "He knew every single plant we came to. I feel like I learned so much in just the ten minutes we spent together."

"That's Ray for you. He says he's retired, but I catch him still reading plant magazines now and again." Mr. Nelson looked longingly at Winnie's remaining parfait. "That was really good, Winnie Girl. How'd you come up with that?"

"It's the same mousse I use in my pastry puffs and it just seemed like it would make a fun pairing with fruit. Today, I made it with blueberries. But I think it would be just as good with strawberries, don't you think?"

Mr. Nelson's eyes lit up. "Perhaps you should try that tomorrow and let us see what we think."

"I might be able to do that . . ." She took one more bite of her parfait and then scooted her glass in front of him. "Why don't you go ahead and finish mine."

"Don't mind if I do, Winnie Girl." Three bites later her dessert was gone as well.

"The bottomless pit strikes again, huh, Bridget?" Winnie joked.

Bridget looked up from her Lovey-topped lap but said nothing.

"Bridget? Are you okay?"

Dropping her gaze back down to the cat, Bridget lifted then dropped her shoulders ever so slightly.

"Is it your stomach again?" Winnie asked.

"No."

"Your ankle?"

"No."

"Your back?"

"No."

At a loss for some of the woman's more common gripes, she finally gave in and looked to Mr. Nelson for help. He, of course, was running his finger along the inside of Winnie's parfait glass trying to get every last drop of mousse he could.

"Your wrist?"

"No."

She rewound back to the previous day when she'd passed her friend on the way to the row of mailboxes that served their section of Serenity Lane. "I know! Your elbow is acting up! It's making a creaking sound when you brush your hair!"

"It is, yes. But that's not what I'm worried about right now."

Suddenly unsure of which body parts she'd mentioned and which she hadn't, Winnie gave up the guessing game. "Then what *are* you worried about, Bridget?"

Bridget pulled her hand from Lovey's back and moved it to the spot between the cat's ears. Sure enough, Lovey began to purr as she did for everyone, except Winnie, who gave her a gentle scratch in that area.

"I'm worried about you, dear."

Winnie drew back. "Me? Why?" And then, like it or not, she was knee deep in a subject she could only parfait away for so long. "Bridget, I'm going to be fine. I didn't kill that girl, so there's nothing to worry about."

"But you love your business, dear."

"You're right, I do." She took a deep breath and plowed on, her desire to be positive rising to the surface once again. "This

Melinda thing has nothing to do with me. The people in this town will come to realize that soon."

"Maybe they already have," Mr. Nelson proposed.

She thought back to Ty's soccer game and the way people had whispered as she passed, and pointed as she drove away. "I wouldn't go that far, Mr. Nelson, but I'm hopeful that will be the case as talk dies out."

"After tomorrow, it's only going to increase, I'm afraid."

"Tomorrow?" Winnie echoed, turning back to her next-door neighbor. "What's tomorrow?"

"The *Silver Lake Herald.*" Bridget stopped scratching Lovey's head and slowly lifted her gaze to Winnie's. "I tried to focus the article in a favorable way, dear, I really did. I even interviewed some of your customers. But Jarod pulled all of that out and focused it more on the crisp."

She felt the parfait beginning to churn in her stomach as Bridget's words took hold. "Meaning?"

"Meaning, any tongues that may have moved on to something else are going to be right back on you and your desserts by tomorrow morning." Bridget reached across the table and covered Winnie's hand with her own. "I'm sorry, Winnie. If I could have stopped it, I would have."

Somehow, despite the renewed sense of dread snaking its way around every positive nugget she'd squeezed from her day, Winnie found herself comforting her friend. "Bridget, I know that. I really do. Please don't look so sad. I'm going to get through this — *we're* going to get through this. I promise."

Bridget squeezed Winnie's hand and then let go. "I know the police have largely left you alone other than a few questions early on, but I'm afraid, after this article, that will have to change."

"I don't understand? What will have to change?"

"The degree to which you've been questioned." Bridget stared down at Lovey, her mouth drooping sadly.

Winnie looked at Mr. Nelson to gauge his reaction to the conversation. The worry she saw in his eyes, though, only made her feel worse. "Why would an article in the paper change that?"

"Because of increased pressure."

"On whom?"

"Mayor Rigsby."

It was official. She was lost. "Bridget, please. I'm not following any of this."

Bridget slowly lifted her gaze to first Mr. Nelson, and then Winnie, her hand beginning to tremble atop Lovey's back. "If Mayor Rigsby gets pressure from the community, he, in turn, will put pressure on the police."

"Okay . . . but what is he going to pressure the cops to do? Question me again?"

"No." Bridget's voice began to shake along with her hand. "To — to charge you."

She saw Lovey's head shoot up in response to her gasp. "*Charge* me? Charge me with what?"

"Now, Winnie Girl, don't go borrowing trouble prematurely —"

Ignoring Mr. Nelson, she continued to stare at the elderly woman seated on the other side of the table. "Charge me with *what,* Bridget?"

"With Melinda's murder."

CHAPTER 23

Winnie was on the front porch, with Lovey in tow (but pretending not to be), when she heard the telltale squeak of the newspaper boy's bicycle. Normally, when she heard that noise on a Sunday morning, she was lounging in bed with a book in one hand and her morning hot chocolate in the other, the comings and goings of Silver Lake something she'd get to at some point.

Today, there was no book. Today, there was no hot chocolate. And today there was no I'll-get-to-it-later attitude regarding the contents of the *Silver Lake Herald.*

No, today she clambered down the steps and onto the stone path that led to the driveway, catching the paper midair as it hurtled in the general direction of the front porch.

Thwump.

"Nice catch, lady!"

Perhaps, on any other day, Winnie might

have responded with a playful curtsy or a dramatic bow, but when she saw her face staring at her from the front page of the rolled-up paper, all she could do was groan.

What the boy did or where he went from that point on was a blur as she slipped the paper from its string-tied embrace and robotically carried it up onto the porch. For a brief second, she considered taking it upstairs and reading it where she could cry or scream when she was done, but she couldn't wait. She had to know.

Sinking onto the top step, she unfurled the paper to find not only a picture of herself, but also the Emergency Dessert Squad, and her delivery stretcher. Positioned inside the triangle layout of the three pictures was a close-up shot of her blackberry crisp. She took a moment to study each and every picture as a way to gain control of her breathing.

First, there was the shot of her standing in her kitchen with her custom-made Emergency Dessert Squad shirt similar in size and color to that of a traditional emergency medical technician, or EMT for short. She remembered the day Bridget had taken the picture, remembered the feeling that had made her smile so big, so genuine. Oh, what she wouldn't give to rewind six weeks to that exact moment and relive the anticipation and excitement that had come with embarking on a new endeavor.

Her eyes moved down and to the left and immediately narrowed in on the Emergency Dessert Squad logo she'd had emblazoned on the side of the vintage ambulance she'd inherited from Gertrude Redenbacher. At the time, she'd been disappointed at the bequest. If it had been money, she could have kept up with the bakery's rent a little longer. But less than twenty-four hours after being given the keys to Gertie's husband's ambulance, Winnie had come up with the idea for the mobile bakery.

Now, of course, she knew she'd made a mistake, but —

"No," she whispered fiercely. "It wasn't a mistake. Being blamed for someone's murder is the mistake."

She looked to the right and felt an instant twinge of nostalgia at the sight of her dessert stretcher. The moment she'd spotted the collapsible model on an ambulance supply website, she'd known it would be the perfect way to continue the emergency theme. And she'd been right. No matter what kind of mood the customer was in when she arrived, the sight of the stretcher, with a dessert on top, made even the brokenhearted smile for at least a little while.

Despair turned to laughter for a few glorious moments as Winnie remembered some of her clients and their specific dessert rescues.

There was the thirty-something guy who'd had one too many bad blind dates, prompting his female coworker to send him Another Bad Date and Nut Bar . . .

There was the teenage boy who'd been cut from his school's lacrosse team. His mom had hoped the Never Give Up-Side Down Cake would provide a lift to his spirits, and it had. By the time Winnie had packed up her rescue bag and turned to leave, he'd been making plans to work on his stick skills during the summer months.

It was a scene that had played out with increasing frequency as news about the Emergency Dessert Squad's existence made its way around town. Some calls were set up by concerned family members, others by friends wanting to tease one another. But whatever the rescue, whatever the reason, the end result was always a smile.

Slowly, she let her eyes move upward to the picture of the blackberry crisp that had been such a crowd pleaser at the bakery — she'd been waiting for just the right rescue to add it to the Dessert Squad's menu.

"Fade to Black-Berry Crisp." She cringed at the name — both in her thoughts and printed below the picture in bold caption font. Bridget was right, the name had been entirely too fitting — psychic almost.

Psychic . . . or coincidence?

The thought gave her pause but it didn't last. She'd stalled long enough. It was time to read the article that went with the pictures and brace herself for the powder keg Bridget seemed certain it would ignite.

The death of Silver Lake College student, Melinda B. Tully, on Monday evening, has rocked the close-knit campus community to its very core. Tully, who was supposed to graduate with her classmates in two weeks, is now gone, and those who knew her best are asking why.

Tully, a journalism major, was looking forward to starting work at the *Cincinnati Ledger,* her hometown paper. In fact, she'd already suggested a number of story possibilities in advance of her first day, according to the *Ledger*'s senior editor, Larry Bryson.

"Tully was a go-getter. I knew it the moment she walked in for her interview. She was determined to get to the truth no matter where it led," Bryson said. "I only hope the Silver Lake Police Department is prepared to do the same in finding her killer."

The path to that truth, it seems, may be as easy to follow as a trail of pie crumbs.

She rolled her eyes and looked away.

Breathe . . .

Breathe . . .

Lovey, who'd been resting underneath Mr. Nelson's rocking chair, vigorously licked her front left paw and then sauntered into Winnie's general vicinity. "Why does everyone keep calling it a pie? It was a *crisp*!"

A window behind her slid open. "Whatcha doin' up so early, Winnie Girl?"

"Nothing much, Mr. Nelson." She shifted on the top porch step just enough to make sure her back was squarely to the house and the man's view. "I'll come see you in a few minutes, okay?"

"I'll put the coffee on."

She waited for the window to slide back down, but the sound of her friend's cane as he thumped his way into the kitchen served the same purpose. Dropping her eyes back to the paper, she continued to read.

While the moments leading up to Tully's death are still the subject of an intense investigation, campus sources tell us that the Emergency Dessert Squad, a six-week-old mobile bakery owned by Silver Lake resident Winnie Johnson, had delivered its popular Fade to Black-Berry Pie to the victim.

Preliminary toxicology reports point to poison. The general consensus points to the Emergency Dessert Squad pie as its likely vehicle. Calls to the victim's family confirmed Tully did not suffer from any food allergies.

"It was a crisp!" Winnie folded the paper in on itself and then tossed it across the porch, narrowly missing Lovey as she licked herself inside a patch of morning sun.

Hisss . . .

"Ah geez, Lovey, I'm sorry." Turning her chin, she looked out over the front yard she shared with Mr. Nelson and tried to harness the sense of peace the view normally provided. This time, however, the sight of a blue jay and a cardinal playing tag at the birdfeeder did nothing. The whir of Harold Jenkins's motorized scooter and the given that Cornelia Wright and Con-Man were in the vicinity did nothing. Even the meticulously attended flowerbed of her late friends, Bart and Ethel Wagner, did nothing.

300

"Coffee is ready, Winnie Girl. You comin'?"

She let her eyes drift upward to the sky. Part of her just wanted to sit there and sulk. Alone. But another part — the part that made her who she was — wanted to carry on. "I'm coming."

"Don't forget to bring in that paper you nearly hit Lovey with when you come, okay?"

She laughed in spite of the article, in spite of Lovey's continued hatred for her, and most especially, in spite of a week that had seen the sinking of her business like a lead-bottomed boat. Trying to pull anything over on Mr. Nelson was an exercise in futility. He knew all, even if he couldn't necessarily always hear all.

"And Lovey?" Winnie asked without turning around. "Should I bring her as well?"

"*Bring* might not be so advisable, but she'll follow. She always does." Once again the sound of the man's cane, thumping against the floor, filtered its way onto the porch. It was a sound she'd grown to love for the person it represented . . .

"C'mon, Your Highness, we're going inside. For coffee." Lovey's ears perked up despite the seemingly indifferent turn of her head in the opposite direction. "Okay.

Pretend you don't care. Mr. Nelson can just toss your treat in the trash, I guess . . ."

Pushing off the top step, Winnie retrieved the paper and carried it over to the front door, glancing back at Lovey as she did. Sure enough, the cat was snaking her way around the table legs trying to make it look like she wasn't going to follow but royally failing in her efforts. "I see you coming. You're not as sly as you think you are."

She opened the door and nearly tripped over the cat. Righting herself against the doorjamb, she looked up to find Mr. Nelson wiggling his fingers at Lovey. "Did you not see the way she just tried to kill me?"

"You're starting to sound like Bridget," he mused as he beckoned her to follow him into his home. "Next thing you know, you'll be telling me that a slight stumble is cause for a brain scan or some such nonsense."

"No, I won't."

Mr. Nelson stopped halfway into his living room and then leaned his cheek toward Winnie for his morning kiss. When she obliged, he continued toward the kitchen. "So how bad was it?" he asked.

"What?"

"I may be hard of hearin', Winnie Girl, but I ain't blind. I saw you readin' that paper before you threw it at Lovey."

When they reached his kitchen, she set the paper on the counter and turned toward the Formica-topped two-person table. The chair with most of its vinyl still intact was reserved for Winnie. The other one — the one with its innards falling out — was Mr. Nelson's beloved chair, Old Faithful. "Tell me you know I wasn't *trying* to hit the cat."

She watched him pour his infamous mud-like coffee into the ceramic cup he reserved especially for her and grinned. There was something comforting about things that never changed, especially when they came against a backdrop that was changing so fast she could barely breathe.

"What I do know is that, with that arm, you should've been on a softball team when you were growing up." He set her mug on the table and then returned to the coffeepot to pour his own. "You'd have made a helluva pitcher, Winnie Girl."

"Mr. Nelson!"

Leaning his cane against the counter, he hobbled over to the table with his coffee. She started to stand and offer assistance, but like the mug and the mud-like coffee, his refusal to accept help inside his home was also one of those things that didn't change. Once his coffee mug was safely in its spot, he braced himself on the edge of the counter and lowered himself on to Old Faithful. "So? How bad was it?"

She followed his gaze to the paper and then looked away. "Bad enough."

"Aren't you goin' to drink your coffee?"

Cringing mentally, she managed to nod. "Uh, sure. In a minute." Maybe, if she were really lucky, he'd excuse himself to go to the bathroom before she had to take a sip . . . "You can tell Bridget didn't write the one I read."

"Oh? How's that?"

"There were mistakes. Several actually."

Mr. Nelson took a sip of his coffee, declared it perfect, and gently scooted her mug into can't-ignore-any-longer territory. "I'll give Bridget that — she is good at what she does."

Desperate to keep from engaging her gag reflex, Winnie wrapped her hands around the mug and pulled it close.

Make it look like you're getting ready to drink it . . .

"She's excellent. She never would have let that story run the way it was."

He stared first at her, and then the mug expectantly.

Stall! Stall!

"Like . . . like the way they kept referring to the dessert as a pie when it wasn't. It was

304

a crisp."

Mr. Nelson took a long gulp of his coffee and then set his mug back down on the table. "I take it there is a difference?"

"Of course there's a difference! Look at the picture! A crisp is a pie without a crust. It's usually baked in a square or rectangular pan and it has a streusel or crumb topping." She averted direct eye contact with the man in the hopes of buying herself and her stomach a bit more time. "And above and beyond that faux paus, the article said the pie — which again, was *a crisp* — was popular."

Twisting his body to the right, Mr. Nelson grabbed a bag of store-bought miniature doughnuts off the counter and helped himself to three. "How is that a mistake? That crisp was popular."

"In its original Delectable Delight form, yes. But in terms of the Dessert Squad, no. In fact, until that call came in that morning, I hadn't yet found the best way to fit it into the emergency theme."

"Melinda named it?" Mr. Nelson asked around his powder-drenched fingers.

"No, I did. I saw what Renee was writing while she was taking the order and the name just came to me. Of course, now I wish it hadn't." She reached for a doughnut, only

305

to have her hand swatted away. "What?"

"I don't want you getting full before you have your coffee."

Thwarted, again . . .

"Oh. Right."

"Maybe Bridget can write a retraction," he suggested.

Mentally weighing her stomach's needs against its well-being, she held her breath, took a sip of the coffee, and reached for the doughnut bag. Again, Mr. Nelson pulled it out of reach.

"I drank some," she protested.

"You were rushing. Take your time. I don't have anywhere pressing to be this morning."

Ugh . . .

Ugh . . .

Ugh!

She revisited the stomach dilemma and held off on taking another sip. "A retraction is shoved on what? Page Two? Underneath the list of the paper's staff? No one reads those anyway. And besides, the less my name appears in the paper right now, the better."

CHAPTER 24

The second she spied the plate of chicken inside the picnic basket, Winnie's stomach began to growl. Not a quiet, dainty growl, but rather the kind that could be heard across a picnic blanket and, likely, beyond.

"Somebody's hungry," Greg joked as he removed the chicken from the basket and set it in the center of the red and white checked oversized blanket they were sitting on in Silver Lake Park. "Did you eat breakfast?"

"Not exactly."

He reached inside the basket a second time, eyeing her curiously as he did. "Weren't you having breakfast with Mr. Nelson when I called?"

"*He* was having breakfast, *I* wasn't."

"Oh?"

"The doughnuts were conditional on drinking his . . . um . . . special brand of coffee."

"Special brand?" His hand emerged from the basket, brandishing a plastic container of macaroni salad.

Again, her stomach grumbled. "That's what he calls it."

"And you? What do you call it, Winnie?"

She took note of the size of the macaroni in the macaroni salad and longed to try some. "I — I call it Mud in a Mug."

"And he makes you drink this stuff?"

Her eyes followed his hand back into the basket. "He thinks I like it."

"And he thinks that because . . ."

"Because I didn't want to hurt his feelings the first time he made me a cup." She felt her lower jaw flap open as he pulled out a bag of potato chips and then a bag of pretzels.

"You were able to drink it that time?" he asked, mid-grin.

She slid her hand behind her back and crossed her fingers, hoping he'd break open the bag of pretzels before she ended up tearing into them like the pretzel monster her parents had always teased her of being. "I took a sip, managed to hide my gag as he poured himself a second cup, and then dumped the rest of it down the sink when he fell prey to the needs of his seventy-five-year-old kidney."

Laughing, Greg reached toward the basket one more time. "And today his kidney behaved?"

"Sadly, yes."

"Well, maybe this will make up for that." He pulled out a brown paper bag and set it next to the chips and pretzels.

"What's in there?" she asked.

"That's for me to know and you to find out." Looking around at the menagerie of items between them, he reached back into the basket and pulled out two sets of napkin-wrapped utensils. He held one out to her and then unwrapped his own. "I'm glad you could come today. I need a little fresh air, you know?"

She tried to hang back in an effort to seem less piggish, but when her stomach growled a third time, she gave up and helped herself to a little bit of everything. "And as you can see, I need a little food."

"A *little*?" he teased as she added a second, slightly larger handful of pretzels to her already brimming plate.

On any other day, she might have been embarrassed, but not today. Today she was simply hungry.

Together, they talked about the weather, Mr. Nelson's coffee, Stan and Chuck's reaction to their unexpected dessert rescue, and even the new shorts Greg was wearing — virtually everything and anything they could think of to avoid the elephant that had surely prompted the picnic idea in the first place.

Bridget was right. Master Sergeant Hottie was nice.

And hot . . .

If it hadn't been for his call and Mr. Nelson's not-so-subtle encouragement in her other ear, she probably would have holed up in her bedroom, imagining herself in an orange jumpsuit.

She was down to a single chip and half a pretzel when she relinquished her hold on her food and smiled across the blanket at her friend. "I know why you did this, and I can't tell you how needed it was. Thank you."

"Why I did what?" He slid his empty plate into the center of the blanket and stretched out on his side, his head propped against his hand.

Winnie popped the last bite of pretzel into her mouth and gestured toward the empty containers and bags with her lone remaining chip. "This — the food, the park, the everything."

"And why do you think I did this?" he asked, studying her intently.

"Because of the article in the paper. Because you knew I needed a pick-me-up."

"You make me sound so gallant." With his opposite hand, he pushed the brown bag closer to Winnie. "In reality, though, it's more a case of my refusal to give up. Especially when my competition has disqualified himself."

He may as well have been speaking Greek, considering how utterly confused she was at that moment. Competition? Disqualified? Refusal to give —

"Open the bag, Winnie."

She tugged the small brown bag closer, unfolded its top, and peeked inside, any resulting moisture in her mouth quickly disappearing.

Uh-oh . . .

Like a traveler equipped with a personal interpreter, the meaning behind his words was suddenly crystal clear.

Refusal to give up meant his refusal to give up on Winnie . . .

His competition's disqualification referred to Jay's inability to know beyond a shadow of a doubt that Winnie was innocent in Melinda Tully's death . . .

Put them all together and garnish them with the chocolate-covered strawberries staring up at her amid a handful of rose petals and, well, she was an idiot — a *blind* idiot.

"Greg, I —"

"I knew you were wrong for him!"

Startled not only by the voice, but also the venom behind it, Winnie turned toward the walking path less than fifteen feet from where Greg had spread their blanket. There, in the center of the path, stood Caroline Morgan, her hands on her hips, the blue-green eyes she shared with her father raging back at Winnie.

She stood up so suddenly, the bag of strawberries toppled over, spewing its contents in a half-dozen different directions. "Caroline! I didn't see you there."

"Well, that's pretty obvious." Caroline gestured toward the blanket and Greg. "So how long were you going to keep stringing my dad along, huh?"

"Stringing your dad along?" Winnie repeated. "What on earth are you talking about?"

Caroline made a wide pass around Winnie and stopped beside the blanket, her anger-filled eyes making short work of Greg before turning back to Winnie once again. "I don't know, Winnie. The picnic blanket? The food? The — the strawberries? The *guy*?"

"The *guy* is my *friend*. Greg."

Greg sat up but not before Caroline stomped back to the path from which she'd come. "Since when do friends have picnics equipped with rose petals, huh?"

Each step Winnie took toward the teenager was counteracted by one from the girl in the opposite direction. "Caroline, please. Stop moving."

"Why? Why should I listen to a thing you have to say?"

Call it the culmination of entirely too much stress. Call it a chance to defend herself against yet another trumped-up accusation. Whatever the reason, though, something inside Winnie snapped. "I don't know, Caroline, it's not like you've listened to a word I've said since the day you realized who I was. *Bam!* I went from being some nice lady in the park to some sort of competition for your father's affections. I get that your mother left you when you were five, but it's not like you were left on the side of a road. You were left in the capable and loving arms of a man who has devoted his every waking breath to you since then."

She sensed Greg's presence at her back even before he touched her arm, but she didn't care. For six weeks she'd been Caroline Morgan's favorite person to hate. For the past five days now she'd been Silver

Lake's most detested resident. And in both cases she'd done nothing to deserve those distinctions. In fact, by her very nature, she'd done everything to earn the opposite. "Your father made you the center of his universe for eleven years, Caroline. *Eleven. Years.* In that time, have you had friends? Have you had boyfriends? You have, and that's great. But your father has had none of that. Because everything has been about you. My being in his life doesn't make you less important. It doesn't mean you're forgotten or loved any less. In fact, because your father finally had something for himself, he had even more to give you. But noooo. You don't give a hoot what your father needs or whether he is truly happy. All you care about is yourself. Maybe I'm supposed to chalk that up to you being sixteen, but I don't. Sixteen is plenty old enough to care about someone other than yourself — especially someone who has done everything for you."

She felt the tears as they slid down her face, tasted them around her angry words, but she didn't care. The flood gate was open and there was no closing the dam now.

"And as for what I am or am not doing here, I'll let you in on a little secret. The people who have taken the time to get to know me — *really* know me — know I'm a good person. You refused to give me a chance, preferring instead to see me as some sort of monster intent on destroying your life. But at least you came by the whole snap judgment thing honestly."

Spinning around, she headed toward the blanket, only to stop and turn back one last time. "Oh, and just so you know, I had nothing to do with Melinda Tully's death. You and Daddy can think what you want, but you're wrong. The people who love and care about me know this. Anyone beyond that no longer matters to me."

CHAPTER 25

Winnie was on her second pass through the baking pantry when she finally let go of the anger that had sent Caroline back on the trail to her house, and Greg practically tripping over himself to get home and cut the grass.

The plus side of her anger's endurance was a clean (and alphabetized) baking pantry.

The negative side was the guilt that was taking up shop in her heart right next to the hurt.

Yes, Caroline had it coming. Yes, the Emergency Dessert Squad was in its final throes of death. And yes, having the whole murderer tag hanging over her head was wildly unfair. But erupting like a volcano wasn't her thing. Baking cupcakes and cookies when she was upset (or happy or frustrated or bored) was . . .

"And so is making things right." She

closed the pantry door and wandered over to the front window. A few feet shy of Lovey's windowsill hammock, she held up her hands. "Please don't hiss, Your Highness. I come in peace."

Winnie closed the remaining gap between them and peered out over Serenity Lane. Halfway down the block, she spied Mr. Nelson, standing in the middle of the street, deep in conversation with Gordon Whipple. Based on the way Mr. Nelson was waving his non-cane-holding hand and Mr. Whipple was pointing in the direction of town, they'd found something to chew on for a while. Closer to home, she smiled at the sight of Peggy London on her hands and knees plucking weeds from the flowerbed outside her front door. The neighborhood's centurion had no interest in letting a number dictate her days.

She wanted things to be like that again — to have life return to normal. She wanted her weekdays to be spent baking and going out on rescue calls, and her weekday evenings to be spent reading quietly on the couch or sitting on the front porch sharing details of her day with Bridget and Mr. Nelson. She wanted her weekends to be about baking, and continuing to fall in love with Jay . . .

"Well, that's enough of *that* daydreaming, isn't it, Lovey?" She hesitated for a moment and then slowly brought her hand down to the spot between the tabby's ears. When there was no rebuke, she turned the touch into a full-fledged pet. "I don't want you to worry, okay? If my business really tanks, I'll still find a way to feed you. I promise."

She paused her hand halfway down Lovey's back and grew silent. Afraid to move any closer, she savored the slight vibration under her fingers and the faintest hint of a motor-like sound tickling her ears.

"But I'm not giving up hope just yet. The truth is out there somewhere, Lovey. It's just up to us to find it." When she reached the bottom of the cat's back, she returned her hand to its starting place for one last scratch. "And when we do, we'll celebrate — tuna for you, and a party with our friends for both of us. Sound good?"

Lovey craned her head around to look at Winnie and then lowered her chin down to her paws for part two of her Sunday post-afternoon nap. Officially dismissed, Winnie wandered over to the table and the order pad that had sat idly for all but two orders the past week.

Two orders.

She couldn't pay rent and buy food on

two orders. Nor could she afford to keep Renee on as an employee. Something had to give, and it had to give soon. Sighing, she swung her leg over the bench seat, sat down, and flipped the order pad's cover up and under itself.

At first, she'd considered putting the triplicate copy in her tax file along with the duplicate, but at Renee's urging, she'd let them remain in the book. It didn't take long to realize Renee's thinking was sound. If they noticed a particular trend in ingredient requests, Winnie could better focus her recipe experimentation.

Page by page she revisited each and every order she'd filled over the past six weeks — from her very first order that led to meeting Jay, to Greg's sweet attempt to help keep her afloat, the book documented every cupcake, brownie, cake, candy, and cookie she'd baked and sold. Each order was placed for a different reason and a different person, but they all succeeded in igniting the all-important word-of-mouth advertising so crucial to any service-oriented business.

She took in the page on which Renee had taken Greg's order.

<u>Recipient</u>: Stan and Chuck

<u>Problem</u>: They need a good swift kick. In

a nice way, of course.

Requested Genre: No

Suggested Rescue Dessert: Butt Kickin' Shoe Fly Pie

Approved: Yes

Location: Silver Lake Ambulance Corps

Time Requested: Lunch-ish (between 11:30 a.m. and 1:30 p.m.)

Payment: Credit card

Note to Recipient: Now, get moving! ~Greg

She giggled at the memory of Stan's glee as he realized the pie was his, too. That's what the Emergency Dessert Squad was all about. Making people happy.

Not killing them . . .

Shaking the mood-ruining thought from her head, she turned the page and stared down at the empty order form and its still intact carbon copies.

Recipient:

Problem:

Requested Genre:

Suggested Rescue Dessert:

Approved:

Location:

Time Requested:

Payment:

Note to Recipient:

No. She needed to wallow in happiness

for a little while longer . . .

Her mind made up, Winnie moved backward through the pad — first Greg's, then Melinda's . . .

Her mouth went dry as she stared down at Renee's handwriting, Winnie's every thought rewinding back to that fateful day.

Problem: Time to hang it up. End of the road.

Requested Genre: A pie.

Suggested Rescue Dessert: Something with blueberries.

Approved: Yes

Location: Silver Lake College, Bryant Hall Dormitory, Suite 218

Time Requested: Deliver after last class (3:30 p.m.)

Payment: Fund Friend

Note to Recipient: None

Oh, what she wouldn't give to go back to that day and tell Renee they couldn't fill the order. But that was the way hindsight always worked.

A muffled ring from somewhere in the living room cut her mental browbeating off at the knees and sent her scurrying to locate her phone. She found it on the floor under the couch and tried not to think of the post-picnic anger that had earned it that spot.

"Hello?"

"Is this Winnie?"

She tried to place the voice, but it was hard. Beyond being female, she was at a loss. "Yes. Who is this?"

"Winnie, it's me, Sam."

Melinda's RA . . .

"Oh, hi. Is everything okay?" she asked. "Did you remember something?"

"The last time you were here, you mentioned leaving messages for Alicia but never getting a call back."

"Okay . . ."

"Well, I thought you might like to know that she's here." Sam's already quiet voice transitioned into more of a whisper. "In the study room at the end of my hall. And judging by the stack of books I saw next to her on the table just now, I'd say she'll be there for a while."

"I'm on my way."

It was hard not to run the moment the elevator doors swished open at the mouth of Bryant Hall's second floor. For nearly a week, Alicia had been unreachable — Alicia, the only other person who had watched Winnie make the blackberry crisp, and the only person who'd been present right up until they relinquished control of the crisp to Sam.

The whole drive over, she kept waffling between Alicia as a suspect, and Alicia as an alibi. If the girl had done something to the dessert, her failure to return to work the following day or to even return one of the half-dozen calls Winnie had left her over the next few days would make sense. But as nice as it would be to have someone else to blame for what happened to Melinda, she knew, in her heart, it made no sense.

Winnie had made the crisp.

Winnie had packaged it for the ride to campus.

Winnie had pushed the stretcher on and off the elevator.

Winnie had been there right up until the moment they'd signed the dessert over to Sam.

Then again, she'd also had to tell Alicia to stop texting a number of times that day. Maybe one of those texts had been to Nina . . .

The squeak of Winnie's sneakers as she stopped outside the study hall room prompted Alicia to look up. The sight of Winnie drained all discernible color from the young woman's face.

Anxious to keep the girl from taking off, Winnie stopped inside the doorway and did her best to eliminate all sign of tension from

323

her stance. "Alicia! I am so glad to see you. I've been so worried about you."

Whatever the girl might have been afraid Winnie would say, it wasn't that, as evidenced by her widening eyes and the return of some color to her face. "You've been w-worried about me?"

Winnie nodded and slowly stepped into the room. "Of course. How could I not?"

Alicia looked down at her hands and then back up at Winnie, the cockiness she'd exhibited during her one and only day on the job noticeably absent. "Because I lied."

She cast about for something to say, but finally settled on the short and sweet version. "I know."

"I figured that's why you left all those messages on my voice mail. To chew me out."

"Nope." Winnie stopped at the edge of the table but remained standing. "I left them trying to find out whether you were going to come back to work."

Alicia stared at her. "Why? You didn't need me the day I was there, so why would you have needed me any other day?"

"Can I handle the baking and delivery on my own? Sure. But that doesn't mean you can't learn something. The whole point of you being there was to get a feel for what

324

it's like to run a small business." When she was sure the girl wasn't going to get up and run, Winnie pulled out an empty chair and sat down. "But since you brought it up, I have to ask, why did you lie to the media? Why did you say you and Melinda were friends when you and I both know that wasn't true?"

Seconds turned into minutes as Alicia sat there in silence. Every time Winnie thought the girl was about to speak, she didn't. Still, Winnie waited. Anything she said to prod the conversation along could potentially give the girl an out.

"I didn't know what else to do."

Not exactly the full confession Winnie was after, but at least it was something . . . "I don't understand. The reporter asks if you were friends and you tell him no. It's not that hard."

"I wasn't sure if she'd turned in her article yet." Alicia fidgeted with the binding on her economics textbook and then moved on to the spiral binding of her notebook. "Look. I can't explain. I just —"

"You mean the article about the papers you and a few of your classmates purchased in order to pass your classes?"

Alicia's hand dropped into her lap. "Y-you know about that? H-how?"

"I just do." There was no need to drag Sam into things.

"Awww, man, do you think they know?" Alicia pushed her chair back and stood, her eyes darting around the room as if she expected someone to jump out at them.

Winnie tried to get a read on Alicia's expression, but anything she was getting didn't exactly mesh with what she'd expected. In fact, instead of anger, there was only fear. Then again, if Alicia had a hand in Melinda's death, fear would make more sense.

"If they don't, they will soon." Winnie patted her front pocket to be sure her phone was within easy reach if necessary and then went for broke. "But if you go to the police *first,* and tell them what you did, maybe they'll cut a deal with you for less jail time."

Alicia backed up so hard, her chair flipped over backward. *"Jail time?* For buying a *term paper?"*

Before Winnie could process what she was hearing, Alicia began to cry. "M-my g-g-grandmother is . . . is . . . go-going to . . . to kill me! She . . . sac-sacrificed . . . everything . . . for . . . for me to go here."

It was official. Winnie was lost with a capital L. "If you weren't talking about the police just now, who were you talking about?"

"N-Nate . . . and Nina. Art. Doug. All of them."

"How could they *not* know, Alicia? They were buying them, too."

Alicia lifted her tear-filled eyes to Winnie's. "*I'm* the one who told Melinda. I'm the one who ratted them out."

"Ex-excuse me?" Winnie stammered.

"A few weekends ago, I went home to visit my grandmother. She told me about the cancer." This time, the tears that fell from Alicia's eyes were driven by grief rather than fear. Any thought to the contrary was wiped away the moment they took a turn toward gut-wrenching sobs. "If . . . if the doctors are . . . are . . . right . . . she will be . . . dead . . . by the middle of summer."

Winnie made her way around the table and began to rub the girl's back, the circular motion one Winnie's mother had used on her many times. "I'm so sorry, Alicia."

"She told me . . . the one thing that was . . . making it all easier . . . was knowing that I'd . . . straightened up . . . that I was living an honest . . . life now."

Suddenly it all made sense. Or at the very least, the part about Alicia blowing the whistle made sense . . .

"But why tell Melinda? Why not tell a teacher? Someone in the main office?"

"Because . . . I . . . didn't want to . . . get . . . kicked . . . out."

"You didn't want to hurt your grandmother," she surmised while continuing to rub the girl's back.

Alicia nodded between sniffles. "Y-y-yes. When I got back to campus that night, I threw away the paper I bought and wrote my own instead."

"That's good!"

"If I was . . . smart . . . the way my grandmother believes I am . . . it would be. But I'm not. I'm . . . stupid."

"Alicia!"

"I am. I got an F on the paper."

"You can't put a grade on honesty, Alicia. At least you did it on your own." As the girl's breathing returned to normal, Winnie pulled her hand away. "I guess I don't get why you told on your friends, though."

"Because what we were doing was wrong. If I kept quiet, it wouldn't matter that I ripped up that paper. I'd still be part of a lie."

"Did Melinda know you ripped up your paper?" Winnie asked.

"She did."

"Was she going to include you in the

article?"

"I don't think so. She said I didn't cheat. She said I simply wasted my money."

It was times like this that Winnie wished life came with a Pause button. If it did, she'd press it and take a few minutes to examine everything Alicia had told her so far and see how it altered things. Short of a Pause button, though, she had to think on the fly and hope that the path her brain was taking made some sort of sense.

"I still don't understand why you'd tell that reporter that you and Melinda were friends. And if you had become friends because of what was going on, why did you tell me you hated her?"

"It was habit. Up until I went to her about this, I *did* hate her. She was Little Miss Perfect. She'd gotten some of my friends in trouble in the past."

Winnie tried Alicia's explanation on for size and decided it worked. To a point. "Okay, so then why tell the reporter you liked her? Where was the habit then?"

"She stuck the camera in my face just after I found out. I was in shock. All I could really think about was how nice Melinda had been to me over the last few weeks. She even tried to help me with my math homework." Alicia bent over, righted her chair, and sat back

329

down, the effects of their conversation clearly taking their toll. "But the second I walked away from the camera, I realized what I'd done. You see, by admitting we were friends, I was pretty much letting my friends know I'd been the one to sell them out. *If* Melinda had turned in her article before she died, that is."

"Would that be so bad?"

Alicia used her top front teeth to stop her lip from quivering. "They're really the only friends I have here. It's like my grandmother always says, you're known by the company you keep. Nice kids, like Melinda, didn't bother with me because they saw me as they saw those guys. And while I realize I've made a lot of bad choices, the fact is that when my grandmother is gone, Nina and Nate and those guys are all I'll have left in this world."

"No, you'll have your integrity." Squatting down beside Alicia's chair, she looked up at the girl. "*That* will bring the right people into your life, Alicia."

Something resembling hope flashed behind Alicia's eyes as she finally met Winnie's once again. "I'm sorry I dodged your calls. Believe it or not, I kind of had fun watching you in action that day. You really love what you do, don't you?"

"I do." Slowly, Winnie stood up straight and wandered over to the window overlooking the Commons. The Sunday prior to finals week had students studying on benches, blankets, and even sidewalks. "That's why I need to figure out who did this to Melinda — so I can *keep* doing what I do."

"Is there anything I can do to help? You know, to make up for being such a jerk?"

There was no mistaking the earnestness in Alicia's voice. The girl was going to be okay. With the right role models and goals, and another year of college, she would make her grandmother proud, even if it was post mortem.

"You can answer two last questions for me."

"I'll do my best."

With one last glance at the vast lawn below, Winnie turned back to Alicia. "Do you think it's possible the others knew Melinda was on to them before she died?"

"I don't know."

"But if they did?" she prodded.

"I wouldn't have wanted to be Melinda."

CHAPTER 26

Winnie had just finished popping her head into Sam's room to say thank you when Nina stepped off the elevator at the end of the hall. In her hand was a piece of apple green fabric rolled into a ball with the outer edges of some sort of logo visible between her fingers.

"Oh, hey there, Nina."

The girl moved toward her while simultaneously removing a lanyard from her neck with her free hand. "Do I know you?"

Winnie stopped at the correct door and stepped aside to let Nina access the lock. "You do. I was here the other day with my friend, Bridget. She was an older woman who —"

"Okay, I remember now. You're the one who made Melinda's pie."

"Crisp," Winnie corrected by force of habit. "And yes, I am."

"You figure out what happened yet?" Nina

opened her dorm room door, tossed her lanyard onto her desk, and then took a moment to unfold the fabric ball and hang it over the back of her desk chair.

Winnie pointed at the apron. "You work at Medders' Fruit Stand?"

"Yup."

"Cool place."

Shrugging, Nina crossed to her bed and dropped onto her back. "If fruit and plants are your thing, then I guess it is."

"I was out there twice over the past two days," Winnie said. "I don't remember seeing you."

"I work every other Monday, and most weekends. Usually I'm out at the stand ringing up customers, or in the greenhouse watering plants, but yesterday they had me up at the house with the kids."

She stepped all the way into the room. "Kids?"

"My cousins."

"You're related to the Medders?"

"Yup. Corey is my uncle." Nina cocked her arm across her face, blocking the room's overhead fluorescent light from her vision. "They moved here to Silver Lake when my aunt's parents passed away and left her the farm."

Winnie sat on the edge of the apron-draped desk chair and took in a framed collage of photographs. A picture on the left-hand side showed the councilman taking his oath of office with his wife, children, and Nina looking on. "Do you like having an uncle that's so visible in this town?"

"I guess. I mean, it definitely has its perks. I know it's gotten me out of two speeding tickets so far this semester."

Speeding tickets are one thing; murder is something completely different . . .

Her mind officially back on task, Winnie took a deep breath and gestured toward the top bunk and its stripped mattress. "How's it going? You know, with everything."

"By 'everything,' do you mean Melinda's murder?"

"I guess. You holding up okay? I mean, regardless of how you felt about her, it had to be pretty unnerving to have someone drop dead in front of you."

Nina shrugged her non-face-covering arm. "Not really. I mean, it's like I told you and that old lady the other day. I was trying so hard to block out her over-the-top chewing noises, it took me a minute to realize she'd fallen out of her chair. And when I did, I thought she was just being weird at first."

"Weird?" Winnie echoed.

"You obviously never met Melinda. Total

and complete geek in her own life, and an annoying snoop when it came to mine and everyone else's." Nina rolled onto her side, keeping her arm in place across her eyes. "Honestly, before it registered what was going on, I actually gave some thought to taking a picture of her staring up at the ceiling with her mouth all blue. I figured my friends would get a kick out of it."

The surge of excitement that coursed through her body was unmistakable. A picture like that could provide clues — big clues. "*Did* you?"

"I said I thought about it, didn't I? That means I didn't do it."

So much for that . . .

She tried a different tactic. "I take it your friends didn't like Melinda, either?"

Something resembling a muffled snort mixed with a laugh made its way around Nina's arm. "That's an understatement of epic proportions."

"I guess that makes sense considering the fact she held all of your graduations in her hand." She hadn't planned to share that tidbit, but the little voice in her head that had been threatening to do it since Nina stepped off the elevator finally won.

Nina's arm moved just enough to provide a clear view of Winnie. "Excuse me?"

"I'm just saying that if she was always creeping around listening to my conversations, I'd have probably felt the same way."

"Anyone would."

Winnie could almost feel her ears perking. "Did you ever think of calling her out on her snooping?"

"All the time." Nina pulled her arm off her face and used it to hoist herself up and onto her opposite elbow. "And I did."

"You *did*?" She tried to steady her voice and her breathing but she hadn't really expected an admission of guilt quite so fast.

"Not at first, of course. I mean, going off on someone isn't necessarily the best way to start off a year together. But after a few weeks, I couldn't hold it in any longer."

"What did you say?"

"I told her she chewed too loud, I told her she snored, I told her that what my friends and I talked about was none of her business, and finally, I told her to just stay out of my way."

Chewing?

Snoring?

Realizing they'd ventured down different paths, Winnie sought to get them back in sync. The only problem, though, was whether to continue with the little pokes or go straight for the sledgehammer . . .

"I was referring to the article she was writing. On you and your friends. Did you ever consider just calling her out on it? Maybe asking her to look the other way?"

Nina drew back, her eyes wide. "Melinda was writing an article on *me*?"

Winnie stood and walked over to the tiny refrigerator across from Nina's bed and hoped the better vantage point would somehow reveal the girl's verbal surprise to be an act. But even from this different angle, Nina's shock and confusion still seemed every bit as genuine.

"She was."

"About what?" Nina snapped.

She took a moment to consider the negative ramifications of tipping her hand prematurely, but there weren't any. If Nina reacted violently, Sam was just down the hall in her room, and Alicia was still in the study lounge . . .

"Your little side business."

"My little side . . ." The rest of Nina's sentence disappeared inside a gasp so loud and so sudden, Winnie's responding gasp nearly drowned out what came next.

"No . . . no . . . no. Tell me she didn't . . ." Nina bolted upright on her bed.

"Didn't *what*, Nina?"

"Know about the" — Nina stopped, swal-

337

lowed, and started again — "papers?"

There were no ifs, ands, or buts about it, Nina was surprised, shocked even. But whether that was genuine or merely an indication the girl should have majored in acting rather than accounting, Winnie couldn't be sure.

Anxious to find out which was the case, she cast the net a little wider. "Oh, she knew about them. She also knew who bought them over the last few weeks, and that you and Nate were acting as brokers for a much bigger fish."

Nina's skin turned a sickly green just before she began to cry. "My dad is going to be so ashamed of me!"

Dusk was settling over Silver Lake as Winnie left the campus and headed through town, the hope she'd had on the front end of the trip virtually smashed to smithereens. It wasn't that she'd necessarily relished the thought of pointing the local police in either Alicia or Nina's direction, but at least then they'd be closer to finding the truth.

She'd been so sure Alicia or Nina had been behind Melinda's murder. But now, after speaking to both of them individually, she was absolutely positive they weren't.

It had, in a nutshell, been a truly lousy

day. And worst of all, she was no closer to proving her innocence to Jay and the rest of Silver Lake now than she'd been when it started.

Her phone vibrated on the passenger seat and she considered ignoring it. After all, the way things were going, it was sure to be bad news. But a quick glance at the screen had her pulling over to the curb and taking the call.

"Hey, Greg. I'm glad you called. But before you say anything, I need to apologize for my behavior earlier today. I guess I just let everything that's going on get the best of me and I —"

"Um, Winnie?"

She pressed her free hand against her heated cheek and berated herself for not going with her initial gut feeling regarding the call. "Aw geez. I saw the number come up and thought it was Greg."

"Nope. Just me — Chuck." The man's initial hesitation gave way to a laugh. "I tried to tell him the chocolate-covered strawberries weren't a good idea, but he didn't listen, I see."

"Could we maybe talk about something else right now?" She shifted the Dessert Squad into Park and threw her head back against the seat.

"Like what?"

"Like the reason you called perhaps?" She heard the beginnings of sarcasm in her tone and silently berated herself for being unkind. Yes, she was under pressure. Yes, her life was heading south at an alarming speed. But that wasn't Chuck's fault any more than it had been Greg's . . . "Is there something I can do for you?"

"No, I just wanted to give you a heads-up about an e-mail I sent to the editor of the *Silver Lake Herald* today. In case he ends up calling you because of it."

"I appreciate it, Chuck, I really do, but I have far bigger fish to fry at the moment."

"I hear you, and I'm sorry you're going through all this. For what it's worth, none of us here think you had anything to do with that girl's death."

She squeezed her eyelids closed against the familiar burn of impending tears and tried to draw some much-needed strength from the man's words. "Thank you, Chuck. That's actually worth a lot."

"I just know that this is not the first time they've put the wrong picture in the paper. And while it might not be a big deal for something like a dessert, one of these days it might really matter and then it's too late to tell them to be more careful."

She wiped a renegade tear from her face and stared out at the passing cars. "If you're talking about the picture of the crisp, it was the right one. It was taken back when I had my bakery, but it's still the same dessert."

"But they used it in conjunction with the story about the dead girl."

"Because that's the dessert I delivered to her."

A sharp intake of air temporarily filled the spot where his voice had been only moments earlier. "But that's not the dessert she'd been eating."

Pulling her gaze back inside the car, Winnie waited for the punch line. But nothing came. "What do you mean, that's not the dessert she'd been eating?"

"It was sitting on one of your fancy little white paper thingies but it wasn't a blackberry crisp, Winnie. It was a blueberry pie."

Chapter 27

Winnie's head was still spinning when she let herself into her apartment twenty minutes later. All the way home in the car she'd replayed Chuck's words over and over again.

"It was sitting on one of your fancy little white paper thingies but it wasn't a blackberry crisp, Winnie. It was a blueberry pie."

"It wasn't a blackberry crisp," Winnie repeated as she sidestepped a clearly irritated Lovey and headed straight for the order pad. "It was a blueberry pie."

Had someone switched her blackberry crisp with a blueberry pie? It was the only thing that made any sense. And if someone had, she was still left with the same two questions.

Who switched them?

And *why*?

On the surface, the answers were simple. The who was most likely the same person who'd killed Melinda, and the why was because they'd *wanted* to kill her.

But why involve Winnie? Why use the logo-emblazoned doily from her Fade to Black-Berry Crisp to legitimize their murder weapon?

She swung her leg over the bench seat and reached for the pad, her thoughts moving so fast she could hardly breathe.

Meow . . .

"Not now, Lovey." Winnie flipped the cover back and began thumbing through the orders. When she reached Melinda's order, she touched her finger to the top of the page and used it to guide her attention across each and every subsequent line, doubling back after each one for a second pass.

<u>Recipient</u>: Melinda B. Tully.

<u>Problem</u>: Time to hang it up. End of the road.

"Time to hang it up," she read aloud. "End of the road." At the time, when she'd read those words over the top of Renee's shoulder, she hadn't put much stock in them. People called in rescue desserts for all sorts of problems. And when Alicia had said Melinda was a senior in college, the reason for the rescue had made perfect sense . . .

<u>Requested Genre</u>: A pie.

Suddenly, any wonder she'd been giving to who might have known Melinda was scheduled to have a dessert rescue disappeared, in its place a certainty that sent a chill down her spine.

<u>Suggested Rescue Dessert</u>: Something with blueberries.

Then again, maybe she was wrong . . .

<u>Approved</u>: Yes

She scanned the next two lines and then stopped on the third . . .

<u>Location</u>: Silver Lake College, Bryant Hall Dormitory, Suite 218

<u>Time Requested</u>: Deliver after last class (3:30 p.m.)

<u>Payment</u>: Fund Friend

The Internet payment service had proven to be helpful since the Dessert Squad's inception, but now, in light of what was in front of her, it also came with pitfalls. Like the ability for a customer to remain fairly anonymous.

<u>Note to recipient: None.</u>

There was a chance the person who'd phoned in the order had no inkling what was to befall their intended recipient less than four hours later, but there was really only one way to find out.

Glancing over her shoulder at the stove clock, she winced. Ten thirty was awfully late to be calling. Then again, considering the circumstances, she was confident her friend would understand.

Meooowww . . .

"Not now, Lovey!" Winnie retrieved her phone from her purse and dialed. Two rings later, Renee's sleepy voice answered. "You better be calling me to tell me you met a really amazing guy and that he has an even more amazing friend."

"I need you to tell me about the person who placed the dessert order for Melinda!"

Renee yawned loudly and then muttered something Winnie couldn't quite catch.

"Renee, please," Winnie begged. "This is really, really, *really* important."

"If it's worth three *really*s in a row, it must be," Renee teased before putting Winnie on hold so she could take a sip of water. When she returned to the line, her voice was void of its previous rasp. "Okay, so what do you want to know?"

"Anything . . . Everything . . ."

Renee yawned a second time. "I don't know. It was almost a full week ago."

"So we'll start with something simple. What gender was the caller?" Winnie asked.

"Oh. That's easy. Male."

Winnie's attention returned to the order pad and the very first line. " 'Time to hang it up' and 'end of the road' — were those your words or his?"

"I always write exactly what they say because that's what usually helps you come up with a name. And it did."

She heard more sipping on the other end and gave her friend a chance to swallow before moving on to the next question. "He specifically requested a pie with blueberries, yet he was okay when I came up with a blackberry dessert."

"Honestly, he seemed kind of distracted, like he just wanted to get the order marked off his to-do list, you know? And there's kind of a chance he heard the black part in relation to the name, rather than the berry, I guess."

"A big chance or a little chance?" she prodded.

"Decent, I guess. But what's with all these questions, Winnie? And why now? At ten thirty at night? I'm gonna be at your place in nine and a half hours."

She half laughed, half snorted. "*Nine and a half?* Really? Because having you here at eight in the morning would be a first . . ."

Renee sighed. Loudly. "Okay. Maybe closer to ten hours . . ."

"*Ten?*"

"Ten and a half." Renee took another,

longer sip, and then exhaled into the phone. "Now, if you don't mind, can we get back to my question about your questions?"

"Melinda wasn't eating my blackberry crisp when she died." There, she'd said it.

The ensuing silence on the other end of the phone was short lived. "What was that?"

"She was eating a blueberry pie."

"And you know this because . . ."

"Chuck, the EMT, said she was eating a blueberry pie." Even now, as she spoke those words aloud, she found her thoughts rewinding to another conversation . . .

"Trust me, the lip smacking was verification enough. And if it wasn't, the blue stain on her lips and tongue when she fell out of her chair ten minutes later sure as hell was."

If she'd been paying attention when she and Bridget had first spoken to Nina, she would have known something was wrong. Blueberries stain blue. Blackberries don't.

"So you're off the hook!" Renee shouted.

"Shhh . . . You don't want to wake Ty." Winnie felt Lovey's head pushing against her leg and glanced toward the food bowl atop the princess placemat — empty.

Oops . . .

"Why aren't you more excited about this, Winnie? You're off the hook! We're back in business."

Oh, how she wished that were true. And maybe it would be. But this business with Melinda's death wasn't over. Not by a long shot. "Someone used me — used *us* — to take a young woman's life."

"Used us how?" Renee asked.

"Whoever did this threw out my crisp and replaced it with the pie that killed Melinda. He put that pie on our Emergency Dessert Squad doily and made that poor girl think someone was doing something nice for her. I'm not okay with that, are you?"

"Maybe Alicia or Nina had a male friend make the call. Maybe it's possible that male friend had no idea why. Or I suppose it's entirely possible he did."

Winnie considered the possibility for all of about a second. "Alicia and Nina had nothing to do with Melinda's death. I'm certain of that."

"Maybe Nate did it."

It was a possibility, but that would mean he knew about Melinda's article and kept that information from Nina. "I don't think that's it, either."

"One of the other students involved?"

"Did it *sound* like a college kid who placed the order?" Winnie posed in response.

"No."

"Then I'm at a loss on . . ." The words petered out as the face of a man she'd seen for the first time that week filled her thoughts. "Renee, I've gotta go. I think the answer is in that last picture on Melinda's camera."

"You mean the guy who sold the papers to the roommate and her friend?"

Even though it was still just a hunch, the fact that Renee's gut took her to the same place was validating. "Yes. But even if we're right, that doesn't mean we can find him."

"Maybe he's the Dave Wright that Melinda mentioned in her notebook."

Dave Wright . . .

"Oh my gosh, Renee. That makes total sense."

"Regardless of whether that's his name or not, the roommate should know how to get ahold of this guy. She was working for him, you know."

"That doesn't mean she'll tell me . . ."

"Then see if you can identify him without the roommate's help."

"But how?" Winnie asked.

"Show the picture to that councilman and see if he remembers anything that could be helpful."

Winnie stood, crossed to the cabinet that held Lovey's food, and quickly poured a serving in her bowl. "Councilman? What councilman?"

"That wiry-looking one with the funky glasses."

"Councilman Medders? How would he . . . wait. You think Nina would have told her uncle what was going on? Trust me, if you saw the way she acted today at the thought that anyone would know what she'd been doing, you'd know she hasn't told her uncle."

Renee's yawns returned, as did the rasp to her voice. "I didn't even know he was the roommate's uncle. I just thought that maybe, since he was sitting two tables over when Melinda snapped that picture, he might remember something that could be useful is all."

"He was there?" she asked.

"Yup."

"And you know that from looking at that picture?"

"Sure," Renee said, mid-yawn. "Why not?

"Wow. Good catch. I'll check with him in the morning. In the meantime, go back to sleep." She started to disconnect but pulled the phone back to her ear one more time. "And, Renee?"

"Yes, Winnie?"

"Thank you. For everything. I don't know

what I'd do without your unwavering support."

"Neither do I."

And then Renee was gone, leaving Winnie alone with her thoughts. She looked down at Lovey, topped off her water bowl, and then headed into her bedroom to locate Melinda's camera.

As she reached for the light switch just inside the open doorway, her eyes gravitated toward the blinking red light on her landline answering machine. Curious, she crossed to the phone, and pressed play.

"Winnie, it's Jay. We need to talk. Caroline told me what happened at the park this afternoon and . . . well . . . we need to talk. You've got all of this completely wrong."

She waited for the Caroline-induced anger to resurface, but it didn't. Instead, a sadness so strong, so overpowering, settled over her being and left her gasping for air. She'd been so intent on proving her innocence to Jay and everyone else, his sudden absence from her day to day life had been stuffed into the deal-with-it-later section of her heart. But now that she was on the cusp of accomplishing her goal, later was getting a whole lot closer.

CHAPTER 28

She was just turning the doorknob on the outer door when Mr. Nelson opened his own and peeked his head into the vestibule. "Is that you, Winnie Girl?"

"Good morning, Mr. Nelson." Doing her best to keep her face concealed from his view, she made a show of trying to locate her car keys in the bottom of her purse. "I really need to clean this thing out one of these days soon."

"I just put on a pot of my special coffee. Can I get you a cup?"

Like Pavlov's dog, the mere mention of Mr. Nelson's liquid mud stoked her gag reflex, a fact she tried to hide with yet another unnecessary pass through her bag for something that was already safely tucked away in the front pocket of her jeans. "Actually, Mr. Nelson, I need to run to city hall this morning, so I'll pass. But maybe, if Renee beats me back, you can offer one to her. But remember, she likes your powder blue clip-on bow tie best."

She knew she was being a stinker, but whatever she could come up with to distract Mr. Nelson from looking too closely at her eyes was fair game at the moment.

"Why are you going to city hall?" Mr. Nelson caned his way closer for a better view of Winnie, but she thwarted his efforts by digging deeper into her purse. "Don't you know they're all crooked down there these days?"

"I just need a moment of Councilman Medders's time. If all goes well, I'll be in and out of there with something useful in a matter of minutes."

Out of the corner of her eye, she saw her friend reach toward her front pocket, a curious expression deepening the lines around his mouth and eyes. "You ain't findin' your keys in your purse because they're right there. In your pocket."

Busted . . .

"Oh. Wow. Good eyes, Mr. Nelson." Reaching into her pocket, she pulled her keys out and jingled them in the air between them. "Well, I guess I better be heading out."

"You must think I'm getting pretty feeble-headed, don't you, Winnie Girl?"

"I don't think that!" she protested, pausing her hand on the door and glancing back at her friend. The moment she did, she knew she'd made a mistake. "Look, Mr. Nelson, I really need to be heading out. The sooner I get there, the sooner I can —"

He reached out, touched the side of her face, and followed it with a sweet, but worried smile. "I heard you crying through the vents last night. Broke my heart hearing you like that."

"Don't you take your hearing aids out at night?"

"I was getting ready to take them out when I heard you."

She knew the tears were still close and knew she couldn't afford to shed any more. She'd had her cry. It was time to move on. "I'm sorry if I worried you, Mr. Nelson, but I'm going to be okay."

"I'm glad to hear that, Winnie Girl."

She returned her hand to the doorknob but stopped shy of actually opening the door. "Hey, Mr. Nelson? Do you happen to know anything about blueberries?"

"I know they taste good. Especially in one of them parfaits of yours."

"I'll make you another one of those this week." She leaned over to kiss him on the cheek but he pulled back just as she got within striking range.

"If you need more than that, I suggest you talk to Ray."

"You mean the man I met the other day?"

"Blueberries come from plants, don't they?"

At her nod, he caned his way into his living room, only to return a few minutes later with his address book and a scrap of paper in his free hand. "His number is in here. Under R. For Ray."

"You don't think he'll mind if I call?"

"He's old like me, ain't he?" Mr. Nelson countered. "Trust me when I say, any phone call is a good phone call when you're as old as we are."

"Miss Johnson?"

Winnie looked up from the men's health magazine she'd opted to read over the latest issue of the *Silver Lake Herald* and smiled at the nervous woman seated behind the desk in the main waiting area of city hall. "Yes?"

"Councilman Medders will see you now."

Returning the magazine to the meager pile on her right, Winnie stood, hiked her purse back onto her shoulder, and headed down the corridor indicated by the receptionist. She tried not to assign too much importance to this meeting, but it was hard. Twenty-four hours earlier, still reeling from seeing her face planted on the cover of the *Herald* in conjunction with a murder investigation, despair had been her overriding emotion. Now she'd have to say it was hope with a hearty side order of determination.

Three quarters of the way down the hallway, the sight of the councilman's name on a door-mounted plate prompted her to run a quick hand through her hair. She'd tried to counteract the lack of sleep and red-rimmed eyes with a bit more makeup than normal that morning, but there was only so much it could do. Still, she didn't want to scare the man . . .

She took a deep breath, squared her shoulders, and knocked on the open door. "Councilman Medders? Your secretary said I could come on back."

The man Renee described as wiry looked up from a stack of papers on his desk, took a moment to assess Winnie, and then stood, holding out his hand as he did. "Miss Johnson. Yours is certainly a name I've been hearing a lot this week."

"I didn't have anything to do with that young woman's death. But that's not why I'm here . . . Well, I guess in a roundabout way it is." She pulled her hand from his and motioned toward the empty chair to her left.

"May I? I won't take too much of your time."

"Yes. Please." He waited until she sat and then leaned his head against laced fingers. "So what can I do for you, Miss Johnson?"

"Does the name *Dave Wright* mean anything to you?"

He cocked his head in thought. "No, I don't think so. Should it?"

"No, probably not." Squaring her shoulders with an inhale, she moved on. "I was hoping you could look at a picture for me."

"A picture? What picture?"

She pulled her purse onto her chair and pulled out Melinda's camera. With a push of a button and a quick tap of another, she found herself looking at the same picture she'd looked at dozens of times over the past few days. "There's a man in this picture that I'm trying to identify and I'm hoping you might be able to help."

"Me? Why?"

"Because you were sitting two tables away with Nick Batkas when this was taken. I guess I'm hoping you might remember seeing him that day." She leaned forward and relinquished the camera to the man on the opposite side of the desk. "Those buttons to the side of the screen? The ones with the arrows? Those will allow you to move around the picture in the event you might find that helpful."

He held the camera close to his face for a few moments and then slowly met her gaze across its top. "Who am I looking at specifically?"

"The man seated at the table across from your niece."

"My *niece*?" he echoed as his eyes darted back down to the screen, and his finger returned to what Winnie assumed was the arrowed buttons.

She took a moment to compose her answer in a way that wouldn't tell any of Nina's secrets. After all, they were Nina's to tell. Winnie's one and only concern at the moment was identifying the man seated at the table with Nina and Nate.

"He's wearing a hat, and if you zoom in, you can see money in his hand."

Seconds turned to minutes as the councilman studied the screen. Eventually, he lowered it back to the desk and shrugged. "I'm sorry, Miss Johnson, but I'm afraid I can't help. I've never seen that man before."

It was the answer she'd expected to hear, but that didn't make it any less disappointing. "Well, thanks for looking. Maybe I'll try to stop back out at the college after work today and see if Nina can give me a name.

Anyway, thank you for your time. I know you're a busy man." They stood in unison but he remained behind his desk. She started toward the door only to turn back and retrace her steps. "Oops, I almost forgot her camera. Sorry about that."

"*Her* camera?"

"Melinda Tully's." Winnie placed the camera inside her purse and then hoisted it back onto her shoulder. "That picture was the last one she ever took and I believe it holds the clue to her murder."

It wasn't until she was back in the car that she realized she'd said the man, and not Nate, was holding money in his hand. For a moment, she considered going back and asking him to look at the picture again, but when she realized he would have known Nate via his niece, she let it go. Money or not, he knew who she'd been talking about and he didn't know the man.

What to do next was the new question.

Did she head out to Bryant Hall now and see if Nina was around? See if she had any information about the man she and Nate were buying papers from?

Or did she stop at the police station, tell them everything she knew, and leave the rest of the investigation to them?

Before she could settle on a course of action, her phone vibrated against the seat, alerting her to an incoming call. A glance at the scrap of paper sitting next to the phone confirmed the caller's identity.

"Thank you for calling me back, Ray. I hope it's okay that Mr. Nelson gave me your number."

"Sure, sure, it's okay. I understand from your message that you have a question about blueberries?"

She looked through the windshield at the side of city hall and decided to go for broke. "Are there poisonous blueberries?"

"Blueberries? No."

So much for that theory . . .

"Berries that *look* like blueberries?" he continued. "Yes."

"Are you sure?" she asked.

"They're from the belladonna plant."

She plucked the sheet of paper containing his number off the passenger seat but abandoned it on her lap in favor of simply listening. "Belladonna plant?"

"That's right. It's one of the most toxic plants found in the Eastern Hemisphere. Every part of the plant is poisonous. Ingestion of a single leaf from a belladonna plant can be fatal."

"And this belladonna plant has berries, too?"

"It does. Eat five or six of those and you're done."

She could feel her hands beginning to shake as the murder weapon solidified in her mind. "Done, as in dead?"

"That's right."

"And it grows around here?"

"No."

Like a balloon pricked by a pin, she felt all the hope rush out of her chest. "Are you sure?"

"Although not original to North America, it was introduced here and can now be found in limited sections of the Northeast, and more widely throughout the Pacific Northwest."

She was back to square one.

Again.

"That said, some greenhouses grow them as a sort of curiosity specimen. In fact, I'm pretty sure they have one out at Medders' Farm. In the next greenhouse over from where I met you on Saturday."

"Medders' Farm?" she repeated, her voice suddenly hoarse.

"That's right."

"And they *sell* these berries?"

"Of course not. That's why it's tucked away in the greenhouse with a sign warning workers and patrons not to eat the berries."

"A sign warning workers and . . ." She sat up tall, the identity of the killer suddenly as clear to her as the sun peeking its way over the top of city hall.

CHAPTER 29

As much as she loved having Renee around, Winnie couldn't help seeing her friend's last-minute decision to take the day off as a blessing. With Renee out of the picture, Winnie could skip the whole maybe-someone-will-call-and-place-an-order thing and instead spend her time concocting the best way to confront Nina.

There was the go-straight-to-the-police option she'd already discarded. That route would entail a certain amount of skepticism and convincing, and thus the passage of time she really couldn't afford.

No, what she needed to do was get the girl to confess, disseminate the details of that confession to the local television news station and the *Silver Lake Herald,* and then beg them to do a piece exonerating both Winnie and the Emergency Dessert Squad.

The key, though, was when to do the confronting. Looking at the digital clock on the stove, Winnie grabbed her phone and dialed Sam's number. Three rings later, the girl picked up.

"Hello?"

"Hi, Sam, it's me, Winnie." She could make out the rumble of voices in the background and guessed Sam was out and about rather than in her dorm room. Still, all she needed was a single answer. "I can tell you're busy, but can I ask a super-quick question?"

"Um, yeah . . . sure. Give me one second." A strange muffling sound was soon followed by Sam's voice and less background noise. "Sorry. I was heading across campus to grab a late lunch and there were too many people around to really be able to hear you. So what's up?"

She considered telling Sam she'd found Melinda's murderer, but after everything the girl had done to help, Winnie wanted to wait to do it in person. "Would you happen to know when Nina is done with classes today?"

"Three forty, I think."

Something clicked inside her head and she felt suddenly foolish for bothering the girl. "Actually, I should have known that since I tried to deliver Melinda's crisp at three thirty last Monday and you hung on to it until Nina showed up ten or fifteen minutes later . . ."

"No problem. As I said, I was just heading across campus. It's not like your call interrupted a class."

"Okay, cool." Winnie eyed the clock again and then gave the girl what she could at that moment. "If you're on your floor in about thirty minutes, I'll be there . . . talking to Nina."

"Wait a second. If Nina was in her room after classes last Monday, she won't be there today."

"Why not?" she asked.

"Because she works every other Monday at her aunt and uncle's farm."

Winnie remembered Nina saying something about that the previous day.

Ugh.

Then again, maybe it would be better to confront Nina at the source. Less chance to claim ignorance and all that . . . Plus, the girls in Sam's wing had been through enough the past week. They didn't need a confrontation and an arrest added to the mix, as well.

"Thank you, Sam. This is very helpful information."

Several beats of silence ticked by before Melinda's friend spoke, but when she did, it was with an air of uncertainty. "Winnie, I'm going to have to ask that you return Melinda's camera and notebook no later than tomorrow afternoon. I really think it's time to hand them over to the police. Whoever did this to her needs to be held accountable."

"And she will be." Then, realizing she'd said more than she intended, Winnie hurried to wrap up things. "As for Melinda's things, I'll be turning all of them over to the Silver Lake Police later this afternoon. You have my word on that."

"Thanks, Winnie."

She ended the call, checked the status of Lovey's bowl, and then took a moment to make sure she had everything she needed . . .

Notebook, check.

Order pad, check.

Camera, check.

All that was left was the confrontation itself and the call to the Silver Lake Police Department. Once that was done, she could return to the life she knew before last Monday.

Minus Jay, of course . . .

She closed her eyes at the sound of Jay's voice in her head — his insistence that they talk resurrecting itself in her mental ear.

Only this time, it didn't send her to bed, sobbing. Instead, it quickened her steps all the way to the door and down the stairs.

If all went as planned, Jay and the rest of the Silver Lake naysayers would be knocking at her proverbial door offering apologies for the error of their ways over the next several days. And Winnie? She'd accept them graciously, of course, but she'd never forget those who'd stood by her through it all — Mr. Nelson, Bridget, Renee, Greg, Chuck, and the rest of her neighbors on Serenity Lane.

In fact, by this time tomorrow, she'd be baking up a storm for a tried-and-true Serenity Lane Celebration.

She stopped at the bottom of the stairs and knocked on Mr. Nelson's door. His rapid-fire response hinted at a man who'd been hovering in anticipation of a certain someone's voice . . .

Nibbling back the laugh she felt brewing, she lovingly greeted the man with a tap on his nose. "Renee isn't coming in today. She's taking a personal day to catch up on the sleep I interrupted with a phone call last night."

He looked as if he was about to say something, but instead merely unclipped his light blue bow tie and tossed it over his shoulder. "You look as if you're feeling a bit more like yourself this afternoon, Winnie Girl."

"I am." She patted the side of her purse and then leaned forward and planted a kiss on the elderly man's forehead. "We're going to have a party here tomorrow afternoon. On the porch. And there will most definitely be a White Chocolate Blueberry Parfait set aside for you!"

"Sounds like a celebration," he said, smiling.

"And that's exactly what it's going to be."

He looked her over from head to toe. "What are we going to be celebrating?"

"The official rebirth of the Emergency Dessert Squad."

His eyebrows nearly shot up in line with the bill of his ball cap. "You've been cleared?"

"I'm about to be." She lifted her wrist, checked the time, and inched toward the outer door. "That's why I've gotta go. To confront a killer and clear the Dessert Squad's reputation once and for all."

Reaching up, Mr. Nelson tugged his hat firmly into place, caned his way into the vestibule, and then turned and pulled his door shut. "Then what are we waiting for? Let's hit the road!"

She'd tried to talk him out of coming, but if she knew one thing about Mr. Nelson (besides his affinity for nosiness, his love of chess, and his fondness for turning off his hearing aid whenever Bridget was near), it was his dislike for being left out of anything resembling adventure.

When it became apparent he wasn't going to let go of the bone she'd mistakenly put within sniffing range, she conceded. The drive to Medders' Farm simply provided the opportunity to get him up to speed on all things Nina.

"You think she was that afraid of people finding out she cheated?" Mr. Nelson resituated the angle of her dashboard vent and then settled back in his seat for the remaining half mile to the farm.

"I most certainly do. I mean, she absolutely freaked yesterday when she entertained the notion of her dad finding out she'd cheated."

Mr. Nelson whistled softly under his breath. "I suspect her father would rather have dealt with that than his daughter as a murderer."

"I know, right?" Winnie let up on the accelerator as they approached the turnoff for the farm. "I just can't believe she tried to use *me* to cover her tracks."

"How did she know about you?"

She turned left onto the gravel driveway and immediately sucked in a fortifying breath of air. "I've made lots of deliveries to the college over the past six weeks, some even to the very dormitory where she lives. I imagine her choice of murder weapon naturally led to thoughts of the Dessert Squad."

When they reached the top of the driveway, she turned into the otherwise empty lot and cut the engine. "Hmmm. Looks quiet around here today. That's probably a good thing."

"If she gets upset and tries to run, I'll trip her with my cane." Mr. Nelson leaned forward, wrestled his cane from its holding spot next to his legs, and then reached for his door handle. "If she puts up a real fight, I'll sit on her."

"Oh no. You're going to wait right here, where I don't have to worry about you." She stopped his protest with a hand to his shoulder. "Look, I agreed to let you come. Don't push it beyond that, okay?"

"What am I supposed to do while I wait?" he asked.

"Listen to the birds, admire the flowers hanging from the eaves of the fruit stand, look at the picture in Melinda's camera, whatever. Just don't get out of the car until I get back." She started to open her door but stopped to smile at her friend.

"What happens if she strikes out at you, Winnie Girl?"

She waved aside his concern and stepped out of the car. "She's twenty-one. How much striking can she really do?"

"She killed Melinda, didn't she?"

Touché.

Still, she wasn't worried. "I'll be okay, Mr. Nelson. Really."

"I have my phone if you need me." He patted his fanny pack and settled back against the sun-drenched front seat, his eyes suddenly droopy with sleep. "Go get your man, Winnie Girl."

She pushed the driver's side door closed and made her way over to the wooden stand and its variety of fruits and vegetables housed in simplistic baskets. The chalkboard sign behind the counter boasted a whole new set of sales from the ones offered over the weekend. A digital scale stood idly by, the absence of customers to blame for the zeros displayed on its small screen.

"Hello? Nina?" she called. "Are you here?"

371

The lack of a response propelled Winnie up the hill and toward the greenhouse. Each actual step she took coincided with the cerebral one that had gotten her to this moment.

Nina and Nate brokering term papers . . .

Nina hating Melinda . . .

Nina finding out somehow that Melinda was onto her and Nate . . .

Nina being alone with the dessert she'd ordered from —

She stopped midway up the hill, her conversation with Renee the previous night replaying in her ear in starts and stops.

"What gender was the caller?"

"Oh. That's easy. Male."

And then . . .

"Did it sound like a college kid who placed the order?"

"No."

The memory gave her pause but she pushed it to the side and kept walking. Voices had nothing to do with age, right? Besides, who else would have access to belladonna berries?

No one . . .

At the top of the hill, a vibration in her back pocket stopped her in her tracks once again. She pulled out her phone, checked the screen, and brought the device to her ear.

"I thought you were going to take a nap," she said by way of a greeting. "What happened?"

"Nick Batkas happened, that's what."

She tried to hold back her groan but was only mildly successful. "Mr. Nelson, can we talk about this later? I haven't found Nina yet."

"I've been saying all along something crooked was goin' on in this town, haven't I?"

"Yes, you have, but can we —"

"Boy, was I right. But at least now there's proof."

She gave up and continued walking. "Mr. Nelson, I —"

"I just never expected it'd be Medders feeding him information. I figured it was that Rawlings, or maybe even Mayor Rigsby."

Medders?

"What are you talking about, Mr. Nelson?"

"It's right here on this camera. You gotta move up a little and then zoom in real close, but all the proof I need is right here on the screen."

"Proof? Proof of what?"

"Medders has been taking bribes from Batkas to show him project bids."

Her footsteps grew heavy as Mr. Nelson's ramblings finally stuck. "Are you talking about the picture at Beans?"

"Looks like the place to me."

"Just because the councilman is sitting at a table with Nick doesn't mean they're doing anything wrong, Mr. Nelson." She stepped into the greenhouse and slowly made her way toward the location Ray had described in relation to the belladonna plant.

"But the stack of bid envelopes in front of them, and the money changing hands between them, sure does."

She froze. "You can see all of that in Melinda's picture?"

"If I can, anyone can."

Suddenly, it all made sense — the gender and voice of the caller who'd placed the order with Renee, the call that had gotten Nina out of her dorm room and away from Winnie's blackberry crisp, the killer's unquestioned presence in a girl's dormitory, Nina's seemingly genuine shock at the thought of Melinda having known about the term paper business, the choice of murder weapon, and finally, the face she knew she'd see when she turned toward the footsteps now headed in her direction . . .

"Mr. Nelson, call the police. Tell them to come to Medders' greenhouse, stat."

The voice in her ear changed — its tone transitioning from anger to worry in under a second. "He's there with you now, isn't he, Winnie Girl?"

"Yes, he is. Call the police."

CHAPTER 30

She tried not to wince as Mr. Nelson removed the bandage from her shoulder and turned her over to Bridget for a swipe of an alcohol wipe and a squirt of antibiotic cream.

"Every time I think of that man chasing you until you fell, my blood boils," he groused. "He's lucky the police got to him first because I would have knocked him senseless if they hadn't."

Placing a calming hand atop his, Winnie smiled up at her housemate and their equally upset next-door neighbor. "I'm here, I'm fine. You can quit worrying now, you know."

"He killed someone's child!" Bridget recapped the cream and stepped aside so Mr. Nelson could apply a new bandage. "And because he did, his own children are going to grow up without a father."

All she could do was nod. After all, Bridget

was right. The true irony in the situation resided in the why. Corey Medders had killed Melinda to keep his dishonesty from being revealed. Yet by killing her, that dishonesty was now the least of his worries. And as for the cheating scandal that had led Melinda to the bigger story in the first place, Bridget and her own nose for news was on the case. Now, it was only a matter of time before the man in the hat was identified and Melinda's final story was put to bed once and for all.

"A-hem . . . There's still a party going on outside."

Winnie stood and gently but firmly herded her elderly friends toward Renee. "Do we need any refills on dessert yet?" she asked.

Renee circled the trio and came up behind Winnie, her version of herding a bit more forceful. "We could invite the entire town of Silver Lake onto this porch and there would still be more than enough desserts, Winnie."

Yes, she'd gone a little crazy making White Chocolate Mousse and Blueberry Parfaits for Mr. Nelson, caramel brownies for Bridget, Bananas Foster for Renee, triple chocolate chunk cookies for Ty, Shoe Fly Pie for Stan, and a variety of other treats guaranteed to please all of her guests, but she couldn't help herself. She'd only baked twice in a week's time and that wasn't okay.

When they reached the outer door, she let Mr. Nelson and Bridget precede them onto the porch so she could have a moment to speak to Renee alone. "Greg approached me earlier about this whole Batkas fiasco. He seems to think that with Nick and his money-grubbing ways no longer a factor in downtown Silver Lake, that maybe we could open up a reborn Delectable Delights in one of the still vacant storefronts."

"Why would we do that?" Renee stared at her, hands on hips. "Why?"

"Because there was never any stigma hanging over the bakery."

Winnie followed Renee's gaze onto the porch and the front lawn beyond, the faces of her friends and supporters warming her from the outside in.

"I don't see any stigma, do you?" Renee countered.

"Here, no. But beyond Serenity Lane, I don't know."

"Councilman Corey Medders killed Melinda B. Tully. With a blueberry pie *he* made, not you. There is no stigma." Renee pushed the screen door open and motioned Winnie to follow, the handful of people milling around the door instantly parting to let them pass. "I'd be lying if I said I didn't love working at the bakery with you. Because I did. It's why I was one hundred percent on board when you came up with the Dessert Squad idea."

"And I'm forever grateful for that, Renee."

Renee stole a chunk of cookie off her son's plate and shook it at Winnie. "I don't want your gratitude, Winnie. I just want to keep doing the dessert dispatcher thing. It's fun, it's creative, and the daily adoration of your downstairs neighbor is good for the ego, you know?"

She did know.

In fact, it was that man's adoration for *Winnie* that had gotten the Silver Lake Police Department, en masse, to the greenhouse in record time the previous afternoon . . .

"We can do this, Winnie," Renee insisted. "Heck, we already were before this whole debacle happened. The Emergency Dessert Squad is going to be just fine. In fact, I think it's going to be a ton better than just fine."

Oh, how she hoped and prayed Renee was right.

Sure, she'd loved her bakery. But the Emergency Dessert Squad was something special.

It brought me Jay . . .

Rattled by the unsettling thought on what was an otherwise perfect afternoon, Winnie excused herself and headed out onto the lawn. She'd been so preoccupied the past few days, she really hadn't given Lovey much attention.

"Lovey?" she called. "Lovey? Where are you, Your Highness?"

"Winnie?"

"Yes?" She turned to see who'd said her name and found herself face to face with a Lovey-holding Caroline. Before she could formulate a response, or even truly process the sixteen-year-old's presence, Caroline set Lovey on the ground and slowly inched her way out from under the protection of the tree on which she'd been leaning.

"I want you to know that you were half wrong the other day," Caroline said, alternating her gaze between her feet and Winnie. "At the park."

A half-dozen or so responses flitted through her thoughts but none of them represented the true Winnie. The person she was determined to be was kind. If others chose to turn a blind eye to that due to their own agenda, that would remain on them, not her.

Breathing in the confidence she needed to get through the moment, she allowed herself a quick scan of the people who'd stood by her the past week and used that to strengthen her resolve to be true to herself. "Actually I was *completely* wrong. I had no right to yell at you the way that I did, Caroline. For that, I am sorry. I never had any intention of taking your father away from you. I simply wanted to love him *with* you."

Caroline's chin quivered before it disappeared from view behind young hands. "No, you had a right to yell. I had it coming to me. I've been a real . . . brat, and I know it. I didn't want to share him. Still don't, if I'm being completely honest.

"It's been just me and Dad since I was five. I haven't had to share him with anyone. He's never had a second date with anyone — until you. Suddenly, he's humming when he's shaving because of you, too. He talks about your desserts just as much as he talks about the ones I make for him. And when I have dance class, he's not reading a book or grading papers at that table on the other side of my studio door, waiting for me to be done so we can be together again. Now, he's looking forward to the time I'm in there so he can be with you."

Winnie took a moment to frame a response even though, in the end, she knew it didn't matter. Not for her anyway. But maybe, just maybe, something she could say would make a difference for the pair in the future.

"But don't you see, Caroline? You just said it yourself — he's humming because of me, *too* . . . he's talking about my desserts, *too* . . . he's still waiting when you get out of dance at the end of the hour; he's just filling the time in between in a different way. Those things don't mean he's forgotten you or pushed you aside for someone else. A person's heart is big enough to love more than one person, Caroline. And the more love a person has coming in *their* direction, the more love they have to give back to the people *they* love."

Caroline slid down the side of the tree until she was sitting crisscross at its base. Lovey, of course, came running back, anxious to claim any lap that didn't belong to Winnie. "A week ago, I didn't buy that crap. But now I guess maybe there's something to it."

Not exactly sure how to respond, Winnie remained silent, the laughter emanating from the yard around her fading into little more than dull background noise.

"I wanted you out of my dad's and my life since the moment it became obvious he liked you. I wish I could say that's different now, but I'm not sure I can. But that's the part that made you *half right* the other day at the park."

Winnie slowly lowered herself to the ground, too, her body still stiff from her fall. There was no two ways about it, she was curious where the girl was going. "Okay, so if my yelling at you and the things I called you out about made me half right, what made me half wrong?"

"The stuff you said about my dad."

Like a vertical Ping-Pong ball, Winnie rose to her feet once again. "You know what, kiddo? How about we shake hands and part ways now, okay? We made some progress and I don't want to see it be derailed. Maybe, if you pass me in town now, you don't have to snarl or glare. We'll just smile and wave . . . like happy people do."

With a gentle push, Caroline dismissed Lovey from her lap and stood to face Winnie. "Not for one single minute did my dad think you had anything to do with that college kid's death. Not. One. Single. Minute."

Winnie didn't mean to snort when she laughed, but it just sort of happened. Falsehoods had a way of making her do that at times . . .

"I'm serious. We even had our first real fight because of that."

"I don't understand."

Caroline held her gaze. "You being tied to a murder helped my case. But instead of getting rid of you, he just got mad at me."

The snort-accompanied laugh was back, and this time she coupled it with a quick stint of pacing that took her no more than a distance of three feet in either direction. "Let's say you are right, Caroline. Let's say he knew I was innocent. Then why did he act so weird every time we talked after Melinda's death?"

"Because he felt bad."

"Excuse me?"

"That whole thing happened the very day Alicia started working for you. He felt responsible."

"So he showed that remorse by shutting me out?" Winnie felt people turning to look at them, but it didn't matter. All that mattered at that moment was calling a spade a spade. "Most people, when they feel bad about something, step up to the plate and correct it."

"Unless they convince themselves that the other person is better off without them."

Winnie spun around to find Jay standing less than two feet away, his blue-green eyes darting from her face to the bandage on her shoulder and back again. "What happened?

Are you okay?"

Mr. Nelson caned his way down the porch steps and over to Winnie, his eyes narrowed on Jay's face. "Corey Medders, the man who killed that young gal out at the college, tried to kill Winnie. He chased her around his greenhouse and knocked her into a table."

Jay fixed anger-filled eyes on his daughter. "Did you know about this, Caroline?"

Caroline nodded but said nothing.

He started to address her, but turned instead back to Winnie. "When did this happen? And why were you *out* there, Winnie?"

"It happened yesterday afternoon. And she was out there because she was trying to prove to you and everyone else who didn't believe her, that she was innocent." Mr. Nelson lifted his cane off the ground and pointed it at Jay for extra emphasis. "You must be blind, young fella, if you think my Winnie Girl could harm a fly, let alone another human being."

"I never doubted your innocence, Winnie," Jay insisted, his voice choked with emotion. "I just felt like I was ruining your life. My daughter was being nasty to you, my indecision on how best to deal with her brought you pain, and then, when you tried to help me out by giving one of my more troublesome students an internship, the bottom falls out of the only thing you've ever wanted to do."

She didn't know what to say. She wanted to believe him, wanted to run into his arms and never move, but she couldn't. Not yet.

"So why are you here now?"

"You never returned my call the other night. I tried to wait you out, I really did, but I just couldn't do it any longer." Jay took a step forward and then stopped, the pain in his eyes raw. "The minute I heard that you'd mistaken my actions as some sort of proof that I didn't believe in your innocence, I knew I had to make things right. I just wish I'd bypassed the phone and come here then."

Winnie turned back to Caroline. "What made you tell him? Especially when you had exactly what you wanted?"

"Because I want my dad back."

"Isn't that *why* you wanted me gone?" Winnie asked. "So you could have him back?"

"It was . . . and maybe it still is, a little. But it's different now than it was before he met you."

"Different how?"

"I'll answer that." Jay reached out, gently took Winnie's hands in his, and pulled her close. "Because *before* you, my life was happy. *With* you, my life was spectacular."

RECIPES

KOOTCHY-KOOTCHY-KOO KUCHEN (APPLE)

Crust:

1 cup flour
1/4 cup confectioners' sugar
1/4 teaspoon salt
1/2 cup butter

Filling:

4 Granny Smith apples (peeled, and cut into
  6-8 wedges each)
2 eggs
1 cup sugar
1/4 teaspoon salt
1/4 tablespoon cinnamon
3 tablespoons flour
1 8-ounce container sour cream

1. Combine all crust ingredients in a bowl
   to form dough. Pat gently into lightly

sprayed 13 × 9 pan.

2. Arrange apple wedges across top of crust.

3. In separate bowl, beat eggs. Blend in sugar, salt, cinnamon, flour, and sour cream. Pour over fruit-topped crust.

4. Bake at 450 degrees for 10 minutes. Then reduce heat to 325 degrees and bake for 30-35 minutes until filling is set.

5. Top with whipped cream if desired. Great warm with ice cream.

6. Store in refrigerator.

FADE TO BLACK-BERRY CRISP
4 cups fresh blackberries
4 tablespoons sugar
2 teaspoons cornstarch
1 cup oats
1/2 cup flour
1/2 cup brown sugar
1/2 cup cold butter
1/2 teaspoon lemon juice
1 teaspoon ground cinnamon

Place blackberries in a greased 13 × 9 pan.

1. Mix cornstarch, lemon juice, sugar, and water. Once smooth, pour over black-berries.

2. Combine flour, oats, brown sugar, and cinnamon. Cut in butter until mixture is crumbly. Sprinkle over berries.

3. Bake at 375 for 20-25 minutes.

Great with whipped cream or a side of ice cream (or both)!

BLACK AND BLUE COOKIES

For Cookies:
1 1/4 cups flour
1/2 teaspoon baking soda
1/2 teaspoon salt
1/3 cup buttermilk
1/2 teaspoon vanilla
1/3 cup unsalted butter (softened)
1/2 cup sugar
1 egg

For Blue Icing:
3 1/3 cups confectioners' sugar
3 tablespoons light corn syrup
3 tablespoons hot water
3/4 teaspoon vanilla extract

A drop (or to desired color) of blue food coloring

For Chocolate Icing:
2 2/3 cups confectioners' sugar
3 tablespoons light corn syrup
3/4 teaspoon vanilla extract
1/4 cup hot water
3/4 cup semisweet chocolate chips, melted.

Cookies:
1. Sift together flour, baking soda, and salt in bowl.

2. In second, smaller bowl, mix vanilla and buttermilk.

3. In still another bowl, beat butter and sugar together until combined well. Add egg and beat until blended.

4. Slowly beat in flour and buttermilk mixtures a little at a time, alternating between each one until all has been added. Mix until smooth.

5. In 1/4 cup serving sizes, spoon batter onto baking sheet lined with parchment paper.

6. Bake in 350 degree preheated oven for 15 minutes (tops will be golden and springy).

7. Allow cookies to cool completely before frosting.

Blue Icing:
1. In bowl, whisk confectioners' sugar, corn syrup, and hot water together.

2. Add in vanilla and mix.

3. Add blue food coloring.

4. Spread blue icing over one-half of each cookie.

5. Set aside.

Chocolate Icing:
1. In bowl, combine confectioners' sugar, corn syrup, vanilla, and hot water. Stir until smooth.

2. Melt chocolate (in microwave or in double boiler — watch carefully to avoid burning).

3. Add melted chocolate to mixture and

stir well.

4. Spread on remaining half of each cookie.

5. Let icing set (at least 30 minutes).

ABOUT THE AUTHOR

Laura Bradford is the national bestselling author of *Éclair and Present Danger,* the debut novel in the Emergency Dessert Squad Mystery series. She also writes the Amish Mystery series. She lives in New York.

The employees of Thorndike Press hope you have enjoyed this Large Print book. All our Thorndike, Wheeler, and Kennebec Large Print titles are designed for easy reading, and all our books are made to last. Other Thorndike Press Large Print books are available at your library, through selected bookstores, or directly from us.

For information about titles, please call:
(800) 223-1244

or visit our website at:
gale.com/thorndike

To share your comments, please write:
Publisher
Thorndike Press
10 Water St., Suite 310
Waterville, ME 04901